DREAMS OF ITHACA

DAVE BRUNETTI

Want another story for FREE?
Read to the end to find out how!

The story of Ithaca continues in *ONE SMALL STEP*, and there's only one way to get it. Flip to the end of the book to find out how to get your copy!

For Amanda
Forever and Ever

CONTENTS

BEFORE THE END OF THE WORLD

1 DECEMBER 2204 CE - TEN YEARS BEFORE DEPARTURE

"In conclusion, people of Earth," Dr. Ramsey lowered his voice, and the hundred gathered journalists duly inched forward in their seats. He let the silence hang, the anticipation build. And then he dropped the bomb. "Our planet is doomed."

Disquieted whispers rippled through the room. He allowed it for just a few calculated seconds, then held up his hand, and silence returned. The room belonged to him.

"And so, in this most desperate hour, as humanity faces down its first true existential threat, I invite the nations of Earth to unite and strive towards the last great achievement of planet Earth: the means of salvation for our species.

"I, Dr. Colin Ramsey, as President and CEO of RamTech Enterprises, along with our Board of Trustees, have begun to liquidate all non-essential assets of my late father's Empire and realign all our resources toward the completion of an interstellar spacecraft within the next ten years."

A louder, longer ripple, tinged with tones of incredulity. Several hands shot in the air.

"The road will be long," Ramsey's voice thundered now, drawing the room back toward himself, back under his authority. The raised hands lowered again. "And there are any number of pitfalls along our narrow path to salvation. But we are the species that built the Great Pyramids and the Great Wall. We traveled to the moon with computers less powerful than today's calculators. We traveled to Mars with the computing power of a modern neural lace. In our own lifetimes, we have built thriving space colonies, such as this one, in orbit around our planet.

"We have always been a species capable of the impossible. And our task has never been more urgent, nor more dire." He raised his hand in both triumph and invitation. "Join me as our species rises to meet its darkest and finest hour. Yes, the age of Earth is ending, but the age of humanity among the stars is only about to begin."

THE SHOUTS OF A HUNDRED JOURNALISTS CHASED RAMSEY through the rear door of the conference room. The door slid back into place and sealed with a hiss. Silence replaced the din. Ramsey took a deep breath and allowed himself to be still for the first time in over forty hours. He loosened his tie and started undoing the buttons on his wrist under his blazer.

"Well, you never were much for subtlety." Dr. Tyson

Daniels leaned against the wall, arms tightly folded against his chest. The disapproving scowl etched on his face complemented the deep bags under his eyes.

Ty was Ramsey's best friend, going back to their early years as the two brightest students at The Fitzpatrick Academy — a preparatory school renowned for churning out top academics in nearly every field. Ty also lived and worked on Troy Orbital Station with his wife and their young daughter, Izzy. Ty headed the operational side of Ramsey's many departments in addition to his work as an Earth Systems Researcher. A waste of talent, in Ramsey's opinion. Ty should have applied his intellect to something more concrete where he could have really pushed the boundaries of scientific knowledge instead of languishing in the analysis of intractable systems that had managed themselves just fine for four billion years.

A damn shame.

Clara, Ty's wife, was a mathematician. Ramsey liked her as well as he liked anyone. Izzy was tolerable for a three-year-old.

"There's no time for subtlety, Ty. You're the one who told me that."

"No, I said there was no time to waste." Ty pushed himself off the wall, moving with familiar ease in the two-thirds-gravity. He had put on some weight ever since the news cycles had first picked up his research, but at thirty-two he still had much of his natural athleticism. "There's always time for more subtlety than that."

Ramsey sighed. "What did you want me to say? 'We're monitoring a potentially dangerous situation and if anyone wants to invest all their resources into our outlandish project that will probably fail, that would be super nice of you?'"

Ty shot him a withering glance. "Of course not."

"Well, what then?"

"For starters, you could have played politics a little to gather some support for the project before unilaterally deciding to tell the whole world that they're 'doomed.'"

Ramsey began the long walk back toward his quarters and motioned for Ty to follow him.

They were in the middle ring of Troy Orbital Station, the crowning jewel of RamTech's space innovations. Home to nearly three thousand permanent residents, plus vacation accommodations for another eight hundred, the space station was the world's first economically viable, permanent, non-terrestrial living environment. Three concentric, wheel-shaped rings, each itself composed of multiple levels and connected through long spokes for transportation between them, made up the bulk of the station, which simulated gravity through its rotation. In some parts of the station, you could leave a room, walk in a straight line, and end up back where you started.

"Politics," said Ramsey, sneering, "are exactly what got us into this mess in the first place. Politicians have always been too concerned about getting reelected to risk anything." He held up his hands in mock contrition. "Fine, I've taken a risk. I admit it. But doing nothing is a death sentence for every man, woman, and child on Earth."

"There will be mass panic. The world wasn't ready to have this slammed down on them." Ty slid behind

Ramsey to avoid three oncoming scientists deep in conversation.

"They've been talking about your research in all the news cycles for the last three weeks," Ramsey said as Ty hustled to catch back up. He adopted a melodramatic tone, "Dr. Daniels' findings paint a bleak picture for the future of the planet. More bad news as independent research groups all-but confirm Dr. Tyson Daniels' apoc-alyptic predictions. World leaders prepare to meet to discuss the Daniels Dilemma."

"Are you done?"

"There's plenty more. Just tell me when you've got the picture." Ramsey smiled as they stopped at large elevator that would take them to the outer ring of Troy.

"I understand your argument, but that's the whole point, Colin. Your point was the only one you considered. You can't just act unilaterally and expect the world to react how you intended."

The cylindrical elevator car, large enough for fifty people, or, more frequently, heavy shipments that needed to be distributed throughout the station, arrived. They entered, and Ramsey pressed the button for the outer rings, where his quarters were. The doors rotated shut and sealed with a hiss.

Ramsey and Ty braced themselves against the side railing. Ramsey's stomach dropped with the car as it began to accelerate with a gentle whir downward along its magnetic track. Almost imperceptibly, the gravity began to increase as they passed through the outer floors of the middle ring, heading for the outermost ring. The main tourist and scientific levels were on that outermost and largest ring, where the station experienced about 80 percent of Earth's gravity.

Between its rings, the wheel of Troy Orbital Station was empty, except for eight spokes connecting the layers together and providing a tether for elevators such as this one to connect the rings. As they entered the spoke between the rings, the elevator car's lights dimmed to black and its solid walls turned transparent.

From here, the infinite black of space expanded in nearly every direction, riddled with shining stars. The very fabric of creation, unfurled and resplendent. A view of space unparalleled in the history of space tourism.

Somewhere out there was the new home of the human race, and Ramsey was going to find it, whatever the cost.

Much closer, filling the foreground, the great wheel of Troy Orbital loomed, shining silver in the rays of the sun. The gods had the cosmos to testify to their greatness, but this space station was exhibit 'A' in the testimony to human greatness.

And it was Ramsey's.

As they approached the innermost layer of the outer ring, the Earth came into view back in the direction of the station's hub.

The dying Earth.

Perhaps Ty was right, and there would be mass panic on the little gray marble. Perhaps RamTech would receive backlash from the weak and short-sighted politicians of Earth. But Ramsey was counting on his speech to force their collective hands into public support and funding of his project. Let their speechwriters find the words to unite

their people behind the noblest of causes: the preservation of the species. That was their job. Ramsey was the
prophet, the speaker of truth, the lighter of fires, the
bringer of knowledge.

It was the only way to save them.

The cosmic vista vanished unceremoniously as they
entered the outer ring and the elevator car's light flickered back to full brightness.

"I never get tired of that view," Ramsey said.

"Don't change the subject."

"Which subject?"

"You. Acting unilaterally. Not taking advice. Being
reckless. Causing panic. Destabilizing governments-"

Ramsey waved a hand. "Et cetera, et cetera."

Ty let out an exasperated sigh and folded his
arms again.

"Look, Ty, I know what I'm doing with this. I already
have my whole plan laid out for CIV. All we need is to
find five thousand people to repopulate the species when
we get to our target world."

"See, this is exactly what I'm talking about!" He began
to count on his fingers. "What the hell is CIV? How are
we going to pick these people? How are we going to get
them to this target world? Where did you get those
numbers from? Does anybody else know about this?"

The elevator came to a stop and began its automated
integrity and pressure balance checks. The doors would
open when those were complete.

"Do you really want those answers or are you being
rhetorical?"

"Well, I was being rhetorical, but sure, why not. Let's

hear it."

Ramsey shrugged. "CIV stands for Colonial Interstellar Vessel, which is what I've named the colony ship, the plans for which are nearly complete, by the way."

Ty's eyes went wide in disbelief.

Ramsey continued. "Whoever wants to live can apply, and if they pass genetic screening and have skills to help a new colony thrive, they will be considered. Our final selections will be run through an algorithm - I have a team that starts development on that next week - to ensure fair representation of all nations and people groups and the best overall genetic compatibility among the population. We'll get them to the target world in cryosleep-"

"Which doesn't exist," interrupted Ty. "Not how you're talking about it, at least."

Ramsey raised his eyebrows.

Ty looked back at him with suspicion. "You don't. You can't."

"Rolling out year after next. Q3, probably."

"Unbelievable."

"Believe it. My father was obsessed with cryo, and we're just working out some kinks now."

"Kinks?"

"Yeah, the chemical makes 25% of the apes we've been testing it on... erm..." he waved his hand idly, "die."

"Killing one in four users is a lot more than a kink!"

"Calm down. We've got time to perfect it."

"You're unbelievable."

Ramsey smiled even though he knew it wasn't meant as a compliment. "Thanks."

Status checks complete, the elevator doors rotated open. Ramsey stepped out and Ty chased after him.

They had entered a long, wide, open court. Hundreds of people speaking a smattering of prominent languages milled about in the nearly Earth-like gravity of the outer ring. Wonderful smells of cuisine from every part of the world wafted through the air. Word of Ramsey's announcement didn't seem to have reached here yet. Most of these people were about to be sent unceremoniously back to Earth. Looking up, a transparent canopy thirty feet or so above the floor revealed another sweeping panorama of space and of the more inward ring groups.

They crossed the courtyard, Ramsey attempting not to draw attention to himself. He loved the public eye, but cared little for the public.

They came to the much smaller elevators used for movement between floors of the outer ring. Ramsey's quarters were all the way out on the outermost floor, where windows in the floor provided views of space and the gravity was closest to that of Earth.

"Two questions to go," Ty sighed as they entered the more traditional elevator.

Ramsey pushed the last button on the panel. "I came up with the five thousand number by calculating how many people we would need to keep the surviving population genetically diverse and how big I think we can build CIV given our ten-year window. And, to answer your last question, no. No one knows much beyond their own projects. No one except for me, and now you."

"Why me?"

Ramsey shrugged. "No one else I trust." It wasn't exactly true, but it was true enough that he could say it convincingly.

The door opened to a white hallway. The curve of the station was gentler here, but the upward curving corridor still vanished after a few dozen feet in either direction. This was the scientific module of the station, where most of RamTech's space-based innovations were tested and studied.

Soon, that description would fit most of Troy Orbital.

Ramsey and Ty were quiet as they approached Ramsey's quarters. Ramsey swiped his right index finger backward across his right sideburn, just above his temple, brushing a strand of dark blonde hair out of his face and activating his neural lace in one motion. The small, subcutaneous transmitter broadcast his arrival and the white plastic door to his studio retracted into the wall.

"I still think you're being reckless," said Ty, following Ramsey into his quarters.

"That's ok."

"You're not perfect, you know. You can make mistakes."

"I'll be sure to mark the calendar when the day arrives." Ramsey loosened his tie and shed the sport coat.

The main living space of his quarters was not much more than ten feet deep by thirty wide. A kitchenette, trimmed in shades of black and white was immaculate, primarily due to lack of use. Meta-material couches were situated around a window in the floor of Troy's outer ring, offering live views of space in lieu of a more traditional area rug. Ramsey rolled his cuffs to his midforearm as he crossed to the kitchenette and pulled a bottle of 2189 Blanton's from the otherwise empty main cabinet. He poured two glasses and passed one to Ty, who took it without objection.

Ramsey invited Ty to join him around the transparent floor panel, and they sat down in the perfectly-conforming comfort of the couches. Ramsey draped his left arm along the top of the couch and crossed his ankle to rest on his knee.

"You're waiting to tell me something you don't think I'll like," said Ty. "The bourbon's a nice gesture, but I'm not touching it until you tell me what you really want me for."

Ramsey took a slow, drawn out sip, letting the aroma and the flavor of the Blanton's fill his senses. He savored the burn as he swallowed. "I work with some of the smartest people in the world, Ty. But, damn, if you aren't the smartest."

Ty failed to stifle a derisive laugh and placed the bourbon on an end table. "No, no, no. Don't waste your flattery. Out with it."

"I'm not flattering you," Ramsey stated.

Ty raised a thick, black eyebrow as he stared Ramsey down.

There was no backing down now. "We've known each other for a long time, Ty. All the way back to the Academy."

"Mmhmm."

"Ever since we graduated and temporarily went our separate ways, I've studied under the most accomplished physicists, mathematicians, and chemists in the world.

From sixteen years old I had an inside view on this organization my father built. He would buy entire companies just to capture their best and brightest minds and add them to his empire. Under my leadership, we've continued that policy. I can look you in the eye and say that there are less than a handful of people in the world who I wish worked for me who don't."

"Don't you think I know that?"

Ramsey took another savoring sip of bourbon. "Do you remember how soon after my father died I offered you a job?"

Ty shifted his weight on the bio-responsive couch. "It was pretty fast."

"He died on a Tuesday. I found out on Wednesday. I called to offer you a job on Thursday. They confirmed me as President and CEO on Friday. You didn't get back to me for over a week."

"Yeah, I was too busy comforting your family, Col." Ty's voice rose to a crescendo. "Your Dad wasn't even in the ground yet and you were already moving to make your mark. I loved him, too, you know. He was a hard man. Ruthless, but good."

Ramsey dismissed the criticism with a dispassionate wave of his glass. "That's not my point, Ty. My point is that you were the first person on my list, even then. Of all the brilliant people I've personally recruited in the last six years, you were the very first name on the list. I made you COO in addition to your scientific responsibilities when I realized how well your baffling choice of specialization prepared you to understand even our most complex systems." Ramsey uncrossed his legs and leaned forward on the couch. "And since that appointment there hasn't been a single day that I have had to worry about the efficiency or thoroughness of this organization's operations."

The tension eased out of Ty's shoulders. His mouth was still set, but the suspicion in his eyes had turned into quiet thoughtfulness. He looked down through the floor window as he rolled up the sleeves of his flannel shirt.

Ramsey eased back in his chair to mirror Ty's shifting posture. "And somehow, despite the near-flawlessness with which you've run the operations, it was still you who had the time and insight to develop the mathematics to model the entirety of the Earth system with an unprecedented level of interconnectivity and precision. If it weren't for that, Ty, we would still be oblivious to how bad things are about to get down there." He motioned to the Earth as it rotated into view again. "So, the point is I really mean it when I say you are the smartest person I've ever met. You're the only person I trust implicitly. You're my only peer."

Ty held up his hand. "You're laying it on a bit thick."

"I'm telling you the truth."

"Really? I don't like it. It's very disconcerting."

"I agree. It doesn't suit me."

Ty laughed. Mission accomplished. Ramsey managed a chuckle.

"You still haven't told me what this is about," said Ty, picking up his glass again. "Although, this is, without doubt, the nicest I've ever seen you, so I guess I should be afraid to ask."

Ramsey took a deep breath. "We have a plan for

almost everything we need to build the ship. The last big hurdle there is the Alcubierre drive, which will allow us to warp space-time and travel at superluminal speeds."

"Wait, wait, wait. Cryo was one thing, now you're telling me you're on the verge of unlocking faster-than-light travel?"

"Well, it's not strictly FTL. The principle is to warp space-time around you and, essentially, ride through it like a relativistically neutral surfboard riding a superluminal wave."

"I didn't think that was really possible. So, you're talking about, essentially, a warp drive?"

Ramsey gritted his teeth, "Yes, essentially, a warp drive. But that's not what it's called. It's called an Alcubierre drive, and I'm in the process of inventing two new kinds of math to make the original idea viable."

"Fine. So, what's the ask? You want me to help you build it? I fail to see how I'm qualified."

"You're not. There are, at most, three other people in the world who might be able to help with this project, and two of them are already on my team." Ramsey cleared his throat. "That is the last major hurdle standing between us and CIV being technologically viable. But there's one more piece of the puzzle that this mission is missing..." He let the suggestion hang.

Ty began to nod slowly. His eyes closed. "The target world."

"Indeed. I want you to lead the team to find it."

Ty chewed on his lower lip, rotating the glass around in his hand. "I hate to repeat myself, but I still fail to see how I'm qualified."

"Our evolution as a species is interwoven with the history of this particular planet. We learned in our attempts to colonize Mars last century that human beings do not thrive long-term in environments radically different from that of our home. We need to find not just any other habitable world, but as damn near to an Earth twin as we can to give the survivors of our species their best chance to thrive."

"Right... so what does that have to do with me?"

"You understand this planet better than anyone in history, Ty. For all the flak I've given you over the years, your understanding of the Earth's systems is almost instinctive. The odds of us finding an exact match are practically nil, so I need you to find and analyze our top candidates with the same level of detail and expertise with which you understand Earth."

Ty smirked. "It took me twelve years to realize that this planet was in trouble, and I could walk on its surface, breathe its air, drink its water, watch its weather patterns shift with my own eyes. How am I supposed to figure out the solution to a problem where I don't even know all the variables from dozens, or hundreds, of light-years away?"

"I've already assembled the team. Experts in spectrography and orbital dynamics, physicists, xenobiologists, et cetera. They'll get you all the data they can. But you're the only one I trust to analyze it and make the decision."

Ty ran his fingers through his short, black hair. "Holy shit."

"I need you, Ty." Ramsey filled his voice with all the sincerity he could muster. "I need you to find Ithaca."

"Ithaca?"

"That's what we're going to call it. The adoptive home of the human race."

"So that makes you, what? Odysseus?"

Ramsey shrugged. "In a manner of speaking."

"Didn't everyone else in *The Odyssey* die?"

"That's not the point."

"Doesn't send a great message, though, does it?"

"People don't read, Ty. Most people these days have no idea what *The Odyssey* is about. We're going on an epic journey across a vast ocean, the victorious survivors. That was all Odysseus wanted -- to get home to Ithaca. But, I suppose, unlike that mythological 'man of twists and turns,' we will lead our people safely home." He stared into Ty's eyes. "If you help me."

Ty sighed and looked away, fidgeting with his watch absentmindedly. He chewed on his lip again, his eyes darting back and forth, searching for the now surely inevitable answer.

Ramsey brushed the edge of his glass with his thumb, his gaze resting on the viscous amber liquor inside of it. He willed the answer to come.

Finally, Ty sighed. "One condition."

Ramsey tried to conceal his anticipation. "Name it."

"Clara and Izzy. Give me your word that they'll be on CIV. That they'll go to Ithaca."

Ramsey smiled and stood, raising his glass. Ty followed suit. "To Ithaca, the future home of the human race. To Dr. Daniels, who will find it. And to his family, the first to be chosen for our great Odyssey across the stars."

"To Ithaca."

2

REACTION

I n the darkness of Ramsey's reawakening mind, an invisible chorus of angels sang a terrible and beautiful melody. Though the words were in no human language Ramsey could identify, he was sure they sang of the beauty of Ithaca, her flowing rivers, grassy plains, and shaded woods.

What else could it be?

In this nowhere place between cryosleep and the waking world, he wasn't sure if he had a body; he could neither move nor speak.

The angel song twisted, and the sound became red. Even in this not-yet conscious state, Ramsey knew that that perception didn't make sense. Nevertheless, the red song continued, like a dawn beginning to break, though there was neither sun, nor landscape for sun to shine upon, nor eyes with which to see it.

A bolt of lightning seared through his emerging

senses. The red grew blacker as the angel song grew more dissonant and sinister.

Ramsey hurt.

The chorus grew louder, more ferocious. White hot irons pierced the body he didn't have in that place that was nowhere.

The structure of the angel song faded and disintegrated until it was no longer a heavenly chorus, but a hellish cacophony.

The black-red burned hotter, until it was like staring into the sun, but Ramsey had no eyes to close against the agonizing brightness.

And then, it stopped. And Ramsey had a body.

It hurt everywhere. The last screeches of his awakening echoed in his ears and the inside of his eyelids danced with blue and yellow dots.

He blinked his eyes open. He was in a vaguely blue, dimly lit cryo tube, propped up almost-vertically, and about as roomy as a coffin. Through the transparent strip of glass in front of his face, a man of about Ramsey's age with pale skin and a thick, blonde beard stared at him. "Are you alright? You seem to be experiencing some discomfort."

Ramsey massaged the pulsating migraine behind his temples. "Just let me out."

A moment later the door to the cryo chamber opened, two halves rotating back against the sides of the vertical chamber. Ramsey buried his face in the crook of his elbow, the flooding light shooting up his optic nerve and exacerbating the fire in his brain. Through squinting eyelids he stepped out into the crew cryo module.

"Before you go, I have tests I need to perform to ensure that the Somnithaw has been flushed from your system," said the man. "It's just standard procedure."

"Not for me, it isn't." Ramsey squinted as he made his way to the door across the undulating floor.

"Apologies, sir, but you can't even walk straight. I think you should let me conduct the test."

Ramsey managed to summon the name, but did not turn to face the man. "Listen, Tyler. I'm not going to do that. Do not ask me again." He found the door and exited into the hallway, the silence that followed carried Tyler's implicit acceptance of Ramsey's terms.

That was good.

He needed space to think without an inferior trying to analyze him.

Whatever had happened, he would deal with it on his own.

Only five hundred years to go, after all.

Everything would be fine... as long as whatever-this-was didn't get any worse.

3

TECHNICIANS

9 MARCH 2205 CE - 9 YEARS BEFORE DEPARTURE

Ramsey was going to kill Ty. There was no way he was actually this stupid. There was no way he actually thought this recommendation was the best option. There was no way he thought this would be possible.

Ty had given up. Already. That was the only reasonable explanation. It was unacceptable. Ramsey fumed with hot fury as he approached Ty's quarters. He pounded his fists on the hard, white, metaplastic door. The overhead light flickered with each strike of his hand. Ramsey paced, muttering curses under his breath. He stopped and smacked his palm against the door in a rapid staccato, and almost fell through the doorway when it opened.

Ramsey drew breath to begin laying into Ty when he realized that it was not his Dr. Daniels, but Ty's wife, Dr. Clara Daniels, wide-eyed, bath-robed, and tousle-haired standing before him. He lowered the accusatory finger he didn't remember raising and fumbled for the proper response.

Clara spoke first, her usually mild French accent slightly more pronounced in her disheveled state. "Colin? What in the world are you doing? It is not yet four in the morning!" The disgust in her voice mirrored the indignation and incredulity in her eyes.

He had forgotten to check the time. "Er... yes. Sorry to bother you so early, Clara, but I needed to discuss something with Ty."

She stared at him, her mouth hanging open in disbelief. "It's 3:54 in the morning! On a Saturday!"

Ramsey had quit clocks when he moved to space. Day and night were arbitrary there, anyway. He trusted his internal clock over mechanical ones. He slept when he was tired, ate when he was hungry, and worked until his eyes went blurry. "I... didn't realize." He stood his ground.

Clara sighed in acquiescence. "Well, come in." She stepped to the side and gestured to the living room.

"Thank you." Ramsey stepped in before she could change her mind.

"Ty is trying to get Izzy back to sleep," said Clara, throwing a sidelong glance of accusation at Ramsey as the door slid shut behind her. "I'll get him."

Ramsey nodded as Clara disappeared into the hallway.

The Daniels' quarters were laid out in a mirror image to Ramsey's. The standard issue furniture and appliances were identical to his, but the homely charm that had been applied to the otherwise sterile environment made it clear that a family, not a bachelor, lived here.

Not that Ramsey minded being a bachelor. In fact, he was decidedly in favor of remaining one forever. He had gone on a few dates every now and then with brilliant and beautiful women, whom he liked well enough. But someone else had always set him up, and he had never been willing to call on anyone a second time. It bored him. His heart belonged elsewhere.

His focus and work ethic had earned him his current position as CEO of his father's company. Some people - jealous people, mostly - accused him of only having achieved success because all of his accomplishments were handed to him. Such was the curse of inheriting a family business. But even at thirty-one years old, Ramsey had proven to himself and to all but the worst of the naysayers that his genius, his vision, his wisdom, and his ambition were his own.

He was going to do it. His confidence increased day by day. CIV would be built. On time. Under budget. Above spec.

Unfortunately, yes, certain nations had destabilized in the aftermath of his announcement. But this was a time in history for the weak to crumble and the strong to show their strength. That meant change, and upheaval for those who lacked the ability to endure it. But such things were natural, and, ultimately, only a minor setback on his path toward immortality.

Yes, immortality. Because that, in truth, was what he was accomplishing. There are those few names nearly everyone knows. Adolf Hitler, Jesus of Nazareth, Julius

Caesar. These rare few men were the only humans who had ever achieved the closest thing to immortality: preservation in history. Preservation that endured beyond their own contemporary context.

And before too long, the first name on anyone's list of key figures in history would be Dr. Colin Ramsey, the man who saved the human race and brought them to their new home world. And in the far future of humanity, when the last memories of the Alexander the Greats and Aristotles and Prophet Mohammeds of Earth faded away, the name of Ramsey would still be sung, remembered, and honored as the one who brought salvation to the human race.

At least, that was what he had thought before Ty's recommendation for a target world had come across his desk.

"What's this about, Colin?" Ty said as he entered the room. The irritation radiated off of him.

Ramsey, suddenly aware of the fact that he had been staring at a dirty pan in the sink while dreaming of his immortalization, turned to face his friend.

It had barely been three months since the announcement, but Ty looked like he had aged years. He had gained a noticeable amount of weight: his long-ago trim physique had previously been replaced over the years with a slightly pudgier version, and that version had now been replaced by a downright husky, unshaven, swollen-eyed man.

"You look awful." Ramsey couldn't keep the hint of disgust from his voice.

"Well, if you wanted to see me at my best, this was not

the time of day to come. Because we human beings are generally, you know, asleep at this hour."

"Clara already said that, and I'm in no mood to be lectured."

Ty crossed his arms. "And I was in no mood to be woken up in the middle of the night."

"Well, you should have thought of that sooner."

Ty raised an incredulous eyebrow. "What the hell are you talking about? How is this my fault?"

"Oh please," Ramsey spat. "You know exactly what I'm talking about."

"Well, I'm assuming it has something to do with the target planet I identified, but-"

"Oh, it's coming to you now, is it?" Ramsey scoffed.

"It's an Earth twin, Colin!" Ty shouted, "Our very first conversation about this you said, 'We need to find as damn near an Earth twin as we can,' and I found it in half the time you gave me for the project. So what's the problem?"

Ramsey found himself breathing hard. He looked away from Ty and stalked through the room, running his hands through his hair. "It's twelve thousand light years away, Ty. Twelve. Thousand. Light years."

"Okay, so it's a little farther away than you were hoping for. So what? We're going to have FTL travel."

"Right, but it's not teleportation. We still have to physically cross the distance."

"I know that."

"It's going to take four hundred years, minimum, to get there at the maximum theoretical output of the Alcubierre drive. More realistically, five or six hundred."

"Right, but it will all feel the same in cryo, won't it?"

Ramsey spun back toward Ty, making every effort to keep his voice level. "Yes, Ty, but not everyone is going to be in cryo."

Ty's eyebrows narrowed. "What do you mean?"

Ramsey chewed on his tongue, then motioned to the couches. "Sit." He rounded the couch and sat himself down. Ty sat on the other a moment later. "When CIV is finished," Ramsey began, "it will be the most advanced piece of technology our planet has ever produced. The math for the Alcubierre drive alone is decades, if not centuries ahead of its time. I barely understand it and I invented it. Add the layers of complexity of radiation shielding, cryogenics, and a rotational axis to keep the simulated gravity going, and it's just not a system you can set and forget for a week, let alone four years, or," he paused and scoffed, "five hundred years."

Ty nodded his dawning understanding. "So what are you going to do?"

"I *was* going to stay awake and monitor the systems. That's why I specifically requested a planetary system as close to Earth as possible. Two hundred, even three hundred, light years would have been acceptable. That's something like ten years on the Alcubierre for someone who's awake. As a society, we are used to building things that can last that long. Even a little longer if needed. We don't even know if it's possible to build a ship that can last for centuries under ambient space radiation and hard vacuum, especially inside the Alcubierre field."

Ty nodded again, chewing on his lip, eyes flitting back and forth through empty space, searching for ideas.

"You need to pick something closer. Much closer."

"I can tell you right now, there is nothing even remotely Earth-like within the radius you're suggesting."

"Well, I'm not immortal, Ty. I can't take care of the ship for five hundred years by myself."

"I'm telling you, there's nothing Earth-like anywhere near to us. This planet is a needle in a haystack. We were lucky to find one as close as this one."

Ramsey scoffed. "Twelve thousand light years is our standard for close now?"

Ty raised his voice defensively, "On the scale of our galaxy, yeah. I'm pretty damn proud of finding one as accessible as this."

"What about the one in the direction of Cygnus? That was a top candidate just last month."

Ty searched his memory, nodding. "That one used to be marginally habitable by human standards. Maybe as recently as thirty thousand years ago. But there's no longer any spectrographic evidence of ongoing photosynthesis. Plus, the magnetic field was too weak."

"And the one in Draco?"

"The days are almost as long as an Earth year, so you'd have six months of constant darkness and temperatures that'll freeze the blood in your veins. Photosynthesis seems to be happening, but how anything could survive there is beyond me."

"How about-"

"Look, Colin. You asked me to find an Earth twin. I found it, closer than was statistically likely. You're asking me to work a miracle far beyond the scope of even your greatest achievements. The one I recommended is our only shot."

Ramsey nodded his acquiescence. "Well, shit. The specs for construction just got a lot stricter. And what I said still stands. We need to figure out how to take care of the ship over half a millennium. She's going to have a lot of wear and tear."

"What are you thinking? Bots?"

Ramsey shook his head. "No, because who is going to maintain them? We've come a long way with AI, but there's still something distinctive about human intelligence that we haven't been able to master yet, even after all this time."

"So, people then?"

"People need to eat. Five or ten years of rations for one person is one thing, but five hundred years of rations is a whole other question. And," he shook his head, "how many people would we need? Even if we had only one person awake at a time for fifty years-"

"They would literally go insane from the isolation."

"Okay, two people at a time," said Ramsey.

"You'll probably want more than that. This is fifty years we're talking about."

"Then make a suggestion, Ty," Ramsey snapped.

"Four people at a time would work better. Every twelve and a half years you'd swap one out for the next guy in line so there would at least be some variety. That would be a better social dynamic."

"Interesting. So, over five hundred years that would be," he did the math in his head, "forty-three people, if you account for partial shifts at the beginning and end. That's way too many. We only have room for five thousand people!"

"And it's actually eighty-six people."

"What? How do you figure?"

"You're going to ask these people - young people, obviously, if they're going to be out of cryo for fifty years - to give up their entire lives to work on this ship. The least you can do is let each of them bring a loved one who gets to stay in cryo."

"Absolutely not. Each and every Ithacan is going to be carefully screened for any disqualifying genetic factors. I can't let these people pollute the population of Ithaca by throwing caution to the wind and allowing just anyone to survive."

Ty crossed his arms. "Pollute the population? Allow them to survive? When did this become about allowing people to survive? I thought we were trying to save the human race?"

"Oh, don't be so naive. We need the very best of Earth to become our Ithacans. We're forcing ourselves into an evolutionary bottleneck. We need diversity. We need quality. We need strength. Nothing can compromise that vision."

"You're talking about eugenics..."

"You can hardly call it eugenics. There's no particular trait I'm selecting for or against. I've been very explicit in my desire for a diverse and representative sample of our planet to go to Ithaca. This is a decision born out of necessity. People can apply for these positions, but I will only accept candidates who pass a minimum level of genetic screening."

Ty held up his hands. "I want absolutely nothing to do with that selection process."

"What am I supposed to do, Ty? Pick the nicest people? The most attractive? Of all the things I could be selecting for, health, strength, and intelligence seem both innocuous and necessary."

"As long as you admit you're selecting for something."

"I'm selecting for survival."

"Fine."

"Fine."

A silence hung over them. The gentle rattle of the life support system kicked on as the uncomfortable moment stretched.

"There's another problem," said Ramsey while Ty was in mid-yawn.

Ty stretched his arms over his head, red pajama shirt rising to reveal the bottom of his rounded stomach as he finished his yawn. "What is it?"

"The systems are going to be too complicated. I won't be able to find forty-three people in the world who can understand the math, let alone that many men in their twenties."

"Or women."

Ramsey shook his head. "No, just men. If you put men and women together, they'll make babies. It's inevitable. That's a risk we just can't take while we're still on the journey. Once we get to Ithaca, we'll need to multiply like rabbits, but on the ship it would be a disaster. Besides, an old man can still make a baby and contribute to our society. An old woman cannot."

"Good luck selling that one to the media."

"If you think I care what they say, you haven't been paying attention."

"No, I'm painfully aware of your stance on the media."

"We're not having this conversation again, Ty."

"It matters, though, Colin. You can't succeed without overwhelming public and private support, especially now that the ship will need to last longer than originally intended."

"That's not my fault, and stop changing the subject. The way I see it, there's really only one thing we can do about the complexity of the systems."

"What's that?"

"You and I will have to take turns waking up, one week per year, to check on the more complicated systems. The ones the technicians won't be smart enough to handle."

Ty sighed. "Colin, how do you expect me to be of any help to you? I barely know anything about the kind of physics you're working with."

"Physics is just applied math, and you are, without doubt, one of the top mathematicians of our generation. Even if you've hidden it behind a veil of planetary dynamics."

"And what about my family? I'm not going to see them for, what..." He paused to do the calculation. "One week every year for five hundred years is five hundred weeks, so about ten years. Five for each of us. I don't know if I can just not see my family for five years."

"Well, if you're sure this planet is our only option, then you don't really have a choice, do you?" The words came out more caustically than he had intended.

"I could say no."

Ramsey looked Ty in the eye, calling his half-hearted bluff. "But you won't, because you're a good man, and I need your help. It's the only way to save Clara and Izzy."

Ty nodded his acquiescence "I'll age five years and they'll stay the same in cryo. That's going to take some time to wrap my head around."

Ramsey scoffed. "This coming from the man who just asked for forty-some technicians to each bring a loved one. They'll age fifty years while their family sleeps. Five years is nothing compared to that."

Ty bit his lip. "Good point. I hadn't thought of it that way."

Clara returned, little Izzy in her arms. Ty stood and lumbered toward them.

"She wouldn't go back to sleep," said Clara, handing the three-year-old to her husband. "She wants you to put her down."

Ty squeezed his little girl tight, and rocked her back and forth, her head on his shoulder. "You ready to go back to bed, sweetheart?"

"Daddy, why is Mr. Coddin here?" She didn't quite have mastery of her 'L's yet.

"Hi, Izzy," said Ramsey, rising from the couch. "I, uh. I'm sorry I woke you up."

Her head perked up off of Ty's shoulder. "That was you? Mommy, Mr. Coddin is the crady person you were talking about! The one who was bane-in on the door!"

Clara opened her mouth to speak, but Ramsey spared her. "It sure was," he said. "I needed to talk to your dad about something very, very important."

"Is Daddy really helping you save the whole world?"

Ramsey glanced at Clara, who avoided eye contact, then to Ty, whose lip curled up in the hint of a smile. "We are all helping to save the world, Izzy. Everyone who lives on Troy Orbital is helping in some way."

"Even me?"

Ramsey couldn't help but smile. "Especially you."

"Wow." She rested her head back on Ty's shoulder, curly brown-blond locks blocking her father's face from view.

"Your dad has a very special job. I'm going to need his help more than anyone else, and it's going to take a long time to finish building the space ship. There might be some really hard times ahead, but with your Dad's help, I know we'll be able to keep you safe. Is that ok if I borrow him a lot?"

She thought about it, then smiled and nodded on Ty's shoulder.

"Thanks, Isabella."

"You ready for bed, Iz?" Ty asked.

"Okay, Daddy."

"Say goodnight."

"Goodnight, Mr. Coddin."

"Goodnight, Izzy," said Ramsey.

Ty kissed Clara on the way towards the bedroom, a droopy-eyed toddler already drifting to sleep on his shoulder.

No sooner had Ty closed the door behind them that

Clara turned on Ramsey. "What do you want from him now?"

"I'm sorry?"

"You never say nice things unless you want something. What have you asked of him?"

"Nothing I haven't asked of myself."

Her words were venomous. "He has a family. You do not."

Ramsey rounded the couch to face her properly. "Look, Clara. We're trying to achieve the impossible. We're trying to advance our technology by fifty or a hundred years over the course of a decade. And more importantly, we're trying to preserve our species. There are going to be a lot of sacrifices, not least by those of us who've found themselves, as Ty and I have, on the front lines of this battle for survival."

She crossed her arms.

"What I am about to tell you is strictly confidential. I know I can trust you."

Her body language seemed unaffected by his promise of confidence.

Ramsey continued. "The closest viable world for our new home is much, much farther away than I had hoped it would be. It's going to take something like five hundred years to get there. It won't have any effect on people like you and Izzy, who will be in cryo, but Ty and I will have to alternate waking up for one week each year to ensure that the ship is running smoothly." He paused, still unable to read any emotions on Clara's usually expressive face. "Each of us will age approximately five years over the course of the journey, relative to the sleepers."

Clara closed her eyes. Her words were icy. "How much will you take from this family before you are satisfied?"

Ramsey cocked his head in confusion. "I really don't know what you mean."

"You're going to work him to death. Leave me without my husband. Leave Izzy without her father. It's already started. We've barely seen him for three months. Izzy will be a teenager by the time we leave for Ithaca, and she'll barely know her father. And then you're going to keep him away from her for five more years?" She shook her head, her mouth open in disgust. "You're despicable."

Ramsey took one step toward her. "Everything I ask of him is necessary," he said through gritted teeth.

"Maybe," she said, her tone cooler than before, "But the ends don't always justify the means."

"When we're talking about the survival of the species, they do. I will do whatever I need to, even if you don't like it."

"We're talking about the love of my life. Your best friend."

"Clara, believe me, I take absolutely no joy in the sacrifices that need to be made. I was hoping to leave Ty out of this, but the planet he identified is so far away, I had no choice but to recruit him, and he agreed."

Ty returned. The room fell into an awkward silence.

"I should be going," said Ramsey. "There's a lot to do today. I have to redesign parts of the ship so the technicians can grow their own food supply. Ty, if you can give me, by noon, a list of the top experts to help with something like that, I would appreciate it."

"It's Saturday," said Clara.

Ramsey ignored her, looked Ty in the eye. "The report, by noon."

Ty hesitated. He glanced at Clara. Then he nodded.

Ramsey turned and marched out of their quarters.

He had a world to save.

4

SICK

S omething was wrong. Worse than before.

Ramsey's stomach lurched as his body came back under his control. He scrunched his eyes closed, gritting his teeth against his writhing intestines. His head dropped to his chest and his arms rotated at the elbows to push against the sides of the tube as he struggled to catch his breath.

A guttural moan snuck from his lips as the door of the tube opened with a hiss, each of the two sides rotating into place outside the tube opening.

Ramsey's head spun with the rush of fresh air as he staggered out of the tube, discovered his leg would not support him, and collapsed at the feet of technician, smacking his head against the floor.

He retched, and his empty stomach had nothing to give but stomach acid and bile. The room went dark around the edges as the technician cursed, and a moment later Ramsey vanished into oblivion.

———

FOUR FACES PEERED DOWN AT RAMSEY AS THE WORLD CAME back into focus. His heavy eyelids pushed themselves back down over his throbbing eyes, but he forced them open again.

"He's coming to. Let him breathe, lads."

Ramsey turned his head to focus on the speaker. An older man, in his late fifties, perhaps, wearing a navy blue jumpsuit. Ramsey's thoughts were trudging through mud trying to form something coherent. Jack. Jim. No, but something with a J. John? John. Definitely John. That was the older man's name. Why was he here?

Where was here?

The other men backed off, hovering nearby as John shooed them away. Technicians. They were his technicians.

His mental acuity began to return.

This was CIV.

They were going to Ithaca.

It had become evident after Ramsey's first few week-years that he was allergic to the Somnithaw. Each week in sequence had been worse than the last, but he wasn't sure if that was objective truth or hyperbole brought on by the misery of his experience.

His cheeks burned as he realized he had... purged... all over Kemal.

"Are you alright, Dr. Ramsey?" asked John.

"Wer..." tried Ramsey. A wave of nausea met him as he opened his mouth.

"I'm sorry?"

He clenched his stomach. "Wah. Ter."

"Oh, of course. Right away." John turned to the youngest technician. "Zeke, get Dr. Ramsey some water."

Zeke waved a dismissive hand, "Yeah, I'm going, I'm going," and hustled out of the room.

After nearly a century of hiding this from the technicians, there was no avoiding it now. They knew he was sick.

And, he supposed, he had to admit it himself now, too.

The room was small. Overhead, two parallel lines of small, bright lights shone out of the grey and white metaplastic ceiling. The medical bay.

His left eye twitched with the effort of staying open, so he let his lids close.

"Does he sleep again?" asked Kemal.

"I think so," said John.

"We should have woken a doctor. He is not well," said Kemal.

Ramsey knew he didn't want that. He had already disabled the bio reader command tree on his cryo pod to prevent the automatic monitoring from flagging him for more detailed followup.

"No, they were very clear. Emergencies only. And he's not dying," said John.

"No, not yet," said Kemal.

John grunted to concede the point.

"The hell is wrong with him anyway?" asked a man with an Eastern European accent. Miroslav. "Why he scream? Why he sick?"

"He's allergic to the Somnithaw, I imagine," said John.

"Pity him, lads. If he's been building up to this the whole time, he's only going to get worse, and there's still more than four hundred years to Ithaca."

"It ees hard to pity him. Cruel, arrogant man," said Miroslav, a snarl in his voice.

"Enough, Mir," said Kemal. "You live, and your nephew sleeps in cryo because of him. We owe him respect."

"The people of my country know not to worship dictators, and he is as bad as any we have endured."

"We do not have countries anymore. We have only us."

Miroslav grunted his derision. "I will always have my country."

Kemal drew breath to respond, but Zeke's return interrupted the men. "I miss anything good?"

"He's resting," said John. "We think he's allergic to the Somnithaw." The dull thud at Ramsey's bedside table told him that the water had been placed on it.

"Oh, the stuff for waking ya up from cryo? That ain't good. What's the treatment?" asked Zeke.

"There isn't any. Guess he never thought he might be allergic to his own creation."

"Oh, man," said Zeke, sounding more excited than concerned, "he is so screwed."

Ramsey cleared his throat and rolled over for his water. He didn't need to hear this.

Zeke's wide eyes registered his surprise. John dutifully helped Ramsey tip the water back.

"Thank you. For the water," Ramsey managed. He decided to pretend he had dozed off and not heard any of the conversation. "I seem to have had an allergic... reaction." He clutched his chest, trying to catch his breath again.

"To the Somnithaw, aye," said John, "Why didn't you warn us?"

"None of your business, technician."

"Well, whatcha gonna do?" John persisted. "You're lookin' at a miserable half-millennium as it stands now."

"Don't you think I've realized that already?" Ramsey snapped, "I'll deal with it. There's nothing else to be done." He ended the line of inquiry with a glare.

John sighed. "Suit yourself, then. Well, dinner's cooking. Green beans are our best crop this year." He addressed his colleagues, "Let's leave him alone for a bit." The four men filed out, whispering and looking over their shoulders at Ramsey. Kemal closed the door and left Ramsey alone in his quarters.

Ramsey tried to sit up, but the room spun again. He cursed himself and lay back down. John was right. He did have a problem. He thrashed around in his bed, unleashing his anger. A moment later, exhausted, he fell asleep.

———

En Route to Ithaca – Year 113 of 504

THE PULSING IN RAMSEY'S HEAD AWOKE HIM. HE WAS IN HIS quarters on CIV, he was pretty sure. But the room swam with floating lights that persisted whether his eyes were open or shut. The ground swayed back and forth like an ocean liner. And the snake that felt like it must be living in his gut writhed and wiggled its nauseating dance through his intestines.

Still, he had enough wits about him to recognize his own room in the middle of the night. He forced his eyes to focus on the clock mounted in the ceiling above him in his bunk. June 7, year 113.

Every week started with June 6. It was the day the ship had departed over two years ago. Ramsey mentally shook his head to adjust his frame of reference. One hundred and thirteen weeks, the equivalent of about two years and two months, was all that had passed for him in his intermittent waking days. But a hundred and thirteen years had passed for the outside world, for the technicians.

Ramsey blinked. The clock must have broken, because it said it was already 0906. He considered whether he might be looking at it upside down and it actually said 9060. That made even less sense. His eyes ached as he struggled to comprehend what he was seeing. It couldn't be after nine already. He was sure it couldn't be anything later than 0300. This was wrong.

Another intestinal spasm provided the needed nudge to move him from his bunk.

His quarters on the ship were not much larger than a decent sized walk-in closet. And as all the quarters on the ship were individual, there were no doors to separate the wash room from the sleeping area.

He crawled and winced his way to the lavatory. His empty digestive system attempted to rid itself of its nonexistent contents.

Thirty seconds later, he sat on the meta-material floor. He leaned back against the wall. His breath was ragged and the echo of his retching still echoed in his ears. He shut his eyes as his head swam with half-formed thoughts of anger and regret.

Was this his punishment for...

No. That implied there was some transcendent force doling out positive and negative outcomes based on the balance of good and evil in one's life. Karmic retribution. Such an idea was so excruciatingly unscientific it wasn't worth considering.

But, even if there were such a force or being, the balance would be unassailably tipped in Ramsey's favor. He had saved five thousand people from a slow and certain death, after all. The only survivors of a dead and dying world. He was the savior of the human race.

If there were such a thing as a god, and if said being were doling out misfortune and suffering on Ramsey's head, that being would be no friend of humanity. To threaten Ramsey was to threaten the success of the Ithaca mission. And to threaten the Ithaca mission was to threaten the human species.

If there were such a thing as God, Ramsey reasoned, its only viable complaint against him could be one of jealousy.

Voices in the hallway recalled him to his present suffering. His eyes flitted open as a series of shadows passed across the tiny illuminated gaps around his door. He wondered what the techs were doing awake at...

His memory failed him. It had been early, though.

Before 0300. He groaned and crawled back toward his bed where he could catch a glimpse of the clock.

0910.

He recognized the numbers but didn't understand them.

And then he understood them.

He was more than an hour behind his carefully controlled schedule that minimized the amount of time he had to spend outside of cryo. He had realized early on that for every hour he could cut out of his awake time each week, he would remove three weeks of total time from his experience of the journey. He had subsequently trimmed down his waking time by sixteen hours per week-year, which left little margin for error in his schedule, but had curtailed his total projected waking time down to less than nine years.

0911.

Ramsey pulled himself to his feet. The room rocked beneath him, and he collapsed back onto the bed, cursing himself. He pulled himself instead toward the shower, where he ordered up another round of heavy detox cleansers and potent stims to rebalance his system. He needed the shower more than he needed the time.

Twelve minutes later, he was at his console on Deck E, running a diagnostic on the Ramsey-Alcubierre Drive. His legs were strong beneath him, his mind sharp and focused.

———

THE MORNING PASSED IN A MOMENT, A COMBINATION OF THE

higher-than-usual volume of work and the condensed timeframe for completing it. Ramsey's hunger from his skipped breakfast, amplified by the empty stomach he had entered cryo with the year before and his body's efforts to eradicate even the memory of food from his system, drove him to the common room for an early lunch.

Kemal was there already, standing by the counter eating his bowl of gruel. His once-black beard was now mostly white, and, from his erect posture, Ramsey suspected that his back was acting up again. Dom, the most recent addition to the crew, chatted with someone Ramsey did not recognize. He wondered if this was one of CIV's medical officers. For the next three hundred and ninety-one years, doctors were his enemies.

Dom was explaining something to the doctor. "It just doesn't make sense, Judah. We didn't evolve to live like that. Besides, changing the length of our days will–"

"Mess up our calendar and desynchronize us from Earth, I know, I know. You keep saying that. But we're traveling at relativistic speeds, so time doesn't pass for us the same as Earth. Just think of everything we could get done with four extra hours every day!" said Judah, whom Ramsey had already decided was too stupid to be a doctor. It was year one-thirteen, which, Ramsey realized, meant that Judah was, in fact, the new junior technician, and Miroslav, the miserable complainer, had finally been put back in storage where he belonged. Good riddance.

"Obviously we would get more done each day," said Dom, running his fingers through his curly Mediterranean hair, "but we would also have the same amount of work to get done in the same amount of time. That can only mean longer shifts, more mistakes, and a slow, spiraling descent into insanity. Besides, we aren't traveling at relativistic speeds. We're riding a space-time wave with relativistically neutral local space... What's that look for? It's in the ship's specs. Just because you don't read doesn't mean I can't. Anyway, I'd rather stay synced with Earth."

"Why?" Kemal spoke for the first time. He sounded older than ever.

"Earth is our home," said Dom.

"Earth used to be our home," said Kemal, "It's an empty rock now. I know it's easy to forget, out here in the black, but everyone you ever knew is probably dead by now. Our home is Ithaca. We should count ourselves lucky to get to see it."

"See, even Kemal is with me, Dom!"

"I am not with you," said Kemal. "Request denied."

"Wait, but you said Dom was wrong!"

"I said Ithaca is our home now, so we shouldn't worry about how things used to be on Earth."

"Right, so you do agree with me then."

"No, because Dom's point remains about the concerns for safety and the danger of longer shifts."

"And," came Dom's smug interjection, "we just didn't evolve for that."

"Look," protested Judah, "I did some research into this back on Earth before we left. A twenty-eight hour day is totally feasible if you lived in an environment where you could control the circadian rhythm. A place like," Judah turned up the sarcasm, "I don't know, a spaceship."

Ramsey had heard enough. He crossed to the dispensary that provided the thick, flavorless, texture-less, gray goo that met all essential dietary needs. The team that invented the stuff had named it Multi-Essential Dietary Balance Control Supplement, or MEDiBaCS.

The technicians had named it gruel.

Gruel had stuck.

"Request denied." Kemal's voice commanded authority, his booming baritone matching his barrel-chested build. With Miroslav back in cryo, Kemal was Senior Technician now. He would do well, provided this new idiot was teachable enough. It also meant he would be able to give his back some better rest as he transitioned to a less physically demanding role on the team.

Judah whined, "But, Kemal, be reasonable. What, just because I'm young you don't think I can get any good ideas?" This did little to assuage Ramsey's assessment of his intelligence.

"This has nothing to do with your age, son," said Kemal. "I have considered your arguments and Dom's rebuttals, as well as a few reservations of my own. My decision is to deny your request. I don't want to hear you ask about this again."

"Thank you," said Dom, throwing his hands wide in appreciation.

Judah mumbled something under his breath and returned to his gruel. Kemal sipped at his tea, his tranquil exterior returning.

Ramsey sat at the far end of the bench, away from the technicians. Kemal and Dom exchanged brief, forced pleasantries with Ramsey while Judah continued to sulk.

Ramsey understood the emotional distance between himself and the technicians. To them, he was the unchanging, nearly immortal supervisor who appeared for a week every year to inconvenience their routine, stretch their resources a little thinner than usual, and point out all of the things they weren't doing well enough. They were smart, though. Some more than others. They were efficient and professional. Part of the screening process for this role was to test for patience and persever-ance, especially in the face of the boredom and mild sensory deprivation they would experience over their half-century of work. But even without the layer of diffi-culty his relative immortality added to their relationship, they were not exactly the sort of person Ramsey was accustomed to associating with. They were some of the best men the Earth had to offer, but they weren't quite to the level of the celebrities and geniuses Ramsey had rubbed elbows with back on Earth.

Earth. Ramsey may have only aged two years thanks to cryo, but everyone alive on Earth – if there was anyone left at all – was a child of the post-RamTech world. A whole century of history in the books, and quite probably the final chapter of the story of that broken planet.

Fortunately, he would be able to write the sequel.

Ramsey refocused his attention on the present and took a bite of gruel as Dom quizzed Judah on the rota-tional coefficients of CIVs ringed structure.

Zeke entered, his bespectacled face intent on the tablet he held in front of him. His bald head bore no resemblance to the thick auburn locks he had started with when he came out of cryo. He looked up just long enough to say a generic hello to no one in particular and grab a bowl of gruel before his attention returned to the tablet. He sat without a word between Ramsey and the other techs at the table.

A small smirk crept onto Ramsey's face. It had been a while since he had really noticed Zeke. He didn't often share a meal schedule with the technicians, and Zeke, as Second Technician - now First Technician with the awakening of Judah - had been very busy with the actual work of maintaining the ship. Even so, based on the motion of the new First Tech's eyes, he appeared to be... reading. Reading intently. Reading so intently, in fact, that his usual overwhelming deluge of meaningless chatter had been silenced.

"What are you reading?" Ramsey asked, trying to keep the skepticism from his voice.

Zeke didn't answer. His eyes continued to dart across the page, lips moving subtly as his eyes tracked the words on each line. Zeke paused, an impressed expression curling his lips into a respectful smile and nod.

"What are you reading?" Ramsey asked again, a little louder.

Dom reached over and tapped Zeke on the shoulder.

Zeke started at the unexpected touch. He seemed surprised to see another human in the room. Dom just pointed at Ramsey and shuffled back to his seat before scooping another tasteless spoonful to his mouth.

Zeke's face flashed with momentary surprise at the sight of Ramsey before something seemed to click in his brain. He smiled genuinely and said, "Sorry, were you talking to me?"

Ramsey breathed a skeptical laugh through his nose. "What book are you reading?"

"Oh, it's *The Republic*."

Ramsey couldn't stop his eyebrow from raising in amused incredulity. "Plato?"

Zeke nodded enthusiastically. "Yeah, I'm partial to the Roman philosophers, to be honest, but so much of their work depends on the philosophical foundation the Greeks laid, I couldn't just keep ignoring Plato forever. Have you read it?"

This had to be a joke. Classic Zeke, trying to pull a fast one over Ramsey. He didn't take well to imbeciles feigning intelligence. "I have. Have you learned anything useful from it?"

Zeke smiled. "I'm not sure how practically applicable three-thousand-year-old political philosophy is to daily life, especially a work as naïve as this one."

"I'm sorry, naïve?"

"Yeah, it's like Plato sees all of human activity as mechanical, that there's no room for nuanced situations or individual actions to change the course of history. Otherwise, according to his arguments, every society would end up in tyranny. History has generally proved the opposite."

Ramsey said nothing for a long moment. He had thought similarly when he first read *The Republic*, and his First Technician's insight had surprised him. Ramsey took in Zeke's features. The immature boy who had been fighting the last years of the battle with acne when CIV left Earth had been replaced by a man with penetrating eyes, a receding hairline, and a gravitas that came with years of hard work and deep study.

This was no longer a child for Ramsey to frown at and scorn.

This was a man, now Ramsey's senior by more than half a decade, he realized, whose intellect had matured and changed as profoundly as his physical appearance. An intelligent man who didn't tolerate being bullied or trifled with.

Where had the time gone?

And although Ramsey was confident that Zeke had taken the idea in the book more literally than intended, that Plato's progression had only meant to serve as an example, there was no point in arguing the point here, where the wit of his intellectual sparring partner had taken him by surprise. He settled on saying, "That's an astute observation, and well said."

Zeke seemed to take this response as sufficient, and returned to his studies.

So Zeke had aged and Ramsey hadn't noticed. So what? He had noticed Kemal's aging. Of course, the bushy white beard was hard to miss.

But Ramsey had neither scars nor gray hair. His eyes were probably tired, but from the burden of leadership and the reaction to the Somnithaw. Not from the relentless turning of the tides of time.

The feeling of immortality suited him, for he was sure there was no one in history as accomplished as Dr. Colin Ramsey.

And yet this development in Zeke was nearly total, a fascinating accomplishment in itself. An unrecognizable transformation. "What changed you?" Ramsey said, his curiosity overcoming his general reluctance to prolong conversations with the technicians.

Zeke wiped the screen blank with a flick of his wrist and set the tablet down. He touched his fingertips together as he chose his words. "Well, I realized I've only got one life to live, and most of it's going to be while I'm stuck in this tube. I figured I may as well better myself, make myself a useful resource for when we get to Ithaca, instead of wasting my one shot. So, yeah. I've read hundreds of books over the last decade or so. Thought about them, wrote about them. Wrote a couple of my own, if you're interested."

"Oh, really? What about?" He asked, his interest genuinely piqued, wondering when the wonders would cease.

"Most of it is pretty philosophical. I wrote quite a bit about Manifest Destiny in the United States in the 1800s and compared it to our own decision to expand to another world."

Ramsey frowned. "Manifest Destiny was the product of pseudo-theistic hyper-nationalism. I don't see how it's the same at all. We're fleeing for our lives."

"True, but without addressing the issues that led Earth into ruin, it won't take long before we're sending another lifeboat to another world or two. And the next thing you know, we're trying to colonize the galaxy because we believe it's some God-given right."

"Hardly God-given, Zeke. No one gives us that right. We take it for ourselves."

"True. But should we? That's the question I ask, and

the exhortation to the people of Ithaca is to care better for our adopted home than we did for the original."

Ramsey gritted his teeth. "But, of course we should colonize the galaxy. Just like the alpha male spreads his seed throughout the population, we must, ultimately, spread ourselves wide and far, to do everything we can to ensure that humanity survives."

Zeke shrugged. "Maybe. Creatures with complex social structures do just what you've said... but, in a similar sense, so do viruses."

"Right, it's a pattern seen throughout nature. You take what you need to make yourself strong whatever the cost to those around you." Ramsey struggled to keep his voice level. Perhaps Zeke was not as wise as he seemed. Too short-sighted and idealistic.

"But are we simply products of nature? I mean, we are, of course, products of nature. But is that all we are? Is doing the bare minimum, selfish thing our hindbrain tells us to do really the best our humanity has to offer?"

"Humanity is the dawning brightness in our galaxy," said Ramsey. "We will bring our knowledge and our science and our will to every planet that can support our survival. And there will be more than just Ithaca. There may have been dozens of other planets closer to Earth where we could have survived, if not thrived. And perhaps our descendants will go there someday. For now, we must be content with our new Earth, until the day we are ready to begin the risky business of true colonization of our galaxy. I thought you would understand that as well as anyone, Ty."

These last words hung heavy in the air. The technicians were silent. Judah stared at him, the others, including Zeke, all looked away.

"Er, sorry. 'Zeke,' I should have said." But the damage was done. Ramsey spooned another bite of gruel into his mouth, but found his ability to swallow disabled. "Excuse me," he said, rising from the table, placing the bowl on the tray for cleaning.

He exited the common room.

The hardest part about being the only immortal in a world of mortals is that, very quickly, you end up all alone.

5

PHYSICIAN

Dr. Serena Miller followed the young technician, Dean, to the Senior Technician's office. She would investigate Dean's concerns about Dr. Ramsey's health after she ate something, and to eat something, she had to register her presence with Harrison, the Senior Tech, so the ship could allocate resources for an extra mouth. That was her habit. If no one was in mortal danger, she ate a meal before treating anyone. She always woke up from cryo hungry.

This was her first time meeting Dean. She placed him in his mid-twenties, so she guessed he was the new Junior Technician. He was short, balding despite his youth, and rather rounder than most of the technicians, with a gentle face. His accent was vaguely Canadian, but she couldn't quite place it.

As they walked along the upward-curving track towards the crew area, Serena couldn't help but notice that the walls seemed grayer than the last time she had been awake. That had been early in Harrison's years of service, and he was now the Senior, so it had been at least thirty-five years. Rationally, she recognized that the walls had probably been tarnishing at a constant rate, and it was only in the time since her last waking that some mental threshold had been crossed which brought the change to her attention. Even so, it was another marker of the ship's age.

"What year of the journey is it, again?" she asked Dean.

"Year of the Ithacan Odyssey number two hundred and eighty-nine," he said with a little flourish of his wrist. He smiled, "Barely two hundred left to go yet!"

As he finished speaking, they arrived at the Senior Technician's office. Dean pressed the comm button on the outside.

"Enter," came the voice from inside, with a tinge of Caribbean warmth that somehow seemed out of place here in the cold, drab featureless-ness of deep space.

Dean swiped the door open. "Hey Harrison, I just wanted to let you know that I have Dr. Miller awake." Harrison looked up from his desk at the sound of Serena's name. His dark eyes found hers with an uncomfortable hunger. Dean continued, "I asked her to examine Dr. Ramsey, what with his issue he's havin'."

Harrison was old. Much older than he had been when she last saw him. His dark skin looked tighter against his frame, which had lost its perfect posture at some point over the years. The navy blue jumpsuit the technicians wore as a uniform seemed to hang off him. His hair had grayed but was still buzzed short. Despite all this, she recognized the man he had been last time she saw him.

That hungry, lingering gaze had become all-too familiar to Serena. She was of average height, brown hair and eyes, and a fit, if not exactly thin, build. She had never considered herself truly beautiful, and so the male attention was as surprising and novel as it was disconcerting.

Of course, the reason was obvious: She was one of the only women a technician was likely to see and speak to over the course of their service. She could only imagine being in Harrison's shoes, going thirty years without seeing a man. She would probably gawk, too.

But that didn't really make it less uncomfortable or off-putting.

Dispassionate civility had been her best tool so far in disarming and distracting these lonely men. "Good to see you again, Harrison. I hope I won't be too much of an inconvenience."

He blinked as his senses returned. "Oh, no, Dr. Miller. Please, please, sit. It is so good to see you again after all this time. Please, sit. How have you been?"

Serena took the empty seat across from the gregarious Trinidadian. Then she caught herself. He wasn't from Trinidad anymore. Everyone was Ithacan, and divisive categories such as nationality were to be discarded. Old habits. "It's good to see you, as well. Although, for me, it has only been a long night's sleep since you last saw me. So, no news, I'm afraid."

Harrison shook his head and smiled warmly. "Of

course, of course. How could I forget? Now, please tell me again, why are you here?"

Serena turned her head to acknowledge Dean.

"It was my idea," said Dean, "Last year when I came out of cryo, Ramsey had just finished his week, so I didn't really understand how bad he was doing. But now that I've seen the state he's in, I couldn't just let him carry on, could I? So, I saw that Dr. Miller here was next on the list of physicians for in-flight emergencies, and I woke her up."

Harrison leaned back in his chair, his fingers tented. He looked back and forth from Dean to Serena, weighing his words. He briefly touched his tented index fingers to his lips before speaking. "Your concern for Dr. Ramsey is... admirable, young Dean, but ultimately misplaced."

"Misplaced?" said Serena. "From what Dean has told me, Dr. Ramsey requires immediate medical intervention."

"Yes, I am convinced of that as well," said Harrison, "but I cannot advise you to follow through on your assessment of him, Dr. Miller."

A long pause filled the too-still, too-clean air that had been recycled through the ancient vessel for nearly three centuries. Serena's eyes narrowed. "I did not think that decisions of medical consequence rested with the Senior Technician. I believe you will forgive me for thinking that responsibility my own, as ranking Medical Officer."

"You misunderstand me. I will not prevent you from pursuing treatment of your patient. I only meant to warn you that you may find the experience... unpleasant." Harrison's eyes turned to Dean even as he continued to address Serena. "Especially considering Dr. Ramsey has expressly forbidden the technicians to pursue medical treatment on his behalf."

Serena kept her gaze on Harrison, but could feel the Junior Technician beside her wilt under the look from his supervisor. "I appreciate your concern, but having been made aware of the issue, it would be neither safe nor ethical for me to renege on my responsibility. I will see Dr. Ramsey after I find something to eat."

Harrison bowed his head in acquiescence. "As you wish, of course, Doctor. There is, then, just the issue of your sleeping arrangement. We do not have an extra room for you, as the visitor's room is currently occupied by your patient."

Dean reentered the conversation, "I thought of that already. I can sleep in the medical room for the next day or two, or however long it takes you to finish your work, Dr. Miller."

"Oh, that won't be necessary. I was with the Global Health Project in Brazil back on Earth. I've dealt with much worse than a cot in my office before. And please, you can call me Serena."

With a smile and a half nod, Dean stepped back toward the door to the office.

"Is there anything else, Harrison?" asked Serena.

His dark eyes met hers, and behind them that hint of longing. "No, that is all. I have registered your presence with the resource distribution system, so there will be enough food and water for you. You may go as you please."

Dean swiped open the door as Serena thanked Harrison, and she followed him out into the hallway.

———

SERENA HAD BEEN AWOKEN IN THE MID-MORNING, AND SO her meal had ended up being somewhere between breakfast and lunch. As much as she disagreed with Harrison's recommendation to avoid examining Ramsey, she did appreciate the warning that he would likely be a hostile patient. And so she decided to wait until after his lunch to examine him. That way he would hopefully be well-fed enough to be civil, and she would avoid an open confrontation with him in front of the technicians.

If you want someone to cooperate with you, talk to them when they are well fed. She had learned that trick from Philippe.

She bit her lip and pulled herself together.

Serena had some time to kill before Ramsey's lunch, so she decided to review the automated health records the ship had kept in her absence over the last thirty years. She walked up-spin around the great wheel to the elevator that took her up to a more inward level of the ring.

The innermost level was where most of the cryo chambers were, as the slightly lower gravity had little impact on persons in cryo sleep and the technicians needed as close to Earth gravity as the ship could generate. She preferred the terminals in this part of the ship. They were more isolated than the ones on the main deck. And even though the crew was sparse, she had learned to appreciate her complete solitude during her final months on Earth.

Besides, these people in cryo were the whole point of the mission. They were the chosen representatives to continue the story of humanity. Each and every person on the ship was a treasure of the species.

As Serena meandered towards the closest terminal, her mind wandered to what life might be like on Ithaca. It had been chosen because its characteristics were nearly identical to Earth; she understood that, but what would it really feel like to have a whole new world to colonize?

There would be new plants and animals, obviously. But they would be from a whole new line of evolution, completely disconnected from that of humanity. She could scarcely imagine the sorts of creatures they might encounter.

Of course, there was also the possibility of convergent evolution - that there were biological forms and ecological niches that were filled so perfectly on Earth that it seemed impossible that they should not evolve similarly again under similar circumstances. Trees came to mind immediately. They seemed pretty inevitable from an evolutionary perspective. And the reports about Ithaca provided proof that plant life, not dissimilar to that of Earth, was present and that photosynthesis was occurring. Or at least a process close enough to photosynthesis that it was spectrographically indistinguishable. That was an encouraging sign.

But her biggest concern of all was about proteins and carbohydrates. The odds of those on Ithaca developing analogously to their counterparts on Earth were astronomical. She supposed this was why there were so many xenobiologists among the chosen, to solve this very problem, but her concern was more medical than agricultural.

They were about to introduce the bacteria of Earth to an alien environment, and in return that alien environment was going to provide the entirety of its own biome to test the endurance of the human creature.

She expected a lot of people to be very sick shortly after they arrived.

Of course, there was always the possibility that the protein structures of the bacteria of Earth and Ithaca were completely non-interactive. That would be best, in many ways.

At least until the first bug mutated and started tearing apart terrestrial biology like scissors through paper.

Arriving at the door for the terminal station she often used, she was surprised to find it closed. She swiped her hand across the sensor to open it, but the backlight switched to red. She ran her hand past it two more times with the same result. She was about to touch her earpiece to ask a technician for assistance with the faulty door when it parted open.

Serena reeled back as a man's voice exploded at her. "I'm sorry, do I need to put up a sign? Don't you people know I'm busy? How hard is it to understand..."

Serena stared at Dr. Ramsey, and he stared back. The next word of his lecture was frozen on his face, his eyes wide with surprise.

"I'm so sorry, I didn't mean to intrude," said Serena.

Ramsey blinked. "Who the hell are you?"

"I'm Dr. Miller, and I..." His eyes narrowed, and she paused to choose her words carefully, "I'm doing some maintenance of the ship's medical records."

"Don't lie, Doctor. You're here for me."

"I-"

"Who was it? Sven?"

"No, he-"

"It doesn't matter. You will not be examining me today, Dr. Miller. Not today, not-" he winced, "- next week, not ever. I am handling my allergy fine on my own. I will not be accepting your help. Now if you will excuse me, I have some incomprehensibly complex systems to analyze, and if you want humanity to survive you will let me get back to it."

"I wasn't-"

"Thank you, Doctor. That will be all."

The door whooshed shut and closed with a click.

Serena blinked. That had gone about as poorly as possible.

She turned to walk down the corridor again, passing by tube after tube of the cryogenically suspended survivors of Earth, searching for another terminal to use.

Ramsey needed her help, that much was clear. His eyes had been sunken, his breath smelled of open wounds. He was very, very sick. And she could tell just from that short of an interaction. If his survival was as key to the success of the mission as he seemed to think it was, it would need to become her primary purpose to keep him alive for the next two hundred-some years. She did a quick mental calculation. About four years remained for

Ramsey, probably a little less based on what she had gleaned about him from the technicians.

It seemed hardly fair that such a prideful, rude, and unappealing man should hold the fate of the human species in his hands, and that all the best people she'd ever known had all died on Earth centuries ago.

And yet, this responsibility had fallen in her lap. She didn't have to like him; she just had to keep him alive long enough to fulfill his usefulness to the survival of the species.

Realizing the implications of her thoughts, she shook her head at herself. It didn't matter how cruel or rude or important or essential Ramsey was. He was, at this moment, the human being most in need of help in the universe. And that task now belonged to her.

The only problem would be getting him to cooperate.

She took an assessment of her situation.

She had no facts about his condition, except that a Somnithaw allergy had been a disqualifying condition during the selection process for CIV. Most of what she knew of Ramsey himself was hearsay from the technicians, not counting the little bit that everyone knew simply from being on Earth in those last years. She knew he had no interest in being examined, which could only mean he was afraid of what she would find.

If he feared what she would find, then either he already knew something he hadn't yet disclosed to any medical staff, or he feared his own mortality.

As she considered what she knew of the brilliant, eccentric, accomplished, wealthy, self-described savior of the human race, her best conclusion was that he feared his own death. Wasn't that common among the wealthy and accomplished? No matter how much money or fame or accomplishment you had, death would come for you eventually. The more you had, the less you wanted to lose it, and death was the ultimate loss.

That assuaged her fear of his impending demise for a moment, until she remembered how terrible he had looked.

Maybe he had a sense of how bad it was and just wanted to accomplish as much as possible in whatever time he had left.

Maybe.

She arrived at the next terminal room, which opened without incident, and logged in to the terminal there. It was a tiny room, just large enough for a woman of average height, like her, to be not quite able to touch the opposing walls at the same time. The terminal was an old style, with a physical screen. They were ugly and bulky, but often more reliable than the more common holographic screens. They were probably cheaper, too, and the budget for building CIV had been tight at the end.

The first thing she checked were the records of Norman, Munir, and Sven, the technicians who had gone back into cryo since her last waking. The automated health system was very reliable for keeping track of that information. All three had finished their respective terms in fine health, so she archived their records.

Then she pulled up Ramsey's file. Apparently Ramsey didn't like anyone, including health AIs, knowing what was happening. The only records in his file were sporadic reports from technicians on Ramsey's mental and physical state in the first twenty-four hours of his annual removal from cryo.

The man was adamant, wasn't he?

As she perused the records, she noticed that the reports on his condition generally got more severe over time, which was expected, but there were no other obvious signs as to what, specifically, was wrong with him.

When she finally logged off of the terminal, she was no closer to an answer.

———

AND AFTER FOUR DAYS OF FRUITLESS ATTEMPTS TO persuade Ramsey, she washed her hands of his fate and went back into cryo.

6

MONEY

S o full had Serena's days been of rushed showers, baggy scrubs, and a distinct lack of time for makeup that she barely recognized the elegant woman gazing back from her mirror.

Her dark brown hair was, for once, not in a ponytail. Instead, it was braided and folded and curled into a complex up-do that she lacked the vocabulary to properly describe. Her dark eyes, so often burdened over the last decade with the exhaustion of medical school and then residency, were highlighted with a gentle blue that brought out the depth and richness of the brown spheres below. And her dress...

Emerald green, golden trim, floor-length, backless, and form-hugging in all the right places.

She hoped Philippe would like it. But, no. She banished the thought. Her duty tonight was to help the Global Health Project secure funding from a big donor at the Miami Charity Gala. Philippe was a master of these sorts of negotiations, and a gala like this was the perfect opportunity to secure the funding for their new operations in Brazil.

Of course, rumor had it that Ty Daniels of RamTech Enterprises was expected to be there, too. How RamTech had managed to meet the eligibility requirements to be allowed into a fund sourcing gala for charities was beyond her comprehension, but all eyes would surely be on the madmen attempting to build a spacecraft capable of bringing human colonists to another world.

She shook her head to snap out of her thoughts, and her crystal earrings glimmered in the mirror.

While her future employment rested on their success tonight, Serena was beginning to allow herself the hope that the future of her happiness rested on her blossoming relationship with Philippe.

A few weeks prior, they had traveled together to Philippe's native Brazil, up into the densely forested area around Fortaleza, to scout the area that would be their home for six years should they receive the funding.

The impoverished area was in dire condition. Like much of the southern hemisphere, the wells were drying up. Dust ripped through village streets, coating everything in a dull, sandy color. Mothers had thrust skinny babies into their arms, but, through tears, they'd been forced to hand the children back. They couldn't do anything to help these people. Not yet. Desperate men had attempted to rob them at one point, but their bodyguards had intervened.

Serena had cried most of the way back to Sao Paolo. These people were desperate. Medicine wasn't the only thing they needed, but they needed it imminently.

Reminding herself that she was trying to secure funding to help them was the only thing that allowed her to feel justified in her emerald green dress and fancy up-do. The wealthy loved to have the appearance of being great benefactors of humanity, but they didn't want to see the ugliness that their dollars were fighting against. Instead, you had to put on a smile and a dress that could be sold to feed an entire village for days.

She couldn't exactly blame the wealthy though. After all, if they were going to open their checkbooks to help the needy, she should be grateful.

Even in Sao Paolo, Philippe's home city, she had already started to distance herself from the horrors of the Fortaleza region. Philippe had shown her the sights, taken her dancing, brought her to the beach.

And then, the night before she was supposed to leave, he had asked her to take a walk with him. They walked down by the water, the three-quarter moon reflecting off the surf, the sounds of beachfront parties serenading their peaceful steps.

And then his hand touched her hand. And hers touched his, too.

His dark eyes had burrowed into hers, his dark locks hanging casually across his brow, his shirt unbuttoned to the middle of his chest. And then his fingers were running through her hair, then across her cheek.

And then his lips were on her lips, her arms were

around his back, her fingers now lost in the curls on top of his head.

It had been the most beautiful night of her life, with the sea and the moon and the sounds of festivity all around, and the hope and promise of a fledgling new love, a spark that fanned quickly into flame.

She had canceled her flight, and stayed with Philippe for another ten days before returning to Los Angeles to visit family for three nights. Then she rejoined him in Miami for the gala.

She took a deep breath to calm herself and focus on the task at hand. She remembered the desperate faces near Fortaleza and set her jaw. With one last look at the beautiful woman in the mirror, the young doctor departed.

————

THE GALA WAS AS BEAUTIFUL AND GRANDIOSE AS ANY EVENT Serena had ever witnessed. Limousine after limousine dropped off the wealthy and powerful, their faces and clothing resplendent in the faint light of that early fall evening in southern Florida.

Inside the Civic Gallery, understated blue and gold lights darted about the room, a carefully controlled and coordinated dance of hundreds of microdrones that cast a fluid, otherworldly luminescence upon the party. A live orchestral performance added to the magic and beauty of the evening, their ancient symphonies bringing out the splendor of the occasion as only classical music can.

As Serena attempted to take in the fullness of the atmosphere, the very tips of Philippe's fingers traced their way up her back, sending shivers through her extremities.

"This is a very beautiful party," said Philippe, casting his gaze heavenward where the dancing lights reflected off the massive crystalline chandeliers.

Serena watched his face as he looked up. "It's one of the most beautiful things I've ever seen," she agreed.

His eyes fell to meet hers. "Do you know what makes it so beautiful?"

"Well, it's the lights, the music, the ocean in the distance. All of it."

"No, no. Those things are indeed lovely, but none of it compares to how you look tonight. I am certain that I have never seen true beauty before this moment."

Serena's heart pounded with delight. She turned up her nose with playful dignity. "You flatter me, good sir."

He took her hand in his as an older couple pushed past them. "I assure you, I do not." He kissed the top of her hand.

She smiled. "Your kindness is well appreciated," she put her mouth close to his ear, "and it will not go unrewarded."

Before Philippe could respond with more than a flirtatious smile, she turned her back on him and pulled him by the hand through the crowd, a giddy grin spread across her face.

———

"...AND THAT'S WHY OUR WORK IN BRAZIL IS SO ESSENTIAL, you see," said Philippe. They were talking with a Canadian businesswoman who had convenient connections to the tourism bureau of Uruguay. "The whole region functions together as one. We've seen it in our history before. That's why we created the *Unión de Naciones Suramericanas* a century ago, because when one country in Latin America falls to chaos, the others around it are likely to follow. Ours is a culture that pollinates across borders, and we must all band together."

The businesswoman frowned. "I suppose that is true, but isn't fighting chaos the job of a soldier? What would be the benefit of setting up medical clinics? Why should I support you, rather than the UdNS military?"

"The situation is severe in Northeastern Brazil, but, as yet, it has not gone so far as real violence," said Serena, her mind pushing down the memory of the men threatening them at knife-point. "However, we must begin soon, or the instability of the region could collapse into chaos. That would be the real threat to your interests in Uruguay, of course. But if we can meet the real needs, the human needs of the impoverished, we can prevent them from radicalizing. But we don't have much time."

The evening was going well. They had passed on contact information from several possible future donors to their home office and secured about eighty percent of the funding they needed to begin their operations in Brazil, and the night was still young.

"And what of these so-called *Ultimas* wreaking havoc in the Amazon? Aren't they the exact thing you are trying to prevent? Aren't you already too late?"

Serena glanced at Philippe, to whom the question had been directed. She had become used to playing second fiddle when Philippe was in the room. Not only would he be the second in command of the entire Brazil campaign should the funding be secured, but his charisma drew people to him like a magnet.

"The *Ultimas* should, of course, be a concern to everyone," said Philippe, his forehead creased with concern. "But if we look back at the history of war, starting in the twentieth century, we will see that guerrilla fighters will always hold the advantage. So, we have a choice. We can accept their foothold and send in a military intervention, making the same mistakes that the Russians, the Americans, the French, the English and the Chinese have famously made in the past. We may be able to eradicate them through force - but we would leave behind a region scoured by war, and we won't have addressed any of the real problems.

Or, we can learn the lessons from the Turkish campaigns in the Middle East, where they destabilized the extremists base by appealing to the needs of the masses. These sorts of rebels can only be stopped by removing their popular support. The best way to do that is through humanitarian interventions, which we will offer to the people of Northern Brazil, if you can give us your pledge of support."

The woman shook her head. "You mean to fight a war without weapons. I'm sorry, but I cannot support you. I admire your idealism, but, it's just not a good investment, you see."

"A good investment?" Serena said before she could

stop herself. "I'm sorry, Miss Tremblay, but I could have sworn this was a charity gala. I didn't realize that the point was for you to make money."

Miss Tremblay's eyes narrowed. "Naive girl. Life is only, ever, all about investment. When I hear a pitch that convinces me it will do some real, quantifiable good in the world, I will happily invest in that endeavor. However, I see no wisdom in giving my money to a couple of idealistic doctors who will be dead six months after they arrive. If anything, young lady, you should be grateful that I've attempted to spare your life."

Serena opened her mouth, but strong fingers closed around her elbow and tugged her away.

"Thank you for your time, Miss Tremblay, we are sorry to have bothered you," Philippe said, then guided Serena away from the confrontation.

"I can't believe that woman!" Serena fumed. "Can you believe what she said to us?"

"You must calm down. She is only one donor. We have plenty of time this evening to find the rest of our funding. But first, you must forget her. Not everyone will see the value of what we do, so all we can do is thank them for their time and move on. We'll find that last bit we need, don't worry."

Serena sucked on her tongue to keep her mouth closed, then, spotting the bar across the crowded room, said, "I think I need a drink," and pulled Philippe by the hand through the crowd of consumerist decadence.

They found a place at the bar next to a pudgy man with short black hair who flitted through correspondence on his tablet, the holographic words and images indecipherable from their position. The last sips of a dark amber drink sat at the bottom of a crystalline tumbler in front of him.

Serena placed her finger on the scanner built into the countertop, which displayed her name in green to indicate her BAC was low enough to order whatever she wanted. "Chardonnay."

"Right away, miss," said the bartender. It had been ages since Serena had seen a live bartender. The gala had truly spared no expense. As much as she understood the extravagant spending to attract the wealthy, it rang of hypocrisy to unnecessarily spend so much money on a glorified charity fundraiser. There was a reason she was a doctor and not an economist.

While she waited for her drink, Philippe introduced himself to the man next to them. "Are you enjoying your evening, my friend?"

The man had the practiced air of one who was used to striking up conversations with strangers. He responded to Philippe equably. "Yes, it's been a lovely evening. Everything has gone just right. How are you?"

"We are well, thank you," said Philippe, glancing for a name tag or some other way to identify the man. "Are you a donor or are you representing a charity?"

"Ah, neither I'm afraid. I'm looking for sponsors, but my organization is not a charity in any traditional sense."

Serena raised a mental eyebrow and regarded the man with as even an expression as she could. He wore a very expensive-looking black tuxedo in the old style, with a vest and bowtie. The distribution of weight on his body suggested he had gained much of it quickly, under stressful circumstances. His build wasn't one where you immediately noticed he was large, but there was no denying that he was significantly overweight. He had the most average face she could imagine: neither round nor thin, medium brown eyes, nondescript nose, and short nearly-black hair. As she caught his eye, the uncanny sense that she had seen him before overwhelmed her.

The bartender reappeared with her wine. She thanked him and turned back to the man, who spared her having to ask the question, "Dr. Tyson Daniels, RamTech Enterprises." He stuck out his hand.

"Ah, a pleasure to meet you, Dr. Daniels," said Philippe grasping the outstretched hand firmly before allowing it to pass on to Serena, "I'm Dr. Philippe Perez, and this is Dr. Serena Miller. We're with the Global Health Project."

If Philippe was feeling any of the same shock she was, he didn't let it show. Ty Daniels was the second in command of RamTech, or, as her father would say, 'those space colony bastards.' Twenty years ago, RamTech had bought out the company her father worked for and hadn't offered to keep him on. He hadn't quite gotten over it.

Dr. Daniels' name and face were all over the nets on a weekly basis, announcing the next steps of construction on that ship they were building, trying to scare people into donating money to their cause. Of course, with how poorly their stock had performed ever since the elder Dr. Ramsey died, leaving his arrogant son in charge of the company, she supposed they had little choice but to seek financial assistance. But, she realized, if RamTech had been invited to this gala...

"How did you manage to get into this gala for actual charities?" she asked.

Ty smiled, "I hate to say it, but, 'friends in high places.'"

"Serena..." Philippe warned, sensing her frustration.

"So you would take money from the poor and needy of the world to fund your vainglorious attempts at galactic colonization? Don't you think we, as a species, ought to focus on meeting the needs of the people living on this actual planet right now instead of worrying about colonizing another one?"

Ty nodded somberly, "I understand how this must look from your point of view, Dr. Miller. But let me assure you, the beliefs Dr. Ramsey and I share about the state of the world are entirely genuine. We would not be planning to evacuate from this planet if we believed there was any chance of saving it in the long run. We are doing the best we can to help the human race survive."

"I don't doubt the sincerity of your beliefs, and crazy as they are, you might even be right about them. My objection is to the funds you're redirecting from the poor of this world by your presence here tonight."

Ty puffed up his cheeks and let the air vibrate out over his lips. "Look, we may not be a charity, but we are doing the most good we can for the human race, and it's come at great cost. Our financial situation is publicly available on the nets, so I'm sure you will believe me when I say we need all the money we can get."

"With respect, Dr. Daniels, you don't need the money."

"With respect, Dr. Miller, we really do. What do you think our motivation could be? Try to find some possible hidden motivation we could have to deceive the world about the danger it's in, intentionally liquidate the empire of the late Dr. Ramsey, all to build a ship that would probably have been built anyway, and under much more stable conditions, sometime in the next fifty years or so."

Serena didn't want to consider his points. She stared at him, silently, willing her mind not to consider his question, lest she allow some foothold for the excuse. But her mind loved puzzles, and this one promised to be important.

She started with what she could observe. Dr. Ty Daniels used a favor to sneak himself into the largest annual charity gala in the world on behalf of RamTech Industries. While there was a lot of money up for grabs, she couldn't imagine that this was the best way for RamTech to go about getting money, so that meant they were resorting to less than optimal tactics to bring in income. And that meant they were actually in financial trouble. She also observed that this was Ty Daniels himself, and not another representative of RamTech who had come. He also had made no effort to hide his identity, so he didn't care if anyone knew he was here. But surely RamTech was powerful enough that it didn't need to come to an event like this. Surely it could organize private meetings with the investors it sought to win. So they must be here for more than the investors.

Serena took a long sip of her wine. "Fine, I believe you. You do need the money. But that's not the only reason you're here."

Ty smiled. "Well done. I don't mind telling you the truth, actually. This will be public knowledge soon enough, anyway. While I am, in fact, here for the investors, I admit I'm more interested in the networking than the finances. Between you and me, Dr. Ramsey is prepared to grind his business into dust if he can only finish CIV in time. But finishing the ship is only a means to an end. Our next phase is to find five thousand volunteers who can pass our genetic screening test and also prove their value to our future life on a colonized world." He tapped a few buttons on the holographic tablet screen. "I've just sent a short-radius data burst, so the contact information should be on any devices you are carrying, or accessible through your neural lace, if you have one. I encourage you both to apply. This world is not going to last for long, and we'll need smart, talented people like you on Ithaca."

"Ithaca?" said Philippe.

"Yes, sorry," said Ty, "That's the code name we've given to our target world. It's a play off of *The Odyssey-*"

"Ah, yes. Odysseus's home town," said Philippe.

"That's right," said Ty, smiling, "The whole point of *The Odyssey* was Odysseus striving to find his home, Ithaca, and that's what we're doing, too."

"The fact remains," Serena interrupted, "that you're trying to solicit business partnerships at a charity event. Why here?"

Ty let out a breathy laugh and shook his head. "Well,

as you pointed out, we do need some money, so this event was an ideal optimization of meeting tough, capable people like you and meeting some of the wealthiest philanthropists in the world. I've been pleased with the results on both sides."

Serena narrowed her eyes. "You've been selling tickets to the new world to the highest bidder. You're cashing in on peoples' fear for personal profit."

Ty laughed again, though there was less genuine amusement this time. "Hardly. I've had a few targeted conversations with some young, healthy donors and encouraged them to apply as well."

"I see," said Serena, unable to keep the bite from her voice. "So if they pay enough, you'll save their lives. And what benefit do they offer to the survival of a new society on an alien planet?"

"All applicants must pass our genetic screening, Dr. Miller. They will be subject to the same level of scrutiny as anyone else. If they are healthy and strong, then their contributions will be among the most pivotal, because they're the ones who are going to help the mission get off the ground in the first place."

"This is flagrantly and unashamedly unethical."

Ty hesitated. "This is ethics on a higher plane."

"Is that what you tell yourself so you can sleep at night? You come here and divert resources that could be used to make the world better and instead doom countless thousands to suffer so you can have your Odyssey." Ty looked away, biting his tongue. She paused. "And then you have the audacity to call your ethics higher than ours?"

Ty let out a deep sigh. "I'm starting to sound like Ramsey," he mumbled. Then, in his normal voice, "Our society has a bent towards immediacy. We use resources in inefficient ways all the time to treat immediately obvious symptoms of issues rather than waiting, identifying root causes, and treating the issues themselves. As a doctor, I'm sure you can appreciate the shortsightedness of that approach. It's the same principle here, except the Earth is dying, we only have so long to save it, and there are no steps that are truly out-of-bounds in the pursuit of our purposes."

Serena's choked on her sip of wine. "So you really think you're above all human standards of morality, then?"

"I am not, Dr. Miller. But, as much as I hate to say it, for a cause as just as this one, the ends really do justify the means. However, before you tear into me for that, let me point out that we have operated above board in everything we've done. Our finances are transparent, as are my purposes here, as are our motivations. We've even made the construction feeds available on nets and neural laces all over the world and colonies. Everyone knows what we are doing and why, whether they believe us or not. And that is far more than you can say of most any other company on or off the planet." He looked from Serena to Philippe and back again. "I'm afraid that I haven't acquitted myself or my company very well in this conversation, but I must say, Dr. Miller, that your insights are incisive. RamTech is always looking to acquire the best talent in the world. I'm sure we could find a suitable position for a mind like yours. I have a division I oversee that's focused on medical preparedness in the face of alien biology. Someone like you would be an exceptional fit."

Serena just blinked at him while she composed a response. "How can you offer me a job when I've just criticized everything about your company?"

"Actually, I found it very refreshing. I'm usually the one pointing out concerns like these to Dr. Ramsey, and he's worse than useless at seeing the other side. He's a brilliant man, but not much for others' points of view when he's set his mind to something. I could use another voice like yours on my team." He tapped on his tablet again. "I've sent out another SRDB to your devices with my personal contact information. I'm sure you'll want to think about it."

"I... I don't know what to say. I appreciate the offer, but I couldn't abandon the people of Brazil. Not all of us have the luxury of being able to ignore the suffering still happening on the planet."

Ty nodded. "I understand. Well, hold on to my information. You have about three years to decide before the hiring cutoff. I must point out that priority selection for Ithaca will be given to RamTech employees who meet the genetic standards to qualify. I should also mention that the selection criteria are very strict. Less than one percent of people meet the standard. But you never know, right?"

Philippe spoke for the first time in several minutes, a rare edge in his voice. "We thank you for the conversation, Dr. Daniels. We will keep all of this in mind as we prepare for our work in Brazil." Then, turning to Serena, he touched her lightly on the inside of her elbow to guide her away from the bar, and said, "We must get back to the donors to secure the last of our funding."

"How close are you?" asked Ty.

Philippe froze for a moment. "Nearly eight hundred thousand U.S. Dollars."

"I'll match that," said the surprising man from RamTech Industries.

Philippe looked at Serena. She didn't know what to say, so she deferred to Philippe with the motion of her eyebrows.

Philippe seemed to understand. He turned back toward Ty. "Are you sure, Dr. Daniels? Don't you need this money for your high moral calling?"

"Our overall budget for this expedition is north of four hundred trillion dollars. We won't even notice the loss. Maybe pass some good press our way, and we'll call it even."

Philippe stood up straighter and extended his hand solemnly. "Thank you, sir. We appreciate your generosity immensely."

Serena followed his lead.

"When do you leave for South America?"

"With the funding secured, as soon as the end of the month," said Philippe.

Ty smiled. "I wish you both well, and I truly hope to see you again on Ithaca." He knocked back the last bit of his drink, placed the empty tumbler behind the bar, nodded at Serena and Philippe, and vanished back into the crowd.

Philippe's impassivity at the beginning of the conversation had now been replaced with the same expression of both joy and shock Serena knew must be on her face. "Well, I guess we're going to Brazil, then," she said.

The look of shock on Philippe's face softened into an enormous smile, and they burst out in laughter together as he covered her face in tender kisses.

7

AWAKENING

Cheng Ahn returned to consciousness peacefully, as a boat drifts inland with the rising tide. As light came into focus, an unfamiliar elderly face appeared on the other side of the glass separating his cryo chamber from the corridor. The seal on his chamber broke. The doors remained closed, but a hissing sound indicated that the Somnithaw had been vented. The old man entered a command. Light flooded in as the doors rotated open. Cheng blinked as his vision adjusted.

"All right, Cheng?" asked the old man.

"Yes. I am well."

"Good. Take your time getting out of there. You've been sleeping for over three hundred years, so you're liable to be a bit stiff."

"Three hundred years," he repeated, "Has it been so long?"

The old man gave him a half-smile out of one side of

his mouth. "'Fraid so. Everything you knew on Earth is long gone by now."

"It has felt like a long, dreamless night of sleep."

"I know what you mean. Same for me fifty years ago when I woke up. I'll be back in cryo in a few days, once we've got you orientated and started in your work. I'm Dean, by the way."

The name was familiar. "Dean... from Winnipeg?"

His face lit up for a moment before the corners of his mouth dropped. "Once upon a time."

"I remember you." Cheng said. "We met the first day in training."

"Sorry. Doesn't ring a bell. That was fifty years ago for me." He tapped his temple. "Memory ain't what it used to be."

"That... that is all right." Cheng studied the lines on Dean's face, the bags under his eyes, the scars on his hands, the ring of grey hair around his head, the curve of his burdened back. The man had been tall, strong, and enthusiastic just the day before. He had lived a lifetime overnight.

Lin.

He would look much like this man the next time he saw her. She would not change. His heart ached. What he would already give for one more day with her. One more moment.

"You ready to get out of that tube?" asked Dean.

Cheng took stock of himself. He felt a little stiff, but strong. "Yes." He grasped Dean's extended hand as he helped him out. The old man did not lack strength in his waning years.

Dean led Cheng to the common room. Three other men greeted him and introductions were made. Cheng recognized two of them from training. These now older men had been his peers such a short time ago.

They shared a meal together to welcome him into their brotherhood. The food was hot, but that was the full extent of its praiseworthiness. Dean explained how recent problems in the hydroponics lab had decimated their vegetable supply, but they hoped to have a new crop in the next two months. In the meantime, everyone had to put up with the flavorless protein concoction they affectionately referred to as 'gruel' for three meals a day.

"Tell us a happy memory from Earth, Cheng," said Manny, after dinner.

The other men focused their attention on Cheng, their eyes pleading, the room suddenly electric with anticipation. He considered for a moment, and began. "My wife and I traveled to Japan for our honeymoon and arrived late at night. The next morning when we woke up, everything was white outside our window. We thought it had snowed, but it was spring. We had not planned it, but we were in Japan in cherry blossom season. Our hotel was in the middle of the largest cherry blossom display in all Japan. The petals were everywhere. It was like a dream. We took the whole day to walk around the city, happy to be married and to start our life together. There seemed a million people, but we did not mind. We had each other, and the whole world was ours."

They received his story reverently. They asked him about the wind and the sun, the feel of grass, the smell of soil. He described it all as best as he could.

"Thank you," said Dean, at last, "It's been so long. Sometimes it's hard to remember."

Cheng inclined his head.

Maurice showed Cheng to his temporary quarters, explaining that Dr. Ramsey occupied them during his waking week each year. Cheng would take over Dean's room when the old man went back into cryo.

———

ON OPPOSITE POINTS ALONG THE PERIMETER OF THE RINGED spaceship called CIV sat the crew module where the technicians lived and worked, and its counterweight, where shuttles and supplies for colonization were stored. The ring itself consisted primarily of the endless circular corridor where most of the chosen slept, side by side, kilometer after kilometer. As the crew and colonization modules circled the ring, different sections of cryo pods became accessible to the technicians, who serviced each section in succession. When they finished one batch, they moved the whole module along the ring to the next section, and the next. It took about six months to complete a circuit of the ship and service all five thousand pods.

By luck, Cheng's waking had coincided with the semi-annual week when the technicians serviced Lin's cryo section. So, before lights-out that first night, Cheng left his quarters. He ascended to the inner ring, where the sleepers rested, walked alone down a distant corridor until he found the upright chamber where his wife had rested in tranquility for over three hundred years.

He gazed upon her face and drank in her features for many moments. She was radiant. Strands of dark hair hung loosely on the right side of her face, obscuring her temple from vision, while the strands on the left lay tucked behind her ear. A gentle hint of a nervous smile rested on the corners of her frozen lips.

"My darling wife," he said in Mandarin, "In my mind, it has only been a few days since we said goodbye, though in truth it has been centuries. I will be very nearly eighty the next time you see me." The gravity of his words weighed on him, real for the first time. "Eighty." He pictured old Dean as he had once looked on Earth.

Closing his eyes, he rested his forehead on the small glass panel in front of her face. His lips were inches from hers. It would be decades before they could touch again. "I know you can't hear me right now, but I hope somehow, deep in your heart, you can sense me. I dedicate these fifty years to you, my Lin. My life will be just a blip in the long night of your rest. But what I do, I do for you. May my sacrifice be worthwhile in your eyes." He kissed the glass, wiping a tear from his cheek as he turned away.

———

It had been a little more than a week since Cheng awoke from cryo. In that time, Dean had gone back to sleep after tearful farewells with the three elder technicians, Manny had moved into the Senior Technician's office, and Cheng's training had begun. He spent most of his time in the simulator, learning the basics beyond what had been covered in pre-launch training, and studying the reports of previous generations of technicians as they encountered anomalies.

He was getting used to the food. It was nothing like the food he was used to eating in China, but it was nourishing, and he chose to be grateful.

The nights were the hardest. He spent long hours staring at the ceiling. After three days, the medical AI had recommended a sleep aid, but he knew he needed that time to process his thoughts. If his mind and body needed to rest, they would rest on their own. In the meantime, he would cope.

On day nine, Santos, the Second Technician, sliced his hand while performing regular maintenance on a cryo pod. It wasn't a serious injury, but the MedAI recommended stitches, which required the direct intervention of a human doctor.

Maurice chuckled as he and Manny examined the wound. "Expertly done, *mon ami*." He patted Santos on the back.

"What do you mean?" asked the surly Greek, pressing the towel tight on the skin between his right thumb and forefinger.

"'What do you mean?'" the Frenchman parroted, "Don't pretend. We all know who the next doctor in the rotation is. And you have injured yourself just enough to wake her up."

A smirk flashed across Santos's face. "I don't know what you are talking about."

Maurice punched him on the arm good-naturedly, smiling.

"I am sorry," said Cheng, "but who is this doctor?"

Maurice chuckled again, his barrel chest booming with laughter. "Oh Cheng, you've so much to learn still. I'm sure it has not bothered you quite yet, but give it a few months, you'll really start to notice the distinct lack of women around here. Now, we've got three doctors who rotate through whenever we have a medical issue, and a certain Dr. Miller is the favorite to look at. Well, Manny prefers Dr. Fernandez. But man or woman, either is fine for him, so he can't complain."

The Senior Technician rolled his eyes. "You didn't need to tell him that."

"I... understand," said Cheng.

"Hey, don't you go judging us, now," said Santos. "When you've been here for a few years, you'll start to get it. You'll miss your - what is she again? - your wife, right? You'll be sad that you're starting to forget her. And then one day, you'll need a medical consult, and it will be Dr. Miller's turn. And her hands will touch your skin, and you'll have forgotten what that felt like, to have a woman touch you, even if it's only for a medical exam. Next thing you know, it's a few years later. You realize that it's Dr. Miller's turn coming up again, and you find yourself a little less careful than usual, and then..." he held up his hand, "you get lucky."

Cheng could only nod noncommittally.

"Santos," said Manny, "Dr. Miller is a medical professional, and you will not do this again."

Santos laughed derisively. "What, Manny? You going to fire me? Put me back in cryo? That'll work fine for me, too. What do I need to do to get you to send me back to cryo?"

"You're not going back into cryo, and you're not getting fired," said Manny. "But you will treat every person on this ship with respect. If I ever suspect that you've done something like this again, there will be hell to pay. Do I make myself clear?"

Santos waved him away. "Yeah, fine. Whatever that means."

"Good. Cheng, come with me. I'm going to walk you through a cryo-extraction so we can wake up Dr. Miller for this imbecile."

Cheng followed.

"Santos doesn't really mean harm," said Manny as they walked down the corridor. "He's just bitter. His girlfriend killed herself 'bout six months before we left Earth. She got rejected from the ship and she just gave up hope. Easy to see how it could happen, but that don't make it any easier."

"It is difficult to lose ones you love," said Cheng, carefully measuring his English word choice. "I have compassion for him from my own life. But bitterness poisons the well. He has no right to treat this Dr. Miller this way. Should we pick a different doctor, to protect her?"

"Your heart's in the right place, young man. I'll have a longer chat with Santos later, though. Don't you worry. May even recommend him for some counseling, depending how it goes. But, no. I know Santos. Open defiance like that, he won't take it too kindly, and the truth is we need to keep everyone on this team happy. He won't do nothing to Dr. Miller but look at her. Besides, there'll be too many questions if we skip a doctor. The AI won't like it, and," he whistled, "you've got no idea what it's like when the AI gets bent out of shape. Thing's pretty basic, but it's also over three hundred years old, and it don't like change much."

Cheng nodded his understanding. Another necessary evil. Like the abandonment of Earth, like the loss of so many billions of people, like the fifty years of labor still before him, like the life with Lin he had foregone to save her.

"While she's awake, we may as well have her examine you, too, Cheng. All the Junior Techs get a manual examination at some point, but not usually in their first month. Maurice went almost seven years before his. We didn't have very many injuries back when Ol' Anuwar was the Senior. Good guy. He ran a tight ship. Dean was no slouch either, don't get me wrong; I knew the guy for almost forty years. But Anuwar was one who just thrived here for some reason, ya know?"

They had arrived in the crew cryo chamber, which, in addition to the technicians, contained ten or so specialists, like Dr. Miller, who could be awoken as needed over the course of the journey to provide skilled assistance whenever the need arose. The chambers lined the room on either side, with another row back to back down the middle from the back wall to the center. On the end of this row, facing the door, one chamber faced out, like a king surveying his courtiers. This was Ramsey's cryo pod. Cheng remembered noticing the peculiarity in the design of the ship when he had first looked at the schematics. Once Ramsey had announced his annual check-in plan to the technicians, the added redundancies and quality control measures on his unit made sense, due to the sheer number of times it would be used. But, practical or not, the configuration of the room did Ramsey no favors in his reputation with the technicians.

Manny approached the third unit on the left and drew out the control panel, which activated instantly. He placed his hand on the panel. "Begin extraction checklist."

The bottom of the pod crept forward about eight inches along a track so that the pod appeared to lean back against the wall. Through the viewport window, a dull blue light within the pod illuminated the frozen features of a dark-haired woman in her early thirties. She looked kind, but something in the crease of her eyes betrayed a great burden in her mind.

The extraction program logged each step of the process on the control panel. Temperature elevation. Neural activity monitoring. Somnithaw mixing. Ventilation calibration. The list went on.

"There are three command trees," Manny explained. "The first one here is for monitoring vitals. When you do Ramsey, these will go all screwy, but don't you worry. That always happens."

Cheng made a mental note to ask why Ramsey's pod didn't function properly.

"The second tree," he pointed to the visual representation on the control panel, "this one here, controls the Somnithaw mixing and administration process. And the last one there is for all the mechanicals. Pretty simple, really, once you get the hang of it." Manny pointed to the visualizer and explained how to watch for errors, but that there had never been an error yet.

"Why does each unit have its own control?" Cheng asked. "Why not one central control hub?"

"Damage control," said Manny, grimly, "If one pod's system goes down, we lose one person. If there's only one system controlling everything and it goes down, we're all dead."

Cheng nodded his understanding.

The cryo pod hummed for a few seconds. "It's venting the Somnithaw, so we're almost done," said Manny.

Through the window, Dr. Miller's eyes opened and shut groggily. Cheng glanced at the first command tree, which glowed bright green, presumably indicating that her vitals were normal. A moment later, the doors rotated open and Dr. Miller held up her hand against the brightness.

"Welcome back, Dr. Miller," said Manny. "How are you feeling?"

Dr. Miller nodded, her eyes still closed. "I'm getting there, thanks." She squinted to look at her welcoming party. "Dean's back in cryo, then?"

"That's right," said Manny, "This here is Cheng Ahn. Only been awake a couple weeks."

Dr. Miller shook off the last of the disorientation. "My wakeup is getting foggier. I may need to take an extended awake time to let myself recover. I hate to be an imposition on your team, though."

"No trouble. Crops are growing well again, and there's always plenty of gruel."

"Good. Thank you." She turned to Cheng. "I think we met before we left Earth. I'm Dr. Serena Miller."

Cheng accepted her hand and bowed his head. "Very

pleased to see you again, Dr. Miller. You may call me Cheng, if you wish. Most people do."

"Okay, Cheng." Dr. Miller smiled, released his hand and turned back to Manny. "So, I suppose I don't need to register with the Senior Tech, since you're the one who woke me up. Can we get something to eat? I'm starving. You can tell me what you need me for on the way."

"Actually, I'm very busy with my transition to Senior. I'll be in my office taking care of that, but I'll get you back in the system. Cheng, make sure Dr. Miller has whatever she needs, then escort her to the medical room for Santos's stitches."

"Yes, Sir."

Dr. Miller tilted her head in confusion. "I don't think I need an escort, Manny. I've logged a few months of awake time since we left Earth. I know the habitat pretty well."

Manny and Cheng looked at each other blankly.

Dr. Miller picked up on the uncomfortable moment. "Okay, someone explain what's going on."

Manny drew a deep breath before he spoke. "Certain crew members have expressed, erm... less-than-professional opinions about you, doctor. I think it'd be best for Cheng here to provide you some companionship, to keep certain crew members in line."

Dr. Miller set her jaw. "I see. You don't think I can protect myself."

"No, it's not that."

"No, it is that, though, Manny." Her voice rose, but stayed under control. "You have no idea what I went through back on Earth, but I assure you, I am not afraid of Santos."

"I didn't say who it-"

"You didn't need to. I've been keeping my eye on him from the first time I met him. If you're going to be afraid for someone's safety, let it be his. Not mine."

She turned and marched out of the cryo chamber.

"I believe her," said Cheng, smiling. "I do not think she needs any help."

"Yeah, just stick by her anyway," said Manny. "Santos is more slippery than either of you realize yet. I'll be in my office." Then he left, tracing the doctor's steps, his gait much heavier and wearier than hers.

Cheng bowed to the now empty room. "Very well," he said, and followed Manny out the door.

He caught up to Dr. Miller quickly, and fell into step beside her.

"You seem like a nice guy, Cheng, but I really, really don't need your help."

"I know. I believe you."

"Ok, good. Then please leave me alone."

"I would, of course, Dr. Miller, but I should not. Manny is in his first week as Senior Tech. It could make my position difficult to defy him."

She sighed. "Fine."

"Do not worry," he teased her, "I am here to escort you, only. I will not protect you, no matter what."

She smiled a little. "How chivalrous."

They walked in silence for several steps.

"Out of curiosity," Dr. Miller said, "What was Santos saying that has Manny so paranoid?"

"He made no threat, so there is that much, at least.

But he said he hurt himself intentionally so you have to wake up for the stitches."

Dr. Miller looked unimpressed. "Well, it's hardly original, but it's effective."

"I am sorry to see you disrespected."

Serena let out a small, appreciative laugh. "Well, thanks. Believe it or not, Santos is not the first. Usually it takes a little longer than it took him. He's Second Technician, only been here twelve years or so. I mean, I get that you guys get lonely. I get that you barely see a woman for fifty years. Your job requires so much sacrifice. I understand that, I really do. But I can't help that I am a woman. Because, more importantly, I'm a damn good doctor. You need me just as much as all five thousand of us need you." She shook her head. "I don't know why I'm telling you this."

They continued the hard work of walking up-spin toward the common room in silence, except for the thousand tiny, ubiquitous sounds of the interior of a space ship. The whirring of the HVAC. The tapping of their heels. The humming of the always-turning wheel. The buzzing of electricity in failing light fixtures. The rattling of doors that no longer closed quite properly after three centuries of use.

They arrived in the common room. Dr. Miller beelined for the dispensaries and swiped her thumb on the panel for the gruel, but it failed to activate.

"Manny must be not back yet," said Cheng. "Here." He swiped his thumb, and a serving of gruel flowed into the top bowl of the stack. He removed the bowl and handed it to Dr. Miller. "Use yours later to cover one for me."

"Thanks," she said, taking the bowl and finding the closest seat. She had barely finished sitting down as the first spoonful shoveled into her mouth.

"I have never known someone so excited about gruel." Cheng tried to conceal his amusement.

Another bite. "Oh, it's as disgusting to me as it is to you, I promise. But I wake up from cryo absolutely ravenous. I can't explain it. It's supposed to take a while before your appetite comes back, but not for me." She swallowed, then quickly replaced the void in her mouth. "Maybe I'm just making up for Ramsey."

"What about him?"

She paused, spoon halfway to her mouth. "They haven't told you about Ramsey?"

"I do not know." He racked his brain. "I know he wakes up one week each year. The others do not like it when he is awake. I understand he can be very cruel, but he would rather be left alone. I imagine he is very lonely."

She shook her head. "I can't believe they haven't told you. Okay," she licked her spoon and put it back in the bowl, "Ramsey is allergic to Somnithaw. Every time he wakes up, he vomits everywhere, and from what I've gathered from past technicians, it makes him totally delirious."

"Delirious?"

"In Ramsey's case, he seems to be talking to people who aren't there, but his words just come out all jumbled. No one knows what he's talking about or who he thinks he's talking to, but it's probably just his brain trying to process the world while he's, essentially, intoxicated. It lasts almost a full day according to the last report I asked to have written."

"Why do you need a report? What about his medical records?"

"He's changed the flight crew medical records system so he can skip the mandatory check-ins."

Cheng frowned. "I thought medical officers had all authority on their ships, even over the Captain. At least for medical issues."

She laughed bitterly. "That's true for virtually every ship that ever sailed or flew. But you've obviously never met Ramsey. He takes full control over everything he can. He isn't concerned about anything but results. I'm sure he has his reasons for not wanting medical attention, but I'm his doctor, and it's my job to make sure he makes it to Ithaca alive."

"I see. When I worked for RamTech Beijing, even there we heard of Ramsey's stubbornness. But I do not think this is Ramsey being stubborn. I think he is afraid."

"I've speculated on this, too. What do you think he's afraid of?" She took another enormous spoonful.

"I do not know. I have some ideas. But my mother always told me that fear makes fools of us all. When someone acts foolishly, either they are a fool or they are afraid. I do not think Ramsey is a fool. Do you?"

"No." She swallowed. "But you're suggesting that if we can determine what he's afraid of, we may be able to help him see reason?"

"Perhaps."

"You said you had ideas…"

"Only the fears common to all men."

"You're going to have to elaborate."

"Shame, failure, and death."

She raised her eyebrows. "So you think he's ashamed to be examined by a medical professional? Or he's ashamed that he's allergic to his own invention?"

"Perhaps."

"You keep saying that."

"I must say it while the answer remains unclear. But I think shame is less likely than the others."

"You think the man who saved the species is afraid of failure?"

"I will not say for certain."

"That's just a fancy way of saying 'perhaps.'"

He couldn't help but smile. "Yes. But, we have not made it to Ithaca yet. So far he has only brought us away from Earth. The hard part is still ahead."

"True, but if he wants to make sure we succeed, he should be willing to do whatever it takes to get there, including agreeing to have a medical exam, or even just the bare minimum of allowing medical records to be created automatically. He had to actively disable the systems in his cryo pod to make it happen. Someone who's accomplished as much as he has isn't going to just lay down and let everything he worked for come to nothing. He has way too much ego for that. He will succeed at all costs."

And then Cheng saw it. "What if his health is the cost he is willing to pay to ensure his success?"

Dr. Miller stared blankly at him for a second.

Absently, she took another bite of gruel. "That makes some sense of what we're observing, I guess. But it doesn't provide a reason why he feels he has to do it."

"We must consider his perspective," said Cheng. "Why does he wake up every year? Why does he continue to torture himself?"

"There are things only he understands, or so he says. There was a technician, Norman. I knew him pretty well not too long ago. Or... wow..." Serena waved her spoon, "I guess that was actually over a hundred years ago. I still haven't really adjusted to this missing-decades-at-a-time thing. Anyway, Norman was probably the smartest technician I've met so far. He tried to learn these systems so he could help Ramsey. Ramsey didn't take it well. Not at all. Norman told me Ramsey doesn't even really trust the diagnostic tools his company developed for the RAD, let alone another person. He uses the tools, but he mostly goes by feel."

"That does not seem safe."

She shrugged, "We're three hundred years in and still kicking."

Cheng nodded to concede the point. "So, he thinks he will lose access to these systems if he allows you to examine him."

"I don't see the connection."

"If you examine him and determine he is dying, what would you do?"

"Dying? I guess I would..." She closed her eyes and nodded, "I would have him stay out of cryo for a very long time, until he was fully recovered, and then I would put him back in cryo for the rest of the journey so he only had to deal with it one more time."

"This is his fear. He trusts no one else to keep the ship working. He trusts no one to realize something is wrong until it is already too late."

Dr. Miller could only nod.

"He believes he is dead either way."

Her brow creased. "But no one said he is dying. We have no way to know what sort of condition he's actually in without examining him."

"True or false, it matters not. It is his belief. It is his fear."

She rolled her neck out and sighed in frustration. "We need to make him submit to an examination."

Cheng shook his head. "No, we must persuade him. Fear makes us animals. Animals do not like to be forced, and an animal as intelligent as Dr. Ramsey will fight to the death to avoid it, and we have just determined he is not afraid to die."

She bit her lip and searched Cheng's eyes. Then she took another bite of gruel.

"I will do everything I can to earn his trust," said Cheng "It may take many, many years, but if I can, I will be his friend. And then, maybe, he will let us examine him. But first, you must make a choice, Dr. Miller."

"At this point, I think you had better just call me 'Serena.' Which choice is that?"

"Will you allow him to die for the good of the rest of us."

"No. I will not." She hadn't even paused to consider.

"Please, take your time. Because if you will not let him

fulfill his destiny, then he is right to fear your interference. If he is dying, you must have a different plan than what you said before. Even if you must let him arrive at Ithaca with death approaching. That is our best guess at his wish."

"You don't even know if any of this is true. This is all speculation."

"If I prove it to you, Serena, will you allow him to die to save the rest of us?"

She hesitated. Then she took a resigned breath. "If you prove to me that he's the only one who can do his job, and that his job is as necessary as he thinks it is, and that his fears and all his reasoning are just as you've said today, then... yes. Yes, I will allow him to die under my care if that is what is necessary and that is what he wants."

He bowed. "I will not let you down."

"It's not me I'm worried about." She took another bite of gruel and chewed it for a long time.

Cheng sat in silence.

"Well, this is a first," Serena said, pushing the nearly-finished bowl toward the center of the table, "I've lost my appetite. If there is a God, Cheng, I pray to it that you're wrong."

"There is, and I am not."

She nodded, then stood up, placing her bowl in the rack. "Come on. I have stitches to complete and I need my bodyguard to protect me from my patient."

8

SAVED

9 FEBRUARY 2214 CE – THE YEAR OF DEPARTURE

C heng Ahn knew the letter had arrived as soon as he entered their apartment. Lin sat on the carpet across the living room, her knees pulled tight to her chest, cheeks streaked from tears she had tried to hide in haste.

"Has it arrived, my darling?" he asked in their native Mandarin.

She nodded and pointed to the kitchen counter. Her lip trembled.

He rounded the bar and pinged the tablet to activate via his neural lace. As the device came to life, the world-famous seal of his employer, RamTech Enterprises, appeared at the top of the screen. He scanned the letter.

He had been accepted as a technician on CIV. He had secured passage to Ithaca.

He had saved her.

Cheng Ahn gazed across the room.

His wife observed him, heartache in her eyes. "I don't know whether to grieve or be grateful."

"Be glad." He crossed the room to sit by her side. He caressed her moist cheek and she held his hand there. "There is no greater honor for a husband than to secure the well-being of his wife."

"What good is my well-being if you will be old and haggard when we arrive at our new home across the stars? How well can I be if I cannot share my life with you? Why not stay and enjoy each other, for whatever time Earth has left?"

He pushed a stray hair behind her ear. "So little time is left, my darling. Perhaps only months." His hands found hers, now folded in her lap. "Please. Let me do this for you. There is no future for us or anyone else on Earth now that Project Artemis has failed. My life is already forfeit." He glanced to the counter where the tablet lay, then back to his wife. "This letter brings us hope. Yes, I must work on the ship for fifty years. But I trade my labor for your life. And when my service is up I will go back to sleep. Then I will see you again, and we will have a new home."

"But when we arrive, you will have the memories of an old man who lost the one he loved long ago. You will be seventy-nine, my Ahn-Ahn. The man you are now will be gone, replaced by a stranger. You will have lived an entire life while I feel as though little more than a long night's sleep has passed."

His lips caressed hers. "It is the only way I can save you."

Her sharp, dark eyes searched his, attempting to

pierce his armor, to find a shred of doubt in him. He gazed back with love and determined certainty. There was no doubt to find. At last, she nodded and laid her head on his chest, silent tears dampening his RamTech uniform.

9

PEACEFUL

D r. Ramsey pushed himself through the familiar cacophony of demons shrieking in his mind and forced the light to appear. He grasped after it until his body returned to his control, then threw himself forward. His legs crumpled beneath him as he fell onto the padding the technicians put out for him each week when they woke him up. The landing got harder every time as the materials degraded over the centuries.

His eyes still burned as he forced them open, searching for the bucket to catch his vomit. Someone held it out in front of him. That was nice. He was used to fumbling for it himself. He tried to take it, but the hands held it firm.

"I have this. You do what you must," said the stranger.

He did. It burned his mouth and his sinuses as much as ever. After three heaves, he knew he had finished. "Ok.

That's it for now," he said, his voice small and hoarse. He slumped down with his legs folded beneath him. The bucket clinked against the floor.

And then, something that had never happened before. The man rubbed his back. Odd, but comforting. Ramsey didn't object. After two or three minutes, Ramsey said, "Thanks."

"You are welcome. Ready to stand?"

"Yeah. I think so."

The man helped him up. "You are very brave to wake up every year and go through that." The mysterious helper was Asian of some description, Chinese probably, based on the shape of his face. Maybe Korean.

"Every week, as I experience it," said Ramsey, "For over six years."

"Even worse. I admire your dedication."

Great. Another fan boy technician. They were somehow worse than the ones who resented him. Ramsey supposed no one had yet warned this new guy not to be friendly with the immortal. "You must be..." he couldn't think of the name of the Senior Technician who had obviously been replaced, "...the new guy."

"Cheng Ahn," he extended his hand.

Ramsey reciprocated. "Dr. Colin Ramsey."

"I did not know you had a first name. Everyone calls you 'Doctor'." Cheng smiled.

Ramsey did prefer his title to his name, but a real fan boy would still have known what it was. He eyed his new technician, assessing him. "Don't spread it around."

"Your secret is safe with me, Dr. Ramsey."

"Yeah. Thanks."

Cheng helped Ramsey to his room, where hot tea, cold water and a meal of clear broth awaited him.

Ramsey slept well for the first time in years.

10

DIAGNOSIS

15 OCTOBER 2209 CE - 4 YEARS BEFORE DEPARTURE

I t was a sign of the times that Ty felt like he was going home as his shuttle departed the atmosphere.

From his window seat aboard the RamTech luxury shuttle, he could now see the Earth falling away below him. In a moment of silent gratitude, Ty thanked whatever deity might be listening for the razor-thin chance that had placed him in the closest circle of influence with Colin, and that it had resulted in the saving of his family from the planet's coming collapse.

The shuttle journey was as uneventful as one could hope it would be. Ty took the rare opportunity to nap, caught up on some correspondence with the contractor responsible for the production of the cryo pods, and napped again before the shuttle arrived at the central hub of Troy Orbital.

After the always-jarring transition to simulated gravity via the spin-lock, and a long series of elevators, Ty found himself alone on an elevator connecting the middle rings with the outer rings of Troy Orbital. In the distance, the Earth shone against the black, rising until it passed overhead and out of sight. From the direction of Ty's feet appeared the skeletal structure of Ramsey's masterpiece.

The work on CIV was progressing according to schedule. However, even with the miraculous advances in planet-to-orbit propulsion that the late Dr. Ramsey, Sr. had innovated during his lifetime, it was still expensive to move all that raw material up from Earth, and so the construction phase had been delayed as long as possible to ensure that the materials that could not be mined from captured asteroids were not brought into orbit wastefully.

The single-ringed structure that the ship would have was already intelligible in the glinting sunlight. Three spokes extended to the ring from a central hub where the Ramsey-Alcubierre Drive would be installed upon its completion. Ramsey was working tirelessly on the RAD, creating and preserving the exotic matter, calibrating the containment fields, seeking optimizations. The current theoretical output would get them to Ithaca in just over five hundred and fifty years. Ramsey had targeted another ten percent improvement in efficiency before they installed the drive. Every twelve years they could shave off meant one fewer technician and their loved one, and that much more room for the truly chosen. At least, that was how Ramsey thought of it.

Darkness returned to the elevator momentarily as it entered the structure of the outer rings and the lights hesitated before flickering back on. With gravity nearly equivalent to that of Earth, the elevator came to a rest and the doors opened.

"Daddy!" cried the little girl with the long, braided, light brown hair, hazel eyes, and her mother's smile.

Izzy ran with long, rambling strides across the courtyard and leapt into her father's outstretched arms. Ty spun her around, cherishing the moment before setting his almost-nine-year-old back down on the floor.

"Did you grow while I was gone, Iz?" he said as he brushed his hand on her freckled face and crouched down to her level.

Izzy smiled, "I'm the tallest in my class this year."

"And the smartest, too, I bet."

Izzy smiled sheepishly and looked away for a moment. "I missed you, Daddy."

His heart soared. "I missed you, too, sweetheart, but I shouldn't have to go away again for a long time. I'll be here with you and Mom." He looked up to scan the crowd for Clara, who stood just a few feet away, forcing a smile for him.

"Welcome home, honey," she said. There was a weight in her voice that he couldn't account for, something pained just behind her eyes. Well, more pained than usual.

Ty spotted an ice cream vendor just across the courtyard. "Hey, Izzy, I think we should have a treat. Don't you?"

A big smile. "I think that would be good."

"Alright, why don't you run over to that ice cream place. You can get anything you want. I'll have cookies and cream, and what do you think Mom would want?"

"Hmmm... chocolate!"

"Good idea. You know our account number, right?"

"Mmmhmm."

He smiled. "Alright, off with you, then. Hurry back." And she scurried away.

As she disappeared into the thin crowd of people, Ty's smile faded as he turned to Clara. She sidled up to him, rested her head just under his chin, where his stubble caught on her thick brown hair.

Ty rubbed his wife's back as he held her "What's wrong? Aren't you glad to see me?"

She nodded, her hair tickling him on the neck. "Of course I am. I'm sorry." She pulled away, her hands still grasping his shirt near his waist.

He disentangled the strands of her hair from his face and pushed them behind her ear.

She forced a smile. "I'm glad you are home."

He bowed his head for a more direct line of sight to look her in the eyes. "But..."

"But," she looked nervously over her shoulder, and her voice dropped to little more than a whisper, "Izzy had her checkup last week and it was the first time that they ran a full screening on her. And she..." Clara's voice caught.

Ty's heartbeat reverberated even down to his toes. His insides screamed for the information, but he forced calm into his voice. "She what, Love?"

Clara pursed her lips, fought back the raw emotion. "She has a genetic disorder... that makes her... ineligible... for Ithaca."

Ty stood in dumb shock, then pulled Clara close as

her tears threatened to overflow. He rubbed her back some more. He glanced over at the ice cream place where his little girl was placing an order for her family. "Is it terminal?" he whispered. His eyes never left his daughter, even as they clouded with moisture.

Clara shook her head in a horizontal motion on his chest. Thank God. Ty let out the air he hadn't realized he'd been holding in. "Does she know?"

Another side-to-side head movement.

"Does anyone else know?"

"Just the doctor, of course." Clara eased away from his arms and wiped her face on her sleeve.

Ty nodded, thinking. The fewer people who knew the better. Ramsey was fanatical in his eradication of any less-than-perfect genes from the applicant pool. Ty himself would have been disqualified based on a few minor markers for things like heart disease. These were genetic trivialities that Ramsey was willing to overlook for the benefit of having Ty's help on the journey, but Izzy's genetic disorder, whatever it was, would remove any shade of gray Ramsey had previously applied to his promise to bring them to Ithaca. There was no room for that in his vision. No, they had to hide this from Ramsey to have any hope.

Ty's chest constricted as his intellect began to catch up with his emotions. The Earth was dying, and unless he could deceive his best friend for nearly five years, Izzy would die with it. Then came the question.

If Izzy is rejected, what will I do?

Unbidden, his mind conjured an image of kissing his daughter goodbye for the last time. Leaving her with his aunt, or Clara's parents, or an orphanage. Looking through the glass of a vehicle as he pulled away, another person's hand resting on his little girl's shoulder as her hazel eyes watched him go. Watching her vanish as the car rounded some corner. Returning to space. Going into cryo. Waking and working, waking and working over and over again for five years during the journey. Seeing Ithaca with his own eyes. Breathing the pure air of a planet untouched by human hands. Setting up a home for himself and Clara. Perhaps having another child. But wondering, always wondering, what had happened to the little girl he had loved with pieces of his heart he hadn't known existed before she came into his life.

And then he saw himself sitting in an apartment on Earth, Izzy and Clara held close, watching the feeds as CIV prepared to depart. Seeing the vids of the ship vanishing into FTL and knowing he would have no further part to play in the story of the human species. And then, what? Killing himself as the conditions deteriorated, the food disappeared, and the violence that was already erupting in many parts of the world reached him? Becoming part of a militant group and causing untold suffering upon countless thousands of innocents? Leading a militant group to save his family at the cost of millions of lives? No, it wasn't in him to use violence, or at least he doubted it was. But what would he do? Watch his family deteriorate slowly over time? Hold his daughter and then his wife as they died of starvation or once-preventable diseases? Look on in horror as his family became victims of human rights atrocities at the hands of desperate and violent men?

Returning to himself, Ty reached out a hand to wipe a tear from Clara's cheek. "Colin can't find out."

She laughed bitterly as she placed her hand on his, guiding it away from her face. "You really think he won't know? Her blood work is in the system. Her file will be flagged as a reject. Even if he doesn't find out directly, someone else will, and they'll stop her."

"I'm the COO. They'll do what I say."

"They'll see through it."

"I have to try."

"There's no point."

"If there's a point to going to Ithaca at all, there's a point to doing whatever it takes to get Izzy there."

"Well, obviously, but there's no point in fighting the inevitable."

"I've seen more impossible things in the last six years than I can count. I have to try, even if I fail."

"You will fail." She almost spat the words.

Ty hesitated. "Clara, why are you doing this? Why won't you let me try."

She briefly glanced over to where Izzy was still waiting for the ice cream, her face pressed up against the glass. "You've barely seen your daughter for the last six years. You work a hundred hours a week. But she still worships you, because you're her daddy. If Ramsey is going to find out anyway, why not just quit? Why not leave Troy, find a quiet place to live back on Earth? You would at least know your daughter, then. Wouldn't that be worth it to you?"

Ty sighed. "Because I want to live, Clara. I want you to live, and Izzy to live. I want to go to Ithaca, the planet that

I found. I want to be a part of the future of the human race, not an anonymous victim of everything that's going to happen down there. And as long as I believe that there's a sliver of hope that I can save her... I will do every single thing in my power to do it. I'll work more, I'll make myself indispensable, I'll use any advantage I have as a bargaining chip to get what I want."

She recoiled, her eyes like a snake ready to strike. "Now you're really starting to sound like Ramsey."

The words were intended to hurt, and they did. His conversation from the previous week echoed in his mind, where that Dr. Miller had told him much the same thing. It was never intended as a positive comparison, but he had to admit that nobody got results the way Colin did. Maybe he needed to be more like his friend to get what he really wanted. "Colin is going to bring the survivors of planet Earth to a new home, and we are going to be there. All three of us."

"And what happens when Ramsey finds out and sends Izzy back to Earth, then? Are you going to come with us, or are you going to stay loyal to your *friend*?" She emphasized the last word passive-aggressively.

"How can you ask me that?"

"That's not an answer."

He wanted to say it. He wanted to promise his loyalty to her. He wanted to show her that his love for them was greater than all his ideals about humanity and the hope of a new future. But his mouth wouldn't open. And after a few seconds, all he could do was look away.

Clara shook her head, too angry for words. She folded her arms and turned away from him just as Izzy returned, tray of ice cream in her small hands, her smile aglow with the innocence of youth and a mind as yet untroubled by the terrors that were to come if Ty failed.

But he wouldn't fail. Whatever it took, he would make sure that they were all on CIV when it departed for Ithaca.

Even if it killed him.

11

DANGER

Morning again. Cheng Ahn awoke to the gradually brightening full-spectrum light in his quarters. The light revealed his uniform, navy blue and firmly pressed, hanging from the hook above his bed. The uniforms at RamTech's Beijing office, where Cheng had worked before his selection as a technician, had always been pressed, and Cheng liked the feeling of precision now as much as he had in his younger days. At first, the other technicians had teased Cheng for the level of attention he paid his uniform, but the jokes had slowed after a few months. Now, very nearly six years later, they had ceased entirely. Besides, Lin liked the way they looked.

Lin.

He sighed, staring at the uniform for a moment longer.

He swung his feet out of bed and began preparing his

shower, willing his mind to escape the depressive rut it had once again fallen into.

Lin slept safely in the ring, oblivious to the relentless passing of time. There she would stay. There she should stay.

But...

He shook his head and tried to think of other things.

Ramsey day. That was today. That was his focus. Cheng made a mental note to make sure Ramsey's quarters were prepared to receive their occupant. Silently, he rehearsed his routine, priming himself to look for any hint of vulnerability in Ramsey that he could penetrate and place himself into Ramsey's circle of influence.

That, of course, was assuming Ramsey was capable of having a circle of influence.

If there was anything Cheng had learned in his week with Ramsey over each of the five previous years, it was that Ramsey's circle of influence contained only one person: himself. He barely spoke to anyone. He ate meals at odd hours to avoid the technicians. He worked at distant terminals, and rarely requested assistance. Other than that first hour of his waking and the last minutes before returning to cryo, Ramsey was inaccessible to Cheng. Two years prior, Cheng had not seen Ramsey at all except for coming out of cryo and going back in, so unyielding was his regimen of isolation.

Cheng let the shower water fall on him for a full minute longer than usual, dried and dressed himself somberly, and headed to breakfast.

Santos and Maurice were already there, spoons deep in their gruel.

"Morning, Cheng," said Maurice.

Santos waved two fingers in a dispassionate mock salute.

"Good morning." Cheng gathered his gruel and sat across from his colleagues.

"So, today's the day," said Maurice.

Santos dropped his spoon into the bowl with a loud clink. "Damn. Is it really? Again?"

"Afraid so."

"Well," said Santos, gesturing at Cheng, "At least Ramsey has his patron saint here to help him out."

Not this again. "It is a privilege to do my duty," said Cheng. "Ramsey's health and comfort is mission-critical."

"You really believe that *malakies*?" said Santos. Cheng didn't know the last word, but it sounded Greek and he could guess the meaning from context. "You really think he's so important?"

"Give it a rest, Santos," said Maurice. "If it weren't for Cheng, you'd still be bitching about having to wake him up every year."

"But doesn't it bother you that he *doesn't* bitch about it?" Santos shot a sideways glance in Cheng's direction, inviting confrontation. "It's almost like he thinks it's fun or something."

Cheng took a bite of gruel to stop his tongue from striking back without thinking. He still had thirty years left of dealing with Santos. Now was not the time to control his temper, not make an enemy. He swallowed. "No, it is not fun. It is difficult and disgusting. But I cannot believe he enjoys torturing himself year after year. If he can endure that, I can endure helping him.

That is all." He didn't dare mention his theories to this audience.

Santos's eyes narrowed.

Maurice gave an impressed nod. "You've got some wisdom in your brain, that's for sure, kid. You're a better man than I."

"There are no better men, or worse men," said Cheng, toeing the line with a glance at Santos, who did not look up. "The only differences between men are the actions they choose to take."

Maurice gave a non-committal grunt.

Cheng returned to his gruel. He needed a plan to gain Ramsey's confidence, and he needed it soon.

———

CHENG STABILIZED RAMSEY AS HE WOBBLED OUT OF CRYO, whispering reassurances. Ramsey's legs shook with each tortured movement. Cheng steadied him, helping him down to his knees where the bucket awaited him. Cheng patted Ramsey's back as it writhed and heaved, holding his breath against the smell. The contents sloshed together in the bucket, and the heaving slowed. Cheng was about to ask if that was the end when Ramsey suddenly went limp, his face plunging into the bucket, tipping it over and spilling its putrid contents across the floor.

Cheng regained his balance and lifted Ramsey's face out of the sick. Stringy tendrils dangled, then dripped from the front of Ramsey's curly blond hair, leaving lines across the floor and across Ramsey's face.

Ramsey's eyes fluttered. He regained enough awareness to realize he was covered in something sticky before he faded back into semi-consciousness. Cheng laid him down on his side, still whispering soothing words as he struggled to keep his own digestive tract in line, and took stock of the situation.

He had one canister of water intended for Ramsey to drink, one small bowl of water he brought customarily in the event that some vomit did slosh out of the bucket, but he had never anticipated a full spill.

If Ramsey had become so unwell that the extraction process was causing him to lose consciousness, the situation might be even more dire than he and Serena had originally evaluated those few years ago. She had not made another appearance in the half-decade since he met her, and there was still Dr. Fernandez to go before Serena had her next turn. It would likely be several more years before they could re-strategize, and Serena would be expecting him to have a close relationship with Ramsey by then to use as a platform.

Any relationship would be a start.

Cheng righted the overturned bucket, grabbed the washrag from the small basin of water, and began to wipe the sickness off of Ramsey's face and hair. The sick man's eyes cracked open, then drooped closed again. This repeated several times as Cheng cleaned Ramsey's face and jumpsuit, neglecting the dark spots that had appeared on his own uniform.

Cheng was far from finished when the water in the canister and the bowl became unusable. He sat Ramsey up, slid his shoulder under the other man's armpit and lifted him off the floor. Ramsey moved like he was drugged, but he kept his legs under him with Cheng's help.

Cheng swore he heard a small, "Thank you," pass through Ramsey's barely parted lips.

He smiled warmly in return.

They arrived at Ramsey's quarters, the door opening with a swipe of the hand. Cheng sat Ramsey down against the wall adjacent to the bathroom and got the shower going.

"Do you need any help, Dr. Ramsey?" he asked. "I believe you should clean yourself before you go to sleep."

"No. I'll be ok," came the small reply.

Cheng bowed. "You know how to reach me if you need assistance with anything."

"Your accent is getting better."

Cheng froze. Ramsey had never said anything about him before. He wasn't sure if the sickness had made him delirious and brought down his verbal filters or if this was trust dawning between them. "Thank you, Dr. Ramsey. I have been using it exclusively for nearly six years now."

Ramsey nodded. "Six years."

Cheng opted to depart on the positive note. "Be well, Dr. Ramsey." With a final bow, he left the room.

Outside, Cheng slid down the hard plastic wall, letting his neck and arms hang limply as they pleased. A heavy sigh. A deep breath. A moment of quiet. A silent prayer that this miserable endeavor would be worth it in the end.

Then he stood, stripped down to his undergarments,

and headed for the supply room to find some way to clean up the mess in crew cryo.

―――――

PRIVATELY, RAMSEY WAS CONCERNED ABOUT HIS... episode... during cryo extraction. Publicly, there could be no sign of weakness, no hesitation to carry on as before, no sign that anything had grown worse.

Undoubtedly, the new technician, Chan, or whatever it was, had told the others all about what had happened, and Ramsey would now be subject to their ridicule for the next several weeks. The key now would be to summon the strength to avoid a repeat the following week, so that it could be written off as a one-time thing.

It would be a one-time thing. A thing of the past.

Ramsey sat on the edge of his bed, his stomach gurgling quietly below. His shower was running, but he didn't remember turning it on, and couldn't think why he would return to his bed after turning it on.

Or, had he already showered and forgotten to turn the water off?

He ran a hand through his hair. Bone dry.

He removed his clothes and shuffled those few feet across the room. He pumped stimulants into the shower cocktail and entered the small stall.

The water was warm, and strong. He savored the millions of tiny impacts splashing off his skin, the roar of the water flowing and splashing and running down the drain.

The stimulants began to take effect, and his thoughts became more acute.

It was Tuesday, or at least the second full day of his waking week, the day Ramsey thought of as Tuesday. Sunday had been wasted in recovery, as usual. Monday had consisted largely of checking the RAD. And today he would oversee the technicians' maintenance of the primary life support system in addition to his normal duties.

The life support system only really needed maintenance every eight years or so, which made it a low-stress system, but also meant that the technicians didn't maintain it frequently enough for even the Senior Tech to be a true expert.

Ramsey admitted he wasn't a true expert on the PLS either. Ty had been influential in the design and implementation of the greenhouse that acted as both the hub of oxygen-carbon dioxide interchange and the hydroponics lab where the crew's fruits and vegetables were grown. The module itself had been built at RamTech's Beijing branch.

The system was a little earthy for Ramsey's liking. He couldn't help but prefer the secondary life support, which was an improvement of his own design over old-fashioned filter-based life support. Ramsey's design was present on the ship, but truly a backup. The expedition would be in serious trouble if the greenhouse were removed from the circulation system for more than a week or so at a time.

He rinsed the soap from his hair, then held his breath

as the water caressed his face for several glorious seconds.

He was ready for the day now. Ready to face the issues in life support, ready to continue his analysis of the RAD output, ready to direct and lead with confidence.

And ready to avoid the technicians if at all possible.

———

It has been known for hundreds of years that true multi-tasking is impossible. A human being only has a certain amount of attention to give, and it has been proven time and again that dividing that attention will adversely affect performance on all tasks.

Ramsey was familiar with the findings, but gave them no credence in his own conduct. And so, while the technicians were maintaining the PLS, he half-listened as he analyzed the latest data from the RAD and compared it against its historical performance.

He failed to register the hesitation in the Second Technician's status report, or the uncertainty in the First Technician's response, or the Junior Technician's question, or the Senior Technician's warning.

And then a distant rumble shook the ship.

And the lights went out.

12

INSIGHT

11 JANUARY 2210 CE - 4 YEARS BEFORE DEPARTURE

I n his office, Ty pored over the specs for the latest impossible assignment from Ramsey. Life Support.

At least it wasn't anything important this time.

He buried his face in his hands. His sarcasm wouldn't help anything, and the stakes were too high to waste his time wallowing in bitterness.

He glanced at the clock. Old habit. Those numbers didn't matter any more, not since he had redoubled his efforts to make himself indispensable to Ramsey. In the three months since Izzy's diagnosis, he had barely seen his wife or daughter. Ramsey's demands were relentless, and he had no problem working any willing victim to the bone. Over half of his senior leadership had burned out and moved on since the announcement of CIV five years ago, including three different CFOs.

Ty had held on out of loyalty and necessity. The ceaseless workload didn't suit him, but the ends justified the means.

Damn. Said it again.

He shook his head and refocused his attention on the Life Support specs.

Mechanical things broke down over time. That was the core of the issue. There had been a massive paradigm shift in manufacturing as an ever-larger share of the things humanity built were destined for space. The wasteful policy of engineered obsolescence, so popular in the preceding centuries, was a thing of the past when it came to space. Things were built to last now, as much as possible. But five centuries would be a long time to keep any system functioning, especially without access to the resources of Earth. And the Industrial Revolution itself was still less than five hundred years old. Nothing from that time remained functioning.

He knew it wasn't a fair comparison. The materials they had to work with then were laughable compared to the hybrids and meta-materials of today. The ship would last.

It had to last.

Ramsey's design for life support was a good one: a definite improvement on the CO_2 conversion systems that existed on space stations like Troy Orbital; but it was designed for efficiency, not longevity. It had to be. It was life support. You can't have inefficient life support.

Ty ran the spec data through the algorithm he had designed. The results returned almost immediately.

Best case scenario, the system would need to be totally reimplemented at least three times. That was far too many for so essential a system. And it would require redundancies. You never could know what might go wrong. He calculated how much space the redundant materials would take up... and his heart sank.

Far, far too much. Life support would need a complete redesign to increase longevity, decrease size, and maintain or improve efficiency.

It was a big ask. For the first time in several years, Ty doubted the mission. Even Ramsey's revolutionary design wouldn't be enough.

Everyone was doomed.

––––––

12 January 2210 CE - 4 Years Before Departure

"AND WHAT, EXACTLY, DO YOU EXPECT ME TO DO WITH THIS information, Ty?"

"We need to redesign the life support again. We need to make it last far longer. Far, far longer."

"This is the best life support system that's ever been designed, and you know it."

"Yeah, I do know it. It's a modern marvel. And if we didn't have to carry the raw supplies for six more copies of it half way across the galaxy, it would be a feasible solution for CIV. As it stands, it is far too resource intensive, there are too many unknowns, and it just won't last long enough."

Ramsey ran his fingers through his hair while Ty clenched and unclenched his jaw. He hated confronting Ramsey like this. Ramsey, for his part, looked almost regal standing behind his desk. His dark blond hair was shorter now, his dark eyes piercing, seeking, observing.

He had the manner of one who had grown accustomed to power, accustomed to getting what he wanted.

"Well then," said Ramsey, pacing out from behind his desk with a slow, methodical gait, "I suppose we'll just have to call off the project." He paced to the window in the floor, just outside of Ty's range of vision, his back to his friend.

Ty swiveled his chair to face Ramsey again and resolved to say nothing in response to Ramsey's antagonizing.

"Or," Ramsey continued, "You can find a solution."

"Me?"

"You."

"Why?"

"I gave it my best go and came up short, by your standards," Ramsey said. The cold calm of his voice made Ty shiver. "So, I'm turning it over to you, Ty."

Ty glared at the back of Ramsey's head. "You know I can't. It's not my area of-"

Ramsey rounded on him, moving with a shocking ferocity. Ty began to recoil, caught himself, stood his ground. Ramsey's face stopped inches from Ty's. His eyes were nearly inhuman, wide in intensity, brow tightly knit with fury, deep, dark bags creasing the sallow skin beneath them. Ramsey raised his index finger to Ty's chest. "You listen to me. You listen." His voice was a whisper laced with poison. "I rely on you, Ty. I count on you to be another me. You see things no one else can, and that is very, very valuable to this mission. But if you ever come to me again, rejecting my work, offering no alternative solutions or lines of inquiry, I swear to God, Ty, I will fire you."

Ty held Ramsey's eyes, clenching his jaw. It was like looking into the sun.

"Do you understand?"

Ty nodded, dropped his eyes.

"Good." Ramsey backed up two paces.

Ty released the breath he hadn't realized he'd been holding. Ramsey wouldn't really fire him, he was pretty sure. But everything he'd done so far would be for nothing if Ramsey sent him away. Somehow it seemed unlikely that Ramsey would honor his promise to Ty's family if Ty lost his job.

The peril of their fragile situation settled on Ty like a sudden darkness. The hours he had worked, the improvements he had made, all the good he had done for the cause of RamTech, for CIV, for Ithaca was, ultimately, insignificant to Ramsey.

Ramsey was no longer a man; he had become a vindictive, narcissistic, capricious demigod. And to a being such as that, the accomplishments of any human, however significant, would always pale in comparison to its own.

The only option left was to comply. To obey. To give in. To remove any cause for scrutiny or disapproval. Maybe, just maybe, he would never notice the truth about Izzy. Ty just needed to make it to the finish line.

But first, he needed to solve the issue at hand: what to do about the life support.

"I'll go see if I can come up with a solution," he said, shuffling toward the door.

Ramsey dismissed Ty with a disinterested wave as he returned to his desk.

———

13 January 2210 CE - 4 Years Before Departure

TY PACED BACK AND FORTH THROUGH HIS LAB. HE HADN'T been to his quarters in nearly forty hours, although he had unintentionally napped for about ninety minutes at some point overnight.

He had written a program years ago for visualizing and analyzing interactions of codependent variables. With a few tweaks, he had applied the program to the life support issue. A giant projection of the output floated in three dimensions from the terminal in the center of the room.

For some reason, the program had rendered the data visually as a spider web-like design, with the bigger variables centralized near the hub and the less significant ones radiating out from the center.

He couldn't make sense of it, but the algorithm had determined this was the best way to represent the data.

Ty deposited himself into a wheeled chair, his mass sending it drifting across the floor until it nudged the opposite wall. He sat there for several long seconds until a chime at the door drew his attention.

"Open," he said wearily.

"Hello?" said a little voice.

His heart soared. "Over here, Izzy."

She skipped around the table and plopped down on

her knees in front of him, her elbows and chin resting on his knees. She looked up at him with those beautiful eyes. "Hi!"

He smiled and put his hand on the side of her face. "Hi, Sweetheart."

"Mom said I could come say hi." She picked her chin up off his knee. "I miss you, Daddy."

He nodded. "I know. I miss you too, Iz. I'm sorry I haven't been home. I just have this problem that I'm working on and it's really important for CIV to work."

"Oh. Mission-critical, huh?"

He laughed, and she laughed too. "Yeah, it is mission-critical."

"Can I see?"

"I don't see why not."

She launched off the floor. "Maybe I can help!"

"Well, I'm glad to have you here then," he said, smiling, "because I really could use some." He stood himself up and led her over to the diagram hovering above the table. "This is a visualization of the problem surrounding the life support system. It's supposed to be arranged in a way that makes it easier to figure out what's wrong, but I can't see the connections yet."

"It looks like a tree trunk if you took a picture of it from above."

"It looks like a spiderweb to me."

She tilted her head. "Hmm... No, I think it's a tree trunk, and the outside ones are the roots." She grabbed his hand. "Daddy, when do you think I'll be able to see some real trees?"

"We have real trees here on Troy, sweetheart." He knew it wasn't what she meant.

"Not very many, though! I want to see a real, live forest someday. They just seem so magical."

"Living here, you have views of the Earth and space that countless generations of people living in the forests of Earth could only dream of."

"But Dad, space is so boring! And all the most interesting places on Troy are places I'm not even allowed to go. Why can't we have a forest in space?"

"Because, sweetheart, we..." he froze.

"We what?"

"Hold on. I'm having an idea."

She tapped her hand on her thigh and looked around the lab melodramatically.

"Maybe," he said at last, "Maybe we could."

"Really?" she beamed.

"Yeah," he was still in shock, "Really. Not here - not on Troy, but on CIV. Trees process carbon dioxide and produce oxygen. It's the life support system for human life on Earth. Why not make it the life support system for human life in space?"

"Cool!"

He picked her up and spun her around as they laughed together. "Izzy, you're a genius!"

She touched down in a fit of giggles. "I think I got it from Mom."

———

14 January 2210 CE - 4 Years Before Departure

"THIS HAD BETTER BE GOOD, TY," SAID RAMSEY.

"It is. I solved the life support problem."

Ramsey raised an eyebrow. "Really?"

"Well, as far as the habitat goes, I solved it. It will require some minor redesigns of the plans for the structure's interior, but I already have some suggestions for your review."

"Let's assess the idea first. We don't want to get ahead of ourselves."

Ty nodded and linked his tablet to the projection deck on Ramsey's desk.

"Throughout the history of humanity's presence in space," Ty began, "we have needed life support. When we first entered orbit in the early second half of the 20th century, the capsules the astronauts went in were tiny, and the tyranny of the rocket equation prevented them from bringing anything unnecessary up there.

"Even the first space stations... you know, those long, modular ones that got popular around the turn of the millennium... were too small and too expensive to launch to consider any solution other than relatively lightweight CO_2 filters.

"It became the de facto and unquestioned standard of how life support was done. The missions were short-term, cramped, and expensive.

"As the first torus-style space stations were built, and gradually got larger, culminating in Troy Orbital, this philosophy continued to go unquestioned. The maintenance is not particularly difficult, and the filters are still lightweight and easily replaceable.

"However, every space structure humanity has built to

date has still fallen under the protection and convenience of relative proximity to Earth. But that is not the case with CIV. Instead, it needs to be a self-sustaining system. There is only one other self-sustaining habitat that humanity has encountered, and that," he pressed a button and a blue-green orb appeared in the projection field, "is planet Earth herself."

Ramsey nodded. "I see. So you want to use photosynthesis to grow plants that will scrub the air naturally?"

"Exactly." God, Ramsey was quick. "I've developed an equation to figure out multiple solutions that would provide other benefits to the crew and the overall health of the space habitat, and we could engineer our specimens not to produce pollen. I have multiple possible configurations on the next slides."

"What about finding space for all this on the ship?"

"I admit that that is a problem, as I'm envisioning a two-story greenhouse. It'll take up a lot of room, but I already have some ideas for how to optimize the crew module without changing its overall dimensions."

Ramsey flipped through the slide show for about an hour, a cautious smile visiting his face on multiple occasions. He asked Ty a few questions, and Ty was well pleased with his ability to respond.

"We're close here, Ty," said Ramsey, "Really close. I have another meeting in just a moment, but let's get back together in twelve hours. I want you to walk me through your math in more detail, and I also want to include a traditional life support as a backup. We do have about five percent wiggle room on the size of the crew module, we'd just need to match it in the counterweight on the opposite side of the ship. See if you can find a way to include both systems. Obviously you can scale my design down as needed to match its reduced role." He disconnected the link between the projection deck and the tablet and handed the device back to Ty. "As you know, I don't say this often, but... I am impressed."

Ty smiled gratefully even as his heart began to pound in his ears. Perhaps this would be the contribution that made Izzy immune to the genetic restrictions. "Thanks, Col." He offered his hand, which was received enthusiastically.

Ramsey's toothy grin faded as he shook Ty's hand. "Are you alright, Ty? Your hands are shaking."

"What? Oh, yeah yeah yeah. I'm fine," he said, his mind racing with the possibility of telling Ramsey about Izzy. But no, better to wait until the plans were finalized, maybe even until the module was built. No point in taking a risk. Not yet.

"Are you sure? Because-"

A chime at the door gave little warning before one of Ramsey's pretty executive assistants entered the room. "The President is here to see you, sir."

Ramsey looked at Ty appraisingly, then back to his XA. "Which President is it, again?"

"The American one, sir."

He turned back to Ty. "Damn. I can't put this one off. I'll see you in twelve hours though, to go over that math, right?"

Ty nodded.

"Ok, good." Then to the XA, "Send her in as soon as

Dr. Daniels is away." In one sweeping motion he was once again poised behind his desk.

By the time Ty had been guided out of the room, Ramsey's projection field was already full of documents and graphs, and Ramsey's focus was so intense that Ty almost thought it impossible that Ramsey had switched gears that quickly.

The trouble with Ramsey was that however hard you worked, he always worked harder. It was like how the very best athletes, apart from the essential hard work to master their sport, always seemed to have some sort of genetic advantage to set them apart from their opponents. For Ramsey it was more than just his raw intellect and ambition; he had a brain capable of much more single-minded focus and determination than the average human. Ty was sure of it.

And that meant that even this accomplishment of Ty's would not be enough.

Nothing would ever be enough. He couldn't believe he had even considered revealing the truth.

As Ty passed into the hallway and back toward his quarters, he began to formulate his lie. Ramsey would ask again what had been on Ty's mind at the end of the meeting, and fortune, in the form of the meeting with the President, had provided an opportunity for him to consider the best possible answer. He would need to learn it, live it, breathe it, and teach it to his family in the exact right proportion. The lie needed to be complete.

It needed to be anything but the truth.

T he warning sounded in a low, melancholy *dwoop, dwoop*.

"No. No, no, no, no, no," Ramsey said aloud despite himself. He fumbled through his jumpsuit's chest pocket, pulling out and discarding the pen and small pad of paper he kept there. A moment later, he found the pressure switch inside the pocket and activated the luminescent patches across his shoulders and collarbones.

The corridor was still dark and bizarrely quiet, but the patches threw enough light to illuminate his immediate surroundings. Ramsey took stock of what he knew.

The station was still spinning, and whatever the extent of the situation, it would continue spinning, so they wouldn't lose gravity. Thank you, Newton.

The fusion reactor was still functioning, because a total failure would have rocked the ship much more than the small tremor he had felt. Thank you, Eddington.

The RAD hadn't failed, or the tidal forces would have pulled the ship apart. Thank you, Ramsey.

The tremor meant the ship was reacting to a reduction in the fusion reactor's output, but it was unclear if that reduction had caused the power failure or if the power failure had caused the reactor to adjust to lower energy needs.

Either way, the technicians had broken something. Incompetent, unprofessional morons.

Ramsey took a deep breath. Now was the time to respond to the crisis.

Heads would roll later.

The terminal he had been working on was dark and unresponsive, but his tablet initiated normally, and was still looped into the ship's diagnostic network. That was good news; there was still power in certain parts of the crew module.

He tapped his ear to try reaching the Senior Technician on the comm, then hesitated. He couldn't remember who was the Senior. "This is Ramsey," he said, quite unnecessarily, "What the hell happened?"

Broken static answered back.

Ok. No technicians. No need to panic. He started sifting through the diagnostic network data and quickly assuaged his worst fears about hull breaches or leaking fuel tanks. Power output was down to about seventy percent, with nearly all the powerless areas in the crew module. The areas that remained with power were short on their energy needs. Pivotally, all five thousand cryo chambers remained operational. Ramsey breathed a sigh of relief and congratulated himself for designing the system well.

The comm crackled in his ear, "-hear us?"

"This is Ramsey, go ahead."

"Dr. Ramsey, this is Manny..."

He was pretty sure Manny was the Senior Technician, and also, apparently, an idiot. "I already said go ahead," he spat, "What's your status?"

"Sorry, sir. No one is hurt too badly. Santos is pretty shaken up, but we're ok."

Ramsey threw his hands in the air in frustration. "I meant the situation with the ship, Manny. What the hell did you do?"

A long pause.

Ramsey continued searching the diagnostics. He grew impatient. "Would someone competent please answer me? We might be on the clock here."

"Dr. Ramsey, this is Cheng," said a familiar voice. Cheng continued without waiting for acknowledgement. "I'm showing a power outage that includes everything on the middle deck, including primary life support, obviously. So, that means no life support for the entire crew module-"

Manny interrupted. "No, we still have the backup. It's down on the outer floor."

"With respect," said Cheng, "the secondary life support is not like the other modules. The scrubber and the filter are on the outer floor, but it shares power with water filtration, which is on this floor, so no power."

"With respect, junior tech, I think I know this ship better than you do."

"No, Cheng is right," Ramsey cut in. He scrolled through the log leading up to the power disruption as he spoke. "The greenhouse was a later addition to the ship's architecture and we had to get creative to power everything." All systems were nominal leading up to the failure. "Cheng, continue."

"In brief, the main power line to the module was severed when we tried to remove a tree root that penetrated between two panels."

Ramsey's hands froze on the holodisplay. The only thing he could manage to say was an icy "Elaborate."

"Yes, sir. When we scoped the access tunnel to make sure it was clear, we noticed that a root had found a hairline gap between two plates in its environment and penetrated into the utility tunnel."

"That shouldn't be possible."

"No," said Manny, "it shouldn't. Maybe it's to do with the genetic modifications to the trees. Could they have made the roots harder, more persistent?"

Ramsey had asked that very question of Ty's team during the process of engineering the specifics of the primary life support module. "Maybe." *Oh, Ty, what have you done?* "But how did power actually fail? Roots where they shouldn't be is a major problem, of course, but why did it fail during maintenance? Cheng said it was severed. How?"

A long pause. Manny spoke again, "The roots were tangled with the main power line, and while we were trying to trim them back, we made a mistake and the power line was cut."

Morons. Absolute, blithering, incompetent morons.

Except, maybe, Cheng. "Manny, you keep saying 'we.' Unless you were all holding the cutters together, one of you is directly responsible. Who did it?"

Another hesitant moment passed. "Yeah, it was, uh, me. Uh, Santos here. Sorry about that."

Ramsey's teeth pressed together hard. "Oh, well if you're sorry I guess it's all fine." His words were venomous.

The incompetent scoffed, sending a burst of static through Ramsey's earpiece. "Well it's not my fault those roots got into the electrical system. And I didn't exactly see anyone else stepping up to volunteer. You were listening to our conversation. If you thought I was doing something wrong, you should have said something then, but where were you?"

"My responsibilities to this ship and the future of the human race so vastly outweigh your own, technician, that I won't dignify that accusation with a response. If you-"

"Your only responsibility is the one you've given yourself for your own vanity. You don't think we see the way you look at us? *If* you even look at us? You've got yourself so deep in your own propaganda you don't even see us, except to cast blame for every little thing that doesn't go perfectly. I didn't design this module, Dr. Ramsey; you did. You didn't wrestle with those roots, trying to do your part; I did."

"This ship has been my vision, my purpose, my life for three hundred and fifty years. In all that time, I've never broken anything. You've barely been here - what, two decades? - and you've jeopardized the entire mission. Everything I've worked for. My legacy."

Silence replied. Ramsey had won.

"Sir," came the tentative voice of Cheng, "If I may, I worked for RamTech Beijing. We built this module, and I can help fix it if we can make a plan together."

Ramsey filed away Cheng's willingness to help should it be required again later. Technicians he could trust were few and far between. In fact, he couldn't think of another he had really trusted. Certainly none of this pathetic batch. He took a deep breath to cleanse his mind of Santos. "Thank you, Cheng." *Show some humility to those who deserve it.* "What was your idea?" *Be ready to listen if the speaker is trustworthy.*

Cheng explained the routing of the power system through the life support and listed all the integrations with other systems. Ramsey ran diagnostics on those systems as Cheng spoke. All systems were green except power supply; everything was running on emergency power. In the end, Ramsey made a few adjustments to Cheng's plan. Cheng took control of the operation from there, while Ramsey completed his own tasks, where possible, and oversaw the impressively-executed repair operation. Under Cheng's direction and Ramsey's authority, even Santos wasn't entirely useless.

———

It took three days to reroute power. And another two to seal off the places where the roots had punctured, and there were several. Maurice and Santos spent thirty hours shuttling back and forth along the rail connecting the crew module with its counterweight on the opposite side of the ring where most of the supplies for creating basic infrastructure on Ithaca were stored. These facilities were normally only inspected once a century, and sat dormant in the meantime, but it took four round trips before the technicians had gathered sufficient microcrete to fill the gaps and prevent future entanglements of natural root and synthetic cable.

The solution wasn't pretty. Cables had been split, supplies had been wasted, the system did not operate as efficiently as it once did. But as the staleness of the air outside the greenhouse was replaced with the first whiffs of the newly operational life support system, nothing else mattered.

CIV had survived its first existential crisis...

And Ramsey felt like he had begun his own.

One could hardly call it a decision; it was more like an instinct, and not one that Ramsey liked: but on his last night before returning to cryo, he found himself summoning Cheng to his quarters.

It was an alien feeling, to see another face in that room that had so long been only his. The accommodations were not meant for hosting others, though, and Cheng stood with as much dignity as possible a few inches from Ramsey's toilet.

"You wanted to see me?" said Cheng.

It was an odd thing to say. Of course he did, that was why Ramsey had summoned him. Perhaps Cheng was not as clever or perceptive as Ramsey had thought. Perhaps this whole conversation was a miscalculation.

And then Ramsey realized that he had been staring at a spot just beyond Cheng for the better part of a minute without speaking. His Junior Technician remained stoic, impassive, enduring the overdrawn moment with poise. His question was one of prompting Ramsey, not of stating the obvious.

"Yes," he said at last, "Thank you for coming."

Cheng inclined his head respectfully, and Ramsey's mind began imagining the cultural mores that would develop among the colonists of Ithaca. Would the microcosm of humanity be heavily swayed by the large populations from South and East Asia? Would the Ithacans of the far future all be bowing to one another?

Focus. Focus. Those questions will be answered in time.

"I wanted to thank you for your assistance with the... issue we had," Ramsey said. "You kept your cool. We were lucky to have you."

"Thank you. I only sought to do my duty for the people of this ship."

"You and I both know it's more than that, Cheng."

Cheng hesitated, but his gaze stayed fixed. "I apologize, but I am not sure what you mean."

"My sickness, obviously. Don't make me spell it out for you. Surely you're too smart for that, and you know I'm too smart to fall for your game."

Cheng considered, then nodded. "I worry."

Smart decision, not to continue feigning ignorance. "Why?"

"You grow worse with each passing year. How you persist, I do not know."

"I know I'm getting worse, Cheng. That's obviously not what I meant. Don't patronize me. I meant why do you care?"

Cheng looked away, then back. "For two reasons. The first is practical. Without you, this ship is in grave danger of failing. If this ship fails, humanity is dead, my life will have been a waste, and I will have failed my wife, who sleeps in the great ring even now. The second is personal. You are a person of great depth and complexity. One who, I think, has never really been known before. Your mind sets you apart from every other person; no one can match your accomplishments. But I believe humans are more than their minds, Dr. Ramsey. You can call it a soul, or spirit, or chi, but it needs to be seen, to be shared with others. I perceive your heart, and it is alone, full of fury and isolation."

Ramsey scratched an itch on his cheek. He really needed to shave. He looked Cheng up and down.

These concepts of 'heart' and 'soul' were, of course, illusions. Illusions cooked up by the ancient, pattern-seeking part of the primate mind. "I do not need your pity, technician. My mind is all that I am. It's my body that betrays me, turning my own creation into a weapon against my mind. My emotions lead to miscalculations. And relationships? Relationships are unfulfilling, shallow, and ultimately pointless, much as this conversation has quickly become. You're dismissed."

Cheng's eyes narrowed. In firm disobedience, his feet remained planted. "You don't really believe that. If mind is all that makes us human, why bring our bodies to Ithaca? Why care about the preservation of the species? Why save us? People have been uploading copies of their neural pathways for nearly a century now. Why not improve on that technology to bring Earth through its existential crisis instead of fleeing to another physical world?"

The conversation had become a battle of wills, and Ramsey could not allow it. "I believe that I dismissed you, technician."

Cheng hesitated, his resolve to remain waned. He had clearly expected his words to have some effect, but instead gathered himself, bowed again and turned toward the door. Back to Ramsey, hand against the opening, he paused and spoke back over his shoulder. "You may dismiss me for any reason you wish, of course, but do not reject my offer of friendship on grounds of fear or suspicion. I believe you will lead us to Ithaca whether or not you survive to set foot on the planet. I seek only your benefit, Dr. Ramsey. Please let me."

Ramsey rose. "Don't tell me what I can and can't do on my ship. Get out."

Three seconds of near-silence, then the door whooshed shut and Ramsey was alone.

Alone.

Alone again.

He shook his head and fell back onto his bed. It was nonsense. Utterly and totally nonsensical garbage. All of those things Cheng had said were cognitional tricks of the light. Everything that made a person who they were was just brain chemistry and gut flora. Modify those and you could control a person's thoughts, feelings, emotions, attitude, everything. Because mind is everything, and everything is mind. Even the illusion of consciousness, which Cheng had tried to use to persuade him otherwise, was an emergent property of mind. There would come a day when synthetic brains could match organic ones. But that was a vision for another day, and for now, weak, fallible human bodies were the only viable vessels for those minds.

That was why he had brought humans, even the inconvenient fleshy parts, to Ithaca.

And the audacity of the Junior Technician! To think that someone so insignificant could actually imagine himself being the confidant of Dr. Colin Ramsey? Even Ty knew he had never really had that place in his life. No one had, and it was by design.

And speaking of Ty, as inspired as his design was for plant-based primary life support, it had almost ruined everything.

It had damn near ended the human species.

Wasn't that the lesson to be taken here? As brilliant and insightful and loyal as people could be, they would always fail you when it mattered most. Sure, Ty had expedited a number of processes, but the Earth wasn't in its death throes yet when they left. It wouldn't have been the end of the world, literally or figuratively, if things had taken just one extra year.

But Ramsey, in his weakness, had allowed Ty into the inner circle with him, allowed him to make decisions, trusted him, and it had almost resulted in the annihilation of the only known sentient lifeforms in the universe.

No, there could be no inner circle. There was Ramsey, and Ramsey alone.

A pantheon of one.

So it must be.

Besides, to allow Cheng access to himself would

accomplish nothing. It was only another ten months or so until Cheng was old and gone, another mortal shell burned through and ready to be discarded in the twinkling of Ramsey's immortal eye.

And his motives couldn't possibly be pure. No *actual* people were actually like that. In all likelihood, Cheng was in league with one of the doctors, probably that woman. Cheng claimed to want to protect him to protect his wife, but Cheng didn't understand what the doctors would do if they had their way. Just one medical exam and it would be all over.

No, isolation was the only way forward.

It was the only way that was safe.

It was the only way.

———

En Route to Ithaca - Year 344 of 504

Ramsey was already waiting by his cryo chamber when Cheng entered crew cryo to prepare Ramsey's pod for the return of its occupant. Cheng had not been expecting him yet, as he had arrived well ahead of schedule himself. The genius demigod who controlled the destiny of CIV flicked through his tablet, oblivious to Cheng's entrance.

It was a rare opportunity to study the man with his guard down, and Cheng visually traced the lines of concern that creased Ramsey's forehead and crinkled around his eyes. Cheng wondered at the hidden secrets that so transparently weighed on Ramsey.

The conversation of the previous night had made it clear that Ramsey's shell was a thick one, and his commitment to his course of action, resolute. Cheng suspected Ramsey hadn't summoned him to his quarters simply to say thank you, but, surely through some misstep of Cheng's, Ramsey had aborted his initial intentions.

The good news was that progress had been made. Ramsey would not forget Cheng week to week. Cheng was named, now. Most technicians couldn't say that much for themselves, that Ramsey knew their names.

Of course, most preferred it that way. Santos surely wished it were still the case.

The next step was pivotal, to press the advantage without spooking Ramsey. Of course, Ramsey was already suspicious of the atypical manner in which he treated him, but that couldn't be helped.

Ramsey winced, his attention drawn to his wrist, which seemed to be spasming. He set the tablet down to attend to his injury. Cheng took the opportunity to close the door behind him and mask his sudden appearance.

"You are here early this week," Cheng said dispassionately as he activated the control panel.

Ramsey glanced at him as he began to recover. "I couldn't sleep." He rolled his wrist out, the joint popping and creaking in protest.

"Cramp?" He reminded himself not to seem too interested in Ramsey's condition.

Ramsey nodded. "It's just acting up a little. Getting older. You know how it is."

It was the closest to permission to have a conversation

Cheng would get. "Even here, every year goes faster than the last."

Ramsey picked up his tablet from where he had placed it on the control panel for his individual pod. "You have no idea what it means for time to pass quickly."

It was the perfect opportunity to restart the conversation from the previous night, for Cheng to prove he understood Ramsey. The comment hung there, like the ripest, juiciest fruit on the tree, there for the picking. Cheng doubted any benefit would come from taking the bait... not in the current circumstances. But in the end his desperation won out over reason. "I guess not. Not like you. Biologically you may still be in your forties, but you have watched four hundred years of history pass by in what must feel like a few moments. I have thought often of how strange it must feel to sleep and wake and sleep and wake and see years and years pass on our faces. How strange and how lonely."

Ramsey was quiet. Cheng held his breath, waiting to see if his gamble had paid off. Then, just as Cheng was about to offer a strategic apology, "Don't pretend like you know. You can't know. You can't imagine what it's like, Cheng."

"I know that I would want someone to talk to, even if it would make it harder in the long run."

"Why would that make it harder?"

"To say goodbye so soon."

"I've said goodbye lots of times to lots of people. I don't mind saying goodbye."

"If not that, then what can I not imagine?"

The look on Ramsey's face said he had an answer, but thought better of saying it.

Cheng thought better of pressing the subject.

He continued to prepare the chamber in the stretching silence.

Then Ramsey slept, and Cheng had another year to consider the way forward.

————

CHENG FOUND SANTOS ALONE IN THE COMMON ROOM, their elder coworkers already finished with breakfast and on to the tasks of the day. Cheng greeted Santos, who fiddled with a spoon in his hand, a half-eaten bowl of gruel pushed toward the middle of the table.

"Is sleeping beauty back in her glass coffin?" Santos said.

"Dr. Ramsey has returned to cryo, yes."

Santos stuck his tongue in his cheek and nodded. "So, what's your deal, Cheng?"

Cheng pulled the lever to dispense the gruel, which oozed out like not-quite—cooked oatmeal. "I'm not sure what you mean," he said, honestly.

"It was one thing for you to enjoy helping Ramsey, but this suck-up know-it-all bullshit has to stop, or I'll stop it for you. *To katálava?*"

Cheng sighed as he sat at the table opposite his colleague. "Santos, my brother, I have no issue with you. All I seek is our survival, and I will do whatever it takes to protect this ship."

Santos stood. Cheng tensed. "Don't make me your enemy," Santos breathed.

"Do not make me into your enemy," said Cheng.

Santos sneered. "You're either on the side of human decency or you're on the side of Ramsey. The rest of the crew knows where they stand, Junior Tech. I suggest you figure it out, too."

Cheng put his spoon down and folded his hands in front of him. "I see. You think that helping a sick man who holds the key to the survival of everyone you care about puts me in opposition to human decency."

Santos wandered to Cheng's side of the table and sat down on the tabletop. "I think bowing and serving and feeding the megalomania of a sociopath puts you in opposition to human decency. Because what's going to happen when we get to Ithaca, Cheng? Have you thought about that? You think Ramsey is going to host democratic elections and listen to the will of the people? He doesn't listen to anyone except himself. He's put himself on track to be an autocratic dictator, and with only five thousand people to feed it won't be too hard to seize absolute control. All he needs," he glared at Cheng pointedly, "is a few. Loyal. Cronies."

"That is not going to happen, Santos. Do not let your anger make you a fool. Ramsey is interested only in his legacy, not in power."

"Oh, I'm nobody's fool. I'm watching out for me and mine. You need to figure out if you're part of me and mine, or if you're Ramsey's man to the end."

Cheng scoffed. "You are creating a distinction that

does not exist! I am loyal to Ramsey equally as much as I am loyal to you-"

"Not at all, then?"

"-And my only concern is getting to Ithaca safely. Do you not see that?"

"I'll tell you what I see." Santos lunged for Cheng, pulling him up from his chair and slamming him into the wall. The air went out of Cheng on impact, but he had already made up his mind not to defend himself this time. He would remain calm and controlled, even if Santos did not. "I see a coward," Santos said, his face inches away. "I see a spineless yes-man riding the coat-tails of a monster for God-only-knows what purpose."

"You have no idea who I am or what my goals are," said Cheng, flatly, "But I assure you that everything I am doing will be of great benefit to you in the long run, Santos."

"Are you trying to bribe me? Or are you actually dumb enough to threaten me?"

"Neither. I bear no ill will toward you. I am only trying to dissuade you from this vendetta born out of embarrassment."

Santos eyes narrowed, and the grip on Cheng's collar tightened.

"We all make mistakes, Santos."

"Shut up. Don't change the subject."

"But is that not the reason for all of this anger and frustration?"

"I said shut up."

"I will not allow you to pursue this path of insanity."

"You think I'm crazy?"

"Look at yourself. Fist raised against a colleague who has done no wrong, accusing a sick and possibly dying man of conspiring to take over a non-existent government two centuries from now." It wasn't quite a fair criticism, but it proved his point. "You tell me, Santos. Are you crazy?"

The fist moved almost too fast for Cheng to see it, and the next thing he knew, he was on the floor, blood gushing from his nose.

"One day soon," said Santos massaging his fist, "there will be a reckoning. I suggest you be on the right side of it."

Cheng grabbed for a towel from the counter as the door whooshed open and Santos' heavy footsteps disappeared into the corridor.

Still seeing stars, and fighting the tears that nose injuries always conjure, Cheng pressed the towel against his face and began making his way back to crew cryo.

14

ABANDONMENT

Dr. Serena Miller gasped for breath as she entered the run-down tent that passed for a command center. Pulling the wrap from her face, and the goggles from her eyes, she fell to her knees and spat the dust and grit onto the dirt floor. She had objected to the extra water Philippe had given her, but she had drunk all of it and was left wanting more. Her saliva congealed into a thick glob that dribbled out of her mouth. Mercifully, Philippe hadn't been there to see that, although it was on his orders that she had come here.

Strong hands helped her back to her feet, and Dr. Allen's very round, very Scottish face appeared inches from hers. "Christ, Miller! What's possessed you? Out in these conditions!"

The dust storm had gotten much worse after she left, but Serena could only hack in response.

"Here, lass, let's get you some water."

He ushered her to the old, wooden chair by the

metal picnic table in the tent. While she spat congealed saliva mixed with dust from her mouth, he gathered a small cup of water - a full, generous ration - and handed it to her. Between coughing fits, she took careful sips, careful to waste none of it despite her parched throat.

It was nine miles to the adjacent camp where she and Philippe had been working with the refugees from further inland. She had run the whole way, despite the conditions. Here in the country, less than an hour from the outskirts of Fortaleza, Brazil, the human-caused pollution was less, but the dust - in your hair, in your eyes, in your food, in your bed dust - was even more dangerous, especially when it was as dry as this.

Serena held up her hand as she hacked and wheezed the dust from her throat. "I came to warn you." Deep breath. "The *Ultimas* are coming." Deep breath. "They know we have wells."

The Scottish doctor stared at her, mouth agape, eyes grim and calculating. "Christ save us."

The *Ultima Milícia Brasileira* called themselves a militia, but to everyone else they were terrorists. They weren't the only group to take advantage of the country's evaporating infrastructure to seize control of the equally evaporating water supply, but they were by far the boldest and the deadliest.

Serena regained her breath. "We were supposed to be safe this close to Fortaleza."

"Aye, lass, that we were. How do you know they're coming?"

"Survivors trickling in. Philippe has been interviewing them. He said it would be hard to draw any other conclusion based on their stories."

Dr. Allen nodded, then sat quietly, fingers pulling at the end of his beard.

There was something odd in Allen's face. His eyes were sorrowful. The sorrow appeared genuine but it was countered with a lack of urgency. "They're looking for wells," she added, hoping to highlight the dire nature of the situation to her supervisor, "and, like I said, they know we have them."

"O'course they're looking for wells. Water's worth its weight in gold, isn't it?" he snapped.

She flushed. "Sorry. It's just that I'm worried about Philippe and Hector, especially with our radio out."

Dr. Allen ran his fingers under his sun hat and through his thin, grey hair. He took a deep breath before reaching a tentative hand for her shoulder. She recoiled slightly at his unexpected touch. "Dr. Miller..." He paused. "Serena." He had never called her by just her first name before.

She rotated her head slightly away, her eyes locked with his, suspicious. "What?"

"Your radio isn't broken, lass." He removed his hand from her shoulder.

She squinted, uncomprehending. "Of course our radio is broken. That's why I had to run here. To warn you." She coughed again.

"Did you see it broken for yourself?"

"No, but why would my fiancé lie to me?"

The corner of his mouth flicked up into a compassionate, pitying smile. "Why, indeed."

She glanced back and forth between his eyes, searching for the answer to this twisted riddle. She replayed the conversation with Philippe in her head.

———

"I'm thirsty," the old woman said, uncommonly strong fingers gripping Serena's forearm.

"I know. I am sorry. There is very not much of water." Serena's Portuguese remained mediocre despite Philippe's lessons and the two years, nearly three, she had spent in Brazil. She rubbed the woman's hand affectionately. "I try to find more for you, I promise."

The woman's grip slowly loosened, more likely from the morphine than from Serena's reassurances, and Serena pulled away. Her gaze hadn't quite left the woman yet as she neared the flap of the canvas tent, and she gasped at the unexpected presence standing in the doorway. The surprise lasted only for the brief moment it took to recognize the tall, curly-haired frame of Philippe.

"You scared me." She rested her hand on his forearm and leaned her forehead against his lips, which obliged with a long, apologetic kiss.

Philippe's typically cheery eyes appeared burdened today. Dozens of villagers had made their way to this camp fleeing from those savage *Ultimas,* who apparently were in the process of expanding their territory closer to Fortaleza. As if the camp's resources hadn't been thin enough.

She understood the burden in Philippe's eyes, but there was something else there. Something even more alert and alive than usual. She supposed 'vivacity' was the word. Perhaps it was simply enough that they were looking upon the object of their affection. Her eyes were a darker brown than his, but he loved to tell her how looking into her eyes made everything in life appear brighter, even in those dark days. She would tell him it only looked that way because he was a fool in love.

She smiled as she kissed him, and his kiss lingered on her lips. "Is everything okay?" she asked, pulling away.

He eyed the woman on the cot, who had drifted off, but lowered his voice anyway. "Unfortunately, no. The *Ultimas* are coming this way."

Her chest constricted. "But... this close to the city? Why would—"

"We have wells, Serena. They are not the deepest or cleanest wells, but we have water. And they know we have it. Close to the city or not, they want it."

"But, how do they know?"

"Think of a gold rush. You cannot keep it secret from everyone when you find such a valuable resource."

He was right. Most camps like this one that lacked a well failed quickly, leaving the patients and refugees to their own devices. If the *Ultimas* knew this camp existed and how long it had been there, they could guess there was water there. "How long do we have?"

He looked at his feet. "A week. Maybe five days. I want us to be gone in three."

"We should be able to do that, right? Have you told Dr. Allen? Is he going to bring the vans?"

His eyes met hers again. "No, I haven't. Hector just

informed me that the radio is broken, and it's thirty hours until our next scheduled check in with base."

She caught his meaning. The only functional vehicles their operation owned were kept at the central clinic, and the main camp wouldn't drive to come check on them until they missed their check in. "That wouldn't leave us with much time."

He nodded somberly. "I know. I must ask something very difficult of you." He took both of her hands in his, his gaze and his fingers resting on the small diamond ring on her left hand. "I need you to go on foot to the command center and tell Dr. Allen what I've told you, so he can organize transportation in time."

Her hands slid out of his. The environment outside the camp was always hostile, but the last week had been flat out dangerous. The dust, the sun, the bugs. There was a reason the refugees needed medical attention when they arrived. "That is a lot to ask."

"You know I would not put you in danger unless it was necessary."

"But, won't you and Hector be overwhelmed here? We're already short-staffed with three."

"We will be, but it is the only way to keep," he hesitated, just for a fraction of a second, "us safe. Everyone safe." His eyes darted away from hers. He licked his lower lip.

Something wasn't quite right, but she didn't press it. Philippe wanted it kept to himself. "Okay. I understand. I'll be back with support as soon as I can. We'll get everyone out of here safely."

He nodded absently, his eyes glassy, his attention

inward-facing on the unstated concern that weighed on him.

She reached out and took his hands back into hers, rubbing her thumbs over his dark, dry knuckles. Whatever was troubling him, she would fulfill her duty to her team lead, and also give her fiancé the space to carry this burden alone. Philippe was a good man, but he kept his own council first and foremost. It made him equally a decisive, inspiring leader and an occasionally distant lover. He was both right now.

Philippe blinked back into the present. "I'm sorry, *meu amor,* I am just feeling overwhelmed with the logistics of organizing this evacuation." He kissed the back of her hands. "You know I would never be separated from you, given any other option."

"Of course I do."

"Good. Then kiss me deeply."

She smiled and leaned in. He pulled her close and kissed her like he had that night in Miami, like he had on the night she had agreed to be his wife, like he had no other source of life in the universe than her lips on his.

When they parted, her eyes fluttered open like she was awaking from another world. Her face was hot, her breath shallow, her soul lost again in those rich brown eyes.

His right hand was still on the back of her neck, stroking the base of her hair. "I love you," he said.

She hadn't regained her voice yet, so she nodded her reciprocation, biting her upper lip.

His hands dropped to her shoulders. "You need to get going. I have your pack."

It was such a sudden change of topic that it took her a moment to remember her task, to remember that there was a band of murderers coming their way, to remember that there were over a hundred sick and dehydrated people in this camp who were depending on her, to remember that people were being killed all over the world for resources that had once been taken for granted, to remember that the Earth was so sick that Ty Daniels of RamTech was preparing to put five thousand colonists on another world. It took her a moment to remember that anything existed outside the arms of this proud, tall, kind man who kissed her like the world was ending. "I'll miss you," she said. "Be safe."

"I will. You be safe, too, *meu amor*." He picked up her pack and helped her shoulder it.

"Why is it so heavy?"

"Extra water."

"No, you need the water here."

"Our camp is about to be overrun with *Ultimas*, so I am not overly concerned with preserving our rations."

"Fair point."

"And I would never forgive myself if something happened to you out there on my orders."

"I said I'll be safe." She smiled. "Don't worry."

"I know you will be safe. I know you will."

She put her goggles over her eyes, then fastened her hood around her head to protect from the swirling dust and the scorching sun. "See you in the morning with a fleet of vans."

"I love you."

She smiled, despite her face being covered, and rested her head against his chest. "I love you, too."

He held her close for a few seconds.

Then he let her go.

———

"I don't understand." Serena breathed heavily. A terrifying idea was forming, and it was twisting her intestines in knots. "I don't understand. If the radio is working, why would he send me away? Why would he lie?"

"I'm so sorry, lass," Dr. Allen said.

"No. No, don't say that." She stood up quickly, knocking the chair back several inches, nearly upending it. "If you're so sure the radio is still working, then call him."

"I don't think-"

"Call him. Now." The words were icy, but her blood was on fire.

Dr. Allen opened his mouth as if he might protest, but ended up giving a grim nod. He led her ten meters or so to the ancient transmitter and turned on the camera at the top of the screen.

Thirty agonizing seconds passed where the entire universe consisted of a screen emblazoned with the word 'connecting...' and a rapid pounding on the inside of her rib cage.

The call connected. Serena lurched forward. "Philippe?"

"I'm here, *meu amor*." He looked like he had aged several years in the hour since she had said goodbye.

"Philippe, what is going on? The radio…"

"I'm sorry. I am so sorry."

"Sorry for what? Talk to me."

He smiled weakly. "The *Ultimas* are coming."

"In a week, Philippe, you said they were coming in a week." Her pulse pounded in her ears.

"I had to lie, Serena. I had to lie to save you."

A burning sensation began behind her eyes. "Save me from what, Philippe?"

"They'll be here by nightfall. The *Ultimas*."

Dr. Allen cursed under his breath.

Serena's fingertips went numb. She covered her mouth with both hands. By nightfall. There was no time. "Why? Why would you send me away alone?"

"I had to keep you safe. I'm so sorry."

The first hot tear ran down her cheek. She asked the question even though she feared she already knew the answer. "How will you escape them?" The last two words came out as a choked breath.

His eyes watered. "I don't think I will, *meu amor*. But I have to try to save our patients. It is my duty."

"Our duty, Philippe. It was our duty. Together… Oh God, how could you do this?"

"My Serena, you must listen to me." He paused, gathering his thoughts. "If I could wish one thing for my life, it would be to spend every moment of it with you. I love you more than anything. But it looks like I have come to the end of my time here." Tears streaked Serena's face as she struggled to keep her composure. She suppressed a sob, her hand over her mouth. Philippe continued, "Should I die tonight," he swallowed, "then I have failed to protect my patients. As a doctor, there is no greater pain than to fail your patients. There is nothing to be done except to try. And I will try. I will try to talk them down and give us time to evacuate. Maybe it will work. Maybe it won't. The *Ultimas* are not well known for their mercy. Either way, I will do my duty as their doctor to the best of my ability."

"But I'm a doctor, too! I have the same duty. I should be by your side. That's the only place I want to be!"

He smiled. "I know. You're so stubborn, and I have always loved you for it. But even if I am to fail as a doctor tonight, I will still have succeeded. I will have protected you. I will have saved you."

"You will have condemned me to a life of misery without you." She was desperate now. "It's not too late, come be with me, or let me come back to you."

He shook his head. "I'm sorry. I can't abandon these people. You are free from responsibility. I sent you away. Whatever happens, these lives are not in your hands anymore. And nothing can be gained from your return."

"I could be with you, you idiot! That's the only thing I want."

"Serena, please try to understand... these people are savages, and you are a beautiful woman. It would not just be death for you, it would be... much worse."

She set her jaw. He was right, of course.

"Saving you was meant as a mercy, *meu amor*. Please, don't take this last gift I can give you away from me."

She paused.

She nodded.

He exhaled. "Thank you."

She breathed deeply and wiped the tears from her face, smearing the mud that had formed from the tears mixing with the dust. "What am I going to do without you?"

A sad smile. "Live. Do something amazing. Remember me. And love again, someday."

New tears replaced the ones she had just wiped away. "No. No, I can't do it Philippe. I can't say goodbye to you. I can't let you go. I can't..." Her breath caught. "I just can't."

He nodded. His rich brown eyes glistened. He reached out to touch the screen. His fingers rested at the center of her viewport. She reached out to touch his fingers.

"I love you," Serena whispered.

"I love you, too." He smiled and almost laughed. "Remember me well."

"I will." The whisper faded to a whimper as her eyes burned hot.

"I know you will." He took a deep breath and let it out slowly. With one last twinkle and crooked smile he said, "Goodbye, Dr. Miller."

And then he was gone.

———

10 December 2212 CE - 17 Months Before Departure

Four weeks.

Philippe had been gone for four weeks.

Serena was back at her parents' house near Los Angeles.

The sky was dark, and the nights were cold.

Already she was forgetting the feel of his fingers touching her face, her hair, her body.

And yet, on the rare occasion that she slept, her dreams were full of her worst fears about how he met his fate.

Her only hope was that it was quick when it happened.

But it had happened.

The *Ultimas* owned that area now.

His body would never be recovered.

———

ONE SUCH COLD, SLEEPLESS NIGHT, SHE BEGAN TO PUT AWAY her things.

The Brazil program in her area had been canceled after the eruption of violence.

She wasn't sure how she could have gone back anyway.

At the bottom of her rucksack, she found an old wrist device she had worn before she went to Brazil.

She plugged it in.

It still worked.

She activated its menu and pulled up her most recent activity.

There was an entry not far from the top of the list with a strange format.

She selected it.

A hologram face materialized.

And a phone number.

She stared at it for a long time.

Then she tethered the wrist device to the wall screen and selected the phone number.

It took several seconds for the connection to be made, which wasn't surprising, considering where it was going.

A round face appeared on the wall.

He didn't look as surprised to see her as she expected him to.

In fact, he looked rather pleased.

"Hi," she said, "I don't know if you remember me… but I was wondering if it was too late to apply for a job?"

"For someone of your brilliance and insight, Dr. Miller, it is never too late," said Dr. Tyson Daniels.

15

PLAN

I t had been twenty-one years since the life support incident. Manny and Maurice had grown old and returned to cryo, and Santos was now Senior Technician. For his part, Cheng was now in his fifties, and not feeling so young himself.

Santos' threats of a coming reckoning had fallen flat, as Cheng knew they would. Ramsey had selected his crew wisely; none of the technicians were much for rebellion, deep down.

The years on CIV had been hard. The monotony of tasks, of food, of locations, of days. It had all taken its toll on Cheng as it did on everyone else. Always the same, always more. He lived for the fleeting days twice a year when the crew module rotated around the ring to where Lin slept. Safe and unchanging in cryo, she grew younger and younger with each passing cycle.

The sister of Fabian Luis da Silva Caceda, the next technician after Cheng, the one who had replaced

Manny, was in a cryo tube not far from Lin due to the alphabetical proximity of their surnames. Cheng and Fabian had formed a firm friendship in the proximity that their loved ones' tubes provided.

Cheng's relationship with Ramsey remained awkward, and Ramsey's skill at endearing himself to his crew had not improved. Ramsey's condition, however, continued to deteriorate, and Cheng had not dared to wake Serena out of turn for fear of the message it would send to the rest of the crew.

It was agony, waiting year after year for someone to hurt themselves severely enough to require medical intervention from a human doctor, especially because the complications of Ramsey's annual appearance justified medical intervention ten times over on their own.

Of course, that was the very thing he could not do. The thing Ramsey would never forgive.

But the necessity for it grew with each passing year.

And so it was that Cheng found himself waiting in the seldom-used medical room, rag tied around the slice on his hand he had connived to inflict upon himself. It stung much more than he had anticipated, and the dull throb pulsed through his whole arm.

The door opened, and she entered. Asahi, the newest Junior Technician, followed close behind.

He stared at Serena, and she stared back. The moment dragged longer than he intended, but the effect was disconcerting. She looked the same as in her previous waking, but younger. She was no longer his peer, but two decades his junior, and he wondered how he had ever come to so mythologize the skill and depth of insight of one so young.

For her part, he realized, she must not have expected him to have aged so much. But she had seen dozens of technicians grow old before him, so why this look of consternation?

"Thank you, Asahi," Cheng said. "Would you please find Fabian and have him join us here? I've already powered down my communicator."

The slim Japanese man nodded curtly and closed the door behind him.

"So, some personnel changes, I see," said Serena.

"Yes, Manny and Maurice have gone the way of all us technicians. I see you have met Asahi."

"He's very quiet. I felt like I was eating my lunch in a graveyard."

"He keeps his own counsel, I admit."

"Let me take a look at that hand."

He offered it to her, and she gently removed the bloody rag.

She examined it briefly, then applied a clean new rag to it, instructing him to maintain the pressure as she prepped her treatment. "So, what did you want to talk to me about?"

Cheng smiled. "Was it that obvious?"

"I've seen a cut like that once before, you know. On Santos, during your first week on the job."

"Really? I don't recall that."

"Of course you do," she protested, "You had just started, and Manny assigned you to be my bodyguard because Santos hurt himself on purpose just so I would have to wake up."

Cheng looked at her blankly. It rang a distant bell of memory.

The smile faded from her face. "You really don't remember that, do you?"

"I remember meeting you, of course, but I couldn't remember the circumstances. It has been a long time, and the battles I have had with Santos are too many to remember on their own."

"Well, it's almost the exact same injury he had, and I bet you got it reaching around the back of a cryo pod without a glove."

"Yes," he smiled, "But I assure you that my motives are pure."

She smiled back as she cleaned the wound, a sadness in her eyes. "That's what all the boys say."

The door opened again and Fabian stuck his head through the door hesitantly. "Cheng?"

"Yes, Fabian," said Cheng. "I want to introduce you to Dr. Serena Miller, one of the three main doctors in our rotation. I believe she is the only one you have not met yet."

Fabian extended his hand warmly. "Fabian Luis da Silva Caceda. A pleasure, Dr. Miller."

"Just 'Serena' will do." She shook his hand, then turned to Cheng. "So, what's this all about?"

Cheng watched Serena prepare the stitching kit for several seconds. He looked over to Fabian, who raised his eyebrows expectantly. "As each of you know, in your own ways, I have spent more time with Dr. Ramsey than any other person has on this journey.

"Fabian, what you do not know is that Serena and I suspect Ramsey is dying. We think he knows it, too. The only difference is that we suspect he might die before we make it to Ithaca, which may have disastrous results for the survival of everyone on this ship."

Fabian nodded slowly, contemplatively.

"Serena," Cheng continued, "You do not know just how bad his awakenings have become over the last twenty years or so. I would struggle to quantify it, but he seems worse by the year."

Serena did not look up from her work, "We suspected the trend would continue."

"Yes, and it has. And that makes what I am about to say all the more difficult. I have dedicated the majority of my adult life here on CIV to befriending Ramsey, and, to my shame, I fear I have made little progress. He knows me by name and face. He respects me as much as I have ever heard of him respecting someone besides himself. But I have still not succeeded in my ultimate goal of becoming a trusted ally, and for that I ask your forgiveness."

Serena had stopped what she was doing.

Fabian looked confused. "I'm sorry," he said, "Why can't we just force him to submit to a medical exam?"

Serena's eyes were still locked on Cheng, but she inclined her head to address Fabian. "Cheng thinks Ramsey fears a medical exam because we'll see how sick he is and force him back into cryo for the rest of the journey, which could doom the ship, in his opinion. Cheng's afraid of what Ramsey would do if we tried to force something on him."

"Indeed," said Cheng. "I know him well, now. His mind, while as sharp and analytical as ever, is as sick as his body. He wants to be isolated. My attempts at closeness have been rebuffed. As soon as I get one finger inside his armor, a new layer, harder than the last appears. But I have still learned much."

"Like what?" said Serena and Fabian together. They exchanged a brief look.

"Most significantly? He sees himself as immortal. A deity, almost. The savior of the human race in a way that transcends the fact that he built this ship."

Fabian scoffed. "Arrogant man. This does not surprise me at all."

Serena's eyes had still barely left Cheng. "He said that to you?"

"Not exactly."

"Then how do you know?"

"Through observation, noticing little things that he says and does that make him different from other people. Savoring the unique details, and allowing them to come together to form a larger, more beautiful picture than he can see in himself. The same way you know things about anyone you have loved for a long time."

Fabian scoffed. "Yeah, but let's not forget this is Ramsey we're talking about. Cruel, unforgiving, pompous, selfish, superior Ramsey. He's barely human, as far as I can see, and certainly not worthy of love."

Cheng's heart ached at that. He spoke quietly. "Everyone is worthy of love, Fabian."

"Not him."

"Especially him. Especially anyone who is hard to love."

Fabian waved him away. "You and your idealism."

"Fabian, I need your help with this. I am telling you that I do not know what to do. I need your insight, and I will need your persuasive skills to help him see his path forward. If you cannot learn to love him, you will need to learn to accept him or we will fail in our goals."

"And what about me?" said Serena.

"What do you mean?"

"When we last discussed this, you said you would prove to me that no one else could learn to do his job, that his job is actually necessary to the degree he thinks it is, and that he is actually rejecting medical treatment because he fears the failure of the ship and sees his involvement as the only way to save it, even if it kills him. So far, all I have heard is more philosophy. At some point soon, one of us doctors is going to decide that enough is enough and run some tests, consequences be damned."

"Serena, you can't do that."

"I can, though. And I think I should. You said yourself that medical officers are supposed to have authority over everyone on the ship, even the Captain. And now you're trying to tell me what I can and can't do?"

Cheng sighed. "You know that's not what I'm saying."

"You've had over twenty years to build your case and prove it to me, but you haven't offered me anything today besides more empty reassurances. What was your goal in waking me up without the information I said I needed?"

"Because I need help!"

The room rang with the echoes of the argument in the silence that followed. Cheng breathed heavily, reigning his emotions back under his control. In. And out.

Serena finally broke eye contact. Her voice was quiet, far away, as she gazed at a nondescript section of floor. "In my life, I've failed enough as a doctor. I've been too weak, too many times. I've let other people make decisions about my life for me. About my job." She looked back at Cheng. The anger was gone, but her eyes were stony, resolute. "The next time I wake up, I will force Ramsey to comply with a medical exam one way or another. Maybe that's the wrong choice, but it's my wrong choice to make."

Cheng considered this for several seconds, then nodded. "Very well. I agree. But in the meantime, will you please help me figure out how to get through to him?"

"You really think we can?" said Fabian, arms crossed.

"I have to believe it's possible." said Cheng. "Let's see what ideas we come up with."

"Fine," said Fabian.

They thought in silence for several seconds.

"You said he wants to be alone?" said Serena.

"Yes, he seeks isolation. His Mount Olympus is wherever he is, and no one else may touch the mountain."

"But even the gods had their own society," said Serena.

"Not to mention Zeus had a thing for mortals," said Fabian.

"The analogy breaks down, I admit," said Cheng. Then he realized something. "But Serena is right, the immortals have their own society." He looked at them expectantly.

Serena and Fabian exchanged another glance. "What's your point?" said Fabian.

"Perhaps I am the wrong person to try to save Ramsey. My very existence reminds him of his separateness. His immortality cannot relate to my mortality. So he-"

"Needs another immortal." Serena's brow was furrowed.

Cheng spoke softly. "I think so."

"Ohh," said Fabian. "I see. But doesn't he want to be alone? Isn't that what you said?"

"I don't think anyone really wants to be alone," said Cheng. "Do you?"

Fabian pursed his lips and shook his head.

Cheng turned back to Serena. "What do you think? Can you do it?"

"I... Honestly, I don't even know how to start thinking about this. What would it mean for resource management? Would I start doing the same thing as him? And, probably most importantly, how in the world would we ever get him to agree to having me as a companion? He can barely stand me, and he's afraid I'm conspiring against him."

"To be fair, you actually are conspiring against him." Fabian grinned sympathetically.

"I'm a doctor. I'm trying to help him."

"No, you can't approach him as a doctor," said Cheng. "That will not work. Your only role with him, at least at the beginning, would be as his friend and companion."

Fabian chuckled. "And you thought being his doctor was hard."

Cheng shot him a glance.

"Calm down, I'm only joking. Look, this is a big challenge. Cheng, we'll need to leverage your knowledge of him to determine the best way to approach this. It will have to look organic."

"I have been trying for almost thirty years to find organic ways to connect with him, and each one has fallen short."

"Because you don't meet his standards of immortality." Fabian said it with bite.

Cheng wanted to defend Ramsey, but conceded the point with a shrug. "Right."

"And what about you?" Fabian asked Serena, "You said he couldn't stand you, but has Ramsey ever even seen you before? Or does he just hate the idea of you?"

"Since we left Earth, I've only seen him once, and it was less than a hundred years ago. When Dean was the Junior."

A brief pang of nostalgia ran through Cheng for old Dean, whom he had only briefly met in his first few waking days as a Technician.

Fabian raised an eyebrow. "Wait, are you saying you knew him before we left Earth?"

"I met him a few times, but I wouldn't expect him to remember. You remember his partner, Dr. Daniels? He got me my job at RamTech after... After I left my previous position."

"Woah, woah, woah. You knew Ty Daniels?"

"Yeah, I did, and that was how I met Ramsey," she stressed, "But that doesn't mean I know Ramsey now."

"No one knows Ramsey," said Cheng. "Not really. There is a depth and complexity to him that I have only glimpsed two or three times in the past few decades, but he reserves that inner world for himself."

"What, are you a psychologist now?" said Fabian.

Cheng smiled, "No, but my life's work is to study this man, and that is about the best I have learned."

"Let's get back on track," said Serena. "I still have no idea how I'm supposed to approach Ramsey or what I'm even supposed to do."

Cheng paused to think. If Ramsey was going to be saved from himself, it would need to be during Cheng's tenure as a Technician. If only Ramsey's fears didn't have such a grip on him.

Come to think of it, why did they have such a grip on him? Cheng had never considered it before. He couldn't possibly think himself powerless if a doctor instructed him to return to cryo. He could overrule their authority and insist on being awoken again on schedule.

But, of course, it was the technicians who actually had to wake him.

If the technicians listened to the doctor and not to Ramsey, Ramsey may never be awoken out of cryo again at all, and then his worst fears would be realized.

"He's afraid of what the technicians would do if they had competing instructions from him and the medical staff. So he refuses to let there be instructions from the medical staff."

"Come on, Cheng, even I don't think he's that petty," said Fabian.

"It may be petty, but what other method does Ramsey have to measure us by? He doesn't know us long enough to get to know us deeply, let alone trust us. Plus, we age ten years every few months of his experience. I know I am not the same as I was ten years ago. There's no consistency."

"And that's why he doesn't want to engage with you, to befriend you," said Serena. "Because it's too hard. He was never great with his subordinates back on Earth, but nothing like the horror stories I've heard over the years here. Most of them weren't as bad as they sound now, though. The stories have shifted over the years."

Fabian stared at her in surprise. "You really are like another immortal, aren't you? All we have are legends of long ago times, but you lived through them."

Serena nodded. "I can understand why he's so lonely. It's not easy watching you guys disappear so soon. The difference is I haven't even been doing this for six months yet, from my point of view."

"So," said Cheng, "he ignores us and is cruel so he doesn't get attached. He hides from medical intervention because the result of ignoring us and treating us badly is he can't trust us to be on his side. And if we are given the choice between listening to him and listening to a doctor..."

"We would choose the doctor every time," said Fabian. "Damn, he's right. I almost feel bad for that guy. So, what do we do?"

Three sets of eyes looked back and forth among each other, each willing the others to have an idea.

Internally, Cheng felt the weight of his failure on his shoulders. His attempts to befriend Ramsey had probably made the whole situation worse. Ramsey probably felt like he was being probed and prodded, Cheng's attempts at camaraderie coming across as violations of safety and self-determination. Cheng cursed himself for his blindness, his foolishness.

"Well, let's start with what we know," said Fabian.

"Think we know," said Serena.

"Ok, fine, what we think we know." Fabian cleared his throat. "Ramsey believes the RAD will fail without the attention he pays to it every year. He believes he is the only one who can do that work sufficiently. He believes the biggest threat to him being able to continue that work is his health, or, more specifically, a doctor's orders regarding his health, because he correctly thinks we technicians will listen to the doctor and not to him. That's his state of mind as far as we can tell, right?"

Cheng nodded. "Which means we have two tasks. We must persuade him of our loyalty and persuade him to receive medical treatment."

"What happened to being willing to let him die?" Serena asked.

"We have no way to know what may happen if he continues as he has, even with your direct, focused medical attention. He may still die, but we must get him treatment. But only after we have persuaded him that we are his allies."

Serena folded her arms. "And I recognize that I may

be the only one who can persuade him of that, but I don't see how I can get close to him when I represent the very thing he fears. Which puts us back at the beginning. What do we do next?"

Fabian raised his hand just above his head. "Sorry, why can't we just strap him down while he's passed out and get a medical scan on him? He's so delirious in those first hours he probably wouldn't know the difference."

"Because, we don't know what that would do to him in his current state of mind," said Cheng. "He is not mentally stable. You can see it when you talk to him. He has become almost animal in his focus and paranoia. We would be winning the battle and losing the war if he caught on."

Serena scoffed. "How do you expect me to befriend a man you've just described as a wild animal? Sugar cube? Salt lick?"

Cheng sighed in frustration. "We need to remind him that he's human. And we must do it in a way that binds him to the others around him."

Fabian began to pace. "Right," he said, "But we keep coming back to the question of how. How are we supposed to do that?"

"I think it starts with us, Fabian. You and me. We will discuss this topic with Asahi; I very much doubt we will make any progress with Santos. But once he's gone, ten years from now, we will teach it to whoever takes his place, and on and on. We will stop telling legends of his cruelty. We will overlook his new offenses. We will endure these things to begin to show him that we are on his side."

"But Cheng," said Serena, "We don't have another century to spare. This needs to get wrapped up soon, or it's all going to be moot and we're going to be on Ithaca already, or else dead somewhere in between."

"Give me a few more weeks with him. Just a few more years. This counsel has given me a new direction to pursue. I just need a little more time."

Serena stared him down again. "You realize that you're gambling with the entire human race, right?"

Cheng met her eyes. He was doing this for Lin, and he would never compromise her well-being. "I do not take this responsibility lightly."

Serena crossed her arms. "But do you really understand the magnitude of it?"

"No, but as a finite being, how could I?" he snapped. "What I can understand is that the love of my life sleeps in cryo. I will do whatever I can to do right by her."

Her gaze did not falter. Fabian blew out a heavy breath.

"I can do this, Serena."

"Next time I wake up, whether it's six months or sixty years, I'm treating him."

Cheng nodded. "So be it. You will not be disappointed."

"We'll see. Let's take another look at that hand."

16

FISSURE

Ty sat in Ramsey's office aboard Troy Orbital. Ramsey sat behind his desk, massaging his face with his hands. Ty knew the feeling.

They'd been working for nearly forty hours straight, trying to solve the problems the MedAI engineering team had brought to them. So far, no solutions for the finnicky program. "Run it by me again," said Ramsey, shifting himself back in his chair, his eyes still scrunched closed.

Ty waved the holographic display back two screens to begin the section again. "Basically, it's a compatibility issue between the gene readers and the blood readers."

"Right. And why can't we just get DNA samples from the technicians at the beginning of the journey and compare against that? Why do we have to keep reading it?"

"Just like any other code, DNA can get corrupted."

"We should just upload our consciousness to a computer. That would get rid of all this unpleasantness."

"A bit too late for that project, I think." Ty forced a smile.

Ramsey actually laughed a little. "Just a little. And we want actual humans on Ithaca, not just copies of their brains." He squinted his eyes open and blinked like he had just woken up from an unexpected nap. "Ok. I'm ok." He made a pulling motion with one hand and the holo-gram inched closer to his face. "Let's take another look."

A few minutes later the comm buzzed. "There's a call for you, Dr. Ramsey."

Ramsey didn't look away from his work. "I'm busy. Unless it's one of the important Presidents, I haven't got the time." His voice sounded too old, too tired for a man who had barely eclipsed forty.

"It's your mother, sir," his assistant said.

Ramsey hesitated. He glanced from the many layers of holograms hovering above his desk to Ty's face.

"Answer it," Ty mouthed.

"Should I put her through?" asked the assistant.

"I haven't got the time," Ramsey said, and turned back to his work.

Ty watched the comm light stay lit for several seconds. Then, presumably, the assistant decided not to argue, and the light switched off with a click.

"Colin, that was your mom."

"We're busy, Ty. I'll call her back when it's less hectic."

"It's always hectic."

Ramsey looked up, danger just below the surface. "I know what I said." He waved to the next page of the holo and worked while he spoke. "There are things in this world that are worth giving up. CIV is the most important

thing to me. Nothing else really matters. Not ultimately."
He scanned back and forth between his personal tablet
and the holo.

Ty resisted pressing back on that statement for several
seconds before his incredulity got the better of him.
"Really, nothing? Or almost nothing?"

Ramsey glared at him. "Literally nothing else."

"What about me?"

Ramsey dropped his tablet onto the desk. "What do
you mean, 'What about you?' Ty?"

"I mean, what if something happened to your best
friend and you were busy working. What would you do?"

"Keep working, obviously. I would be of no use
to you."

"Come on, Colin, it's obviously a hypothetical."

Ramsey stared for what felt like an eternity, but was
probably only three seconds. "CIV is the most important
thing to me. And it should be the most important thing to
you. Without it, all other human endeavor or meaning is
lost. I would sacrifice anything, and I mean anything, to
get that ship to Ithaca safely."

Ty raised an eyebrow. "Even basic human social
responses? Even sympathy?"

"Please, if I were still playing the sympathy game I
wouldn't be able to do what I'm doing. I'd be obsessed
with trying to save more and more people and the ship
would never get done. Sympathy..." he scoffed, "It's hard
to keep up the sympathy when you know that almost
everyone is about to die. What do their cultures, their
traditions, their concerns mean to me or you?"

"Isn't that what we've been working to save - some

remnant of our shared humanity? If we sacrifice what makes us human to get there, have we even saved the species?"

"Yes. Objectively, yes. Of course we have. The strongest, healthiest genes we've got from all over the world will be passed on to countless future generations. What other definition can there be for saving a species?"

"There's a difference between passing on genetic code and preserving the values and communal directives that make our species worth saving in the first place. Yes, CIV will shelter *homo sapiens* on its journey to the new world, but is being *homo sapiens* the same thing as being *human*?"

"Ty, you're losing me in this philosophical muckraking. What does this have to do with anything? I have one mission: Build CIV, choose the best and brightest, get them to Ithaca. I don't have to choose between you and CIV. We'll have all the time in the world when we get to Ithaca. But right now, we're on a deadline." He turned back to his work.

Ty's mind was in a fog, probably from the exhaustion. He wasn't sure Ramsey had really done anything wrong, even if this outlook was problematic at best. And everything he said made a lot of sense. It did go against human nature to die with integrity when there was even a chance at life if you sacrificed everything.

No species survives that's willing to die happily.

Still, Ramsey's callousness bothered him. Ramsey had always said that the ends justified the means. It was an ancient cliché. Ty had assumed Ramsey's philosophical adoption of it extended no further than to the construction of the ship. But these comments seemed to indicate a shift in Ramsey's psychology, and suddenly Ty wasn't sure what Ramsey's ends were anymore. After all, he was the one who wrote the algorithm to select the chosen survivors. He could have selected for anything. The only exceptions to the verdicts of the algorithm were Ramsey himself and Ty's family.

"When you select the chosen," Ty tested, "Will you force parents to leave their children behind? Will you separate husbands and wives?"

"Depends."

"On what?"

"If the loved ones are also suitable. And how badly I need certain skills. Ideally, the entire population would be of child-bearing age. But I'm a realist; I understand that I may have to accept some children to recruit my most desired candidates."

"I'm sorry, candidates? I thought we were calling them applicants."

"Yes, over a billion applicants, but I've now whittled it down to around one hundred thousand true candidates."

Ty raised an eyebrow in surprise. Even now, Ramsey played his cards close to his chest. "Is that including the preference given to RamTech employees?"

"What do you mean?"

"Just that, since the beginning, you've said that any employee or contractor of RamTech who meets the minimum criteria would be given preference over applicants from the outside."

"Of course," said Ramsey.

Ty breathed an internal sigh of relief.

"But, don't forget that I'm the one who sets the criteria, and it's ultimately up to my discretion. Most of the people who work for us are remarkable in one way or another, but few of them will truly be of use to me on Ithaca."

Ty's blood ran cold.

Ramsey looked up. "Don't worry, Ty. I already told you that you're coming. I couldn't do this without you. And besides, I won't tell them until CIV is basically done and all that remains is testing. Another five months or so."

"How many?"

"How many what?" Ramsey ran a calculation on the holo.

"How many RamTech employees are candidates?"

"Oh. Not sure. Maybe five, six hundred?"

"RamTech has over a million employees. You only found one in every two thousand employees suitable?"

Ramsey looked up, catching the note of criticism. "Better than the one in twelve thousand outsiders. I'm spoiled for choice, Ty. Of course I'm going to pick the best available."

"If you're spoiled for choice, then start with our people. Start with the people who made this possible."

"Why? They had a duty to the human race to build CIV. I am not obligated to allow them to come to the planet. Is it right of me to take an electrical engineer with good genetics over a molecular biologist with even better genetics simply because the engineer worked for me? Isn't that favoritism?"

"You gave them your word."

Ramsey rolled his eyes. "Don't be naïve. My word is breakable. My word is malleable. I will do whatever it takes to see humanity succeed, Ty. How many times will we go over this? The-"

"-Ends justify the means. Yeah, I've got it."

"...You think I'm a monster."

Ty scoffed. "A little, yeah."

"Don't conflate strength with cruelty. I am not vindictive. I never have been. I am only practical."

"Tell that to the million families who gave their last years together in the hope of a ticket to Ithaca, only for you to tell them that their sacrifice meant nothing to you."

"They did what was necessary, just as I am. They can die secure in that knowledge."

Ty's heart seemed to stop. "Can... can you not hear yourself?"

Ramsey's temper flared and he stood up behind the desk, pushing the holo images violently aside. "I can hear myself just fine, Ty. But you don't seem to be listening. This," he motioned vaguely to everything around them, "is mine. All of it. I did this. I built this. Me. Not the species. Not the company. Not even you. Me. Just me. The Earth is no longer our home, understand? It is a holding pen for ten billion animals, ready to be slaughtered. They, and their lives, belong to me, and me alone. I will choose some to save, and the others I will condemn to death. That is the hand fate has handed me, and I intend to play it well."

Ty whispered, "You're insane," but Ramsey didn't hear or see. His mind was elsewhere.

"In the place of this desiccated, dying world, I will build a new creation, a new Eden for a better humanity. And when all other names from this rotting rock are long forgotten, mine will not be. And so," his attention snapped back to Ty, "you will forgive me for slighting the feelings of these unimportant people who would have been equally dead had I done nothing."

Ty fumbled for words, and settled on repeating himself. "You're insane."

"On the contrary, I am the only one who sees things clearly."

"You're playing God."

Ramsey shrugged. "Maybe." He leaned across the desk, weight resting on his closed fists. "But I defy you to name a way in which I am not like one."

"You really don't think you sound insane?"

"Tell me how I'm wrong."

He wasn't wrong, Ty realized. He was like a god, but not a good one. He looked away.

"Thank you," said Ramsey, and he actually sounded relieved. He took his seat again. "Look, this isn't personal against these people. I understand your point about them, but there is no room for compassion to cloud judgments for decisions as fundamental as this one. I must pick the right people. There's no second chances. That's why I'm willing to do whatever it takes, even pull families apart if I need to."

"Would you pull my family apart?"

Ty regretted the question almost immediately. It hung in the air for several seconds. The silence saying more with each passing moment.

"Come on, Ty, what do you want me to say?"

His pulse pounded in his ears. "I just want you to answer it. Because you gave me your word, just like you gave them your word, and I want to know if you're good for it."

Ramsey sighed heavily. "Look, you got unlucky with Izzy..."

Veins turn to ice.

"...but the fact is, she won't be able to have children..."

Neurons blaze with fire as they forge new neural paths.

"...I'm willing to work with you on Clara, though. The doctors said you should be able to have another child or two without risk of another complication..."

He knows about Izzy. He knows. How does he know? How does he know about Izzy?

"...But, no. Izzy will not be allowed to come to Ithaca."

The words fell like a building collapsing on its foundations. Like a star collapsing into a black hole. Ty clung to the little composure that remained available to him. "How long?"

"How long what?" Ramsey remained in his seat, impassive, unfeeling.

"How long have you known?"

Ramsey shrugged. "Maybe three years."

"Why didn't you tell me?" Ty whispered.

Ramsey's eyebrows shot up. "Really? You're asking *me* that question? You're the one who's been trying to hide it, Ty."

"Because I was afraid you would do something idiotic, like you're doing right now!"

Ramsey's eyes turned cold. He set his tablet down. "Idiotic?" A long pause.

Ty thought of rephrasing to soften the sentiment, but his resource-starved mind would not cooperate.

"Idiotic." Ramsey reiterated, nodding his head in mock agreement. "Yes, I can see how my vision for saving the human race could seem '*idiotic*.'"

"The vision itself isn't idiotic-"

"Let me finish!" Ramsey shouted, standing and slamming his tablet on the floor. Ty froze. He had never seen Ramsey in a wild fury like this. "My vision, as ambitious and calculated as it is, is a gambit, Ty. Do you not understand that? I've gambled my entire life, my family's fortune and legacy, and the future of my company on your models being right. I've gambled the fate of the colonists of Ithaca on the calculations you ran to determine the best candidate world. I've trusted your designs for the life support of the technicians who will hold the fate of the human species in their insignificant hands. YOU are the one who showed me the genetic models, Ty. *You* know how small our margin for error is. Every man, woman, and child who sleeps in one of those pods must, out of necessity for the survival of the species, be able to reproduce. You *know* that."

"But she's one person, Colin!"

"She is not!"

A thick silence hung in the air. Ty remained in his seat. Ramsey towered above him, his eyes bored into Ty, but they weren't really seeing him.

Ty looked away as Ramsey spoke. "Every person on that ship represents all of their future descendants. The mission cannot tolerate bringing someone who is just a passenger. Maybe some will fail to reproduce anyway, but we can't bring someone like that on purpose."

Ty breathed heavily. Ramsey wouldn't budge.

"As I said, you are free to bring Clara, who, by the way, will probably be the oldest woman left alive when we get there."

"How gracious." His voice was barely more than a whisper.

"Hey. Look at me."

Ty lifted his twelve-ton head up.

"Every single person who gets on that ship is leaving behind someone, or something, that they love. Brothers, mothers, friends, spouses. Everyone has to say goodbye to someone. Even the technicians only get one person, as long as they meet the minimum standards. No one else got two spots, Ty. All you're doing is making the same hard choice as everyone else."

"But this is *me*, Colin. This is me. How can you make *me* choose?"

"I haven't changed anything on you Ty. This has always been the deal. You could bring them both, provided they met certain genetic minimums. Clara passed. Izzy didn't. It happens."

"'It happens?' Colin, you're condemning my daughter to death."

"No. I'm allowing you to save your wife."

"This is me, Colin!" he tried again, pleading. "Doesn't it mean *anything* to you, after all I've done, all I've sacrificed for you?"

Ramsey looked him in the eye, and took his time

before speaking. "No. It doesn't. Each of us has a role, Ty. You did yours exceptionally, but the vision is bigger than any of us."

"What am I supposed to say to her?"

"She'll be thirteen this year. She'll understand."

"She is a child!" Ty stood up, slamming his tablet down on Ramsey's desk.

Ramsey was defiant. "She is a hindrance to the vision."

"Would you stop it with 'the vision' already? Huh? What vision? Of a genetically pure master race living on a distant paradise, with you as their savior, prophet, and king?" Ramsey reeled. "Is that what you want, Dr. Ramsey?"

The cold fire was rising in Ramsey again. "Is that what you think? That this is all about me? I'm not a god, Ty."

"Oh, well that's good news," he spat.

"I am so much more than that. I offer a real salvation, not naïve, deceptive, manipulative wish fulfillment."

Ty's stomach churned. "You're a monster."

"I'm a savior."

Ty laughed bitterly. "Not to Izzy, you're not."

"Should I break some other family's heart instead? Should I tell them how sorry I am that their little girl was next in line to go to Ithaca, but I showed favoritism to my friend's daughter instead? Would that really be right of me, Ty? Would it?"

"Maybe not, but it doesn't change anything. You lied to me, you betrayed me, you used me. And do you know what? The ends don't always justify the means, Colin.

Sometimes you lose your humanity in the process. I don't know who you are, but you aren't the same man I knew when this started."

"And what is that supposed to mean?"

"It means I'm done. I'm going to go enjoy whatever time I have left with my family. Good luck with your spaceship. I'm out."

"Ty."

"And, hey, what a relief for you." Ty's voice cracked as he fought the emotion. "Now you have two more spots to fill. I'm sure you'll find someone smarter, better and more useful to take my place."

"Come on, Ty, don't do this. I need your help."

"The conditions of my help were the safe passage of my wife and daughter to Ithaca. You have severed the terms of that agreement, and I am no longer bound to you."

"This is the survival of the human race we're talking about!"

Ty shrugged. "What do I care? I'll be long dead when you get there."

Ramsey was insistent, but calm. "You're making a mistake. I want you by my side."

"All I want by my side is my little girl."

He turned and marched out of the room without a backwards glance.

17

SACRIFICE

EN ROUTE TO ITHACA - YEAR 382 OF 504

Ramsey ran the system diagnostic again at the remote access terminal. The results, although obscured by hundreds of dead pixels and two white bars running across the screen, indicated nominal functionality for the RAD. He clenched his jaw. The raw data indicated a major discrepancy that the diagnostic kept failing to identify. It would have destroyed their propulsion system if he hadn't caught it. A death sentence for the human race, narrowly avoided.

On days like today, though, he wondered if it was even worth it. Seven years of Somnithaw and isolation had taken a toll. His resolve had weakened, the joy of immortality staled. He keyed in the command to run the diagnostic again.

He had fainted. More than once. He hadn't told anyone, of course. There was no need to risk losing everything now. Not when they were more than three quarters of the way to Ithaca. The finish line felt like it was finally coming into view.

Just a few more lifetimes to go.

The results came back. System nominal. As the only person in the universe who understood why that was a problem, the continued necessity of his eternal torment made itself clear. He would have no respite, no relief.

He ripped his tablet from the interface and stormed off to try another terminal.

Further down the always-uphill corridor, a figure leaned against a cryo tube, obscured by shadow. Ramsey wondered what they were doing away from their post during working hours. As he approached, he recognized the curve of the back and the wiry, salt-and-pepper hair of Cheng Ahn, his Senior Technician.

Cheng.

He had gotten so old. He'd be back in cryo soon, no doubt. Someone new would wake Ramsey from cryo each week. His anxiety spiked inexplicably, so he forced the thought down.

"Everything all right, Cheng?" Ramsey asked as he approached.

Cheng started, but relaxed when he saw it was Ramsey. "Hey, Colin."

Ramsey still hadn't quite become accustomed to being called "Colin" regularly. Cheng had started it, a couple months - a decade - ago. He tolerated it, as long as they weren't working. The Technicians these days didn't seem quite so hostile as previous generations, and he wondered if the familiarity had anything to do with it. Sometimes Fabricio would sit quietly with Ramsey and share a meal, despite Ramsey's intentionally irregular eating pattern. Not Fabricio. What was his name? Fabian? Yes, Fabian.

It was obviously the influence of Cheng that had revitalized these relationships, but Ramsey knew everything would go back to normal when Cheng went back to sleep. And the time was getting close. Just a few more week-years.

"What's going on here?" Ramsey asked.

"Oh, just visiting my wife." The old man smiled sheepishly, bringing out the wrinkles around his eyes and mouth. He gestured to the woman in the chamber. "My years have only increased her beauty."

Ramsey thought her average.

Cheng nodded and gazed on his wife. "She was right, you know."

"About what?"

"About me. She said I would be old and haggard when we got to Ithaca. That she would be a memory of a long-lost love. I told her it was the only way I could save her."

"You were right, obviously."

"I know. I did the right, the honorable, thing. I saved her life." His voice caught. "It's just... Oh, God, Colin... I miss her so much."

Then he broke down. Ramsey had not expected that. Cheng fell to his knees, struggling to keep his shaking body from crying out.

Something caught in Ramsey's throat. He knelt down beside his Senior Technician and slowly, tentatively laid his arm across the old man's shoulders. He searched for words, but found none.

What was there to say? *"Don't worry, she'll still love you?"* *"The ends justify the means, and your life has been sacrificed upon that altar?"* *"My vision is grander than your tiny concerns?"* *"Thank you for your service?"*

No, all wrong. But for the first time in many years, Ramsey caught himself wondering how to help. It was a disorienting moment to realize he cared what happened to this man.

It was a terrible moment.

———

CHENG REGISTERED THE ARM ACROSS HIS SHOULDER WITH some surprise. Even in the midst of his mourning over the life he had burned through, that he and Lin would never share, part of his mind latched onto this small grain of hope.

Ramsey was having a moment of sympathy for him. It was not something he had thought his employer capable of. After forty-five years, had Ramsey's unintended intrusion on Cheng's semi-annual private moment with Lin finally been the catalyst to spark true companionship?

"I'm sorry," Ramsey said. Mumbled, really. But it was just right, it was just enough to confirm what Cheng had been working toward all those years.

The tears kept flowing, but no longer out of sorrow.

After several more seconds, they subsided, and Cheng took a deep breath. "Thank you, Colin."

Ramsey wouldn't make eye contact for more than a

moment at a time. "Yeah. Don't worry about it." A little smile flickered across his face. "Seriously."

Now was the time to play the cards, but it had to be done carefully. Cheng had nearly given Ramsey up for lost, admitted defeat, and allowed Fabian, Serena, and the others to pursue medical intervention, whatever the cost.

But now, maybe. Just maybe.

"It has been difficult, these years without her," Cheng tested.

Ramsey nodded noncommittally.

"She was my anchor. My friend since childhood. We knew each other our whole lives."

"You'll see her again, though. You keep talking about her in the past tense."

Cheng nodded. "You are right. She is not lost to me." He thought about it for a moment. "But I am lost to her. After forty-five years, she is a ghost from another lifetime."

Ramsey looked unsure of what to say, and turned to leave.

Cheng grasped for words to keep the conversation going. "I think often of how difficult it will be for the loved ones of the technicians." Ramsey turned back toward him. "They will not have changed at all, and we will all be very old," Cheng continued. "I imagine it will be difficult, to arrive in a new place, knowing no one except this one person, who is not really the same person any more."

Ramsey's body language was pulling him away from Cheng, his patience wearing out. Cheng had to try again, and quickly.

"I imagine it's the same feeling for you."

Ramsey half raised an eyebrow, then returned his beleaguered face to normal. "How so?"

"You are not avoiding aging, not like them, but you are experiencing it very slowly compared to real time. You not only see the result of the aging of us technicians, you watch it happen week by week. How do you endure?"

"I do what I must."

Cheng nodded. He had Ramsey talking, at least. "I have always admired your perseverance. I know the rest of the crew does, too."

"What do you want, Cheng?" Ramsey didn't yell the question, but it felt like an explosion nonetheless. He stared at Cheng with fire in his eyes, an implicit challenge to all comers.

"I don't-"

"Don't lie."

Cheng shut his mouth. The bluff had been called, and it was time to play the cards. So he played them. "When I say I admire your perseverance, what I really mean is, I'm not sure how you are still alive, medically."

"You're not a medic. What would you know about it?"

"I don't need to be a medic to understand the reaction your body is having to the Somnithaw every year. Every week. Your body can't process the toxins, so it purges them, but not all of it gets out, does it? Some stays in your bloodstream, some in your lungs, some in your brain. Every year, you get a little bit sicker and your recovery is a little bit harder. You can only take so much."

"My health is fine, and no concern of yours."

"You know that is not true. Your health is objectively not fine, and if you die, we all die. As someone who sacrificed his whole life to get this ship to its new home, that concerns me, my wife, and the last humans in the universe, all under your care."

"You know nothing of sacrifice. You have no idea what I've done, what I've suffered, what I've given up to bring us this far. This achievement is mine. This ship is mine. Your *life* is mine, Cheng. Everything you've done on this ship belongs to me."

Cheng kept his wits about him enough to follow his own protocol and ignore the megalomania. "If you want me to know what you've suffered, what you've lost, then tell me. I've spent four decades trying to find a way to befriend you," he confessed, "No one should have to be alone. Not like you have been. I watch it tear you apart year by year. Well, you don't have to suffer in it alone! I've wanted nothing more than to be your friend, and you have denied me at every turn. Think about what I've suffered for a minute and you will see the truth; you're not as alone as you thought."

"Don't be pathetic. Talking about friendship and loneliness like they're these deep forces of human nature? It's absurd. It's childish."

Childish? Cheng paused. Humanity was born out of social connection, community, togetherness. Ancient ancestors thrived because they watched out for each other, the development of communication enabling the transfer of increasingly complex ideas was itself only advantageous because we needed each other. Ramsey could think it childish if he wanted, but Cheng called it human. "I disagree. These are the building blocks of society. We want to be connected, not alone. It's hardwired into us."

"I don't need your help, or your friendship."

The cards had not been played well, or had at least come up short. "I regret that you feel that way. And it means that, despite my best efforts, I have failed."

Ramsey folded his arms. "Yeah, I guess so. Are we done here? Because I actually have important things to do."

"If you will not hear me as your friend, and I am your friend, even if you are not mine, then hear me as your Chief Technician." He looked Ramsey in the eye. "Sir, you need a medical assessment or you are going to die."

"No. Forget it. I'm not getting one." He stormed away.

"You are afraid we don't trust you," Cheng blurted out. "You're afraid of what the doctor will say, that you'll be stuck in cryo because the technicians won't wake you up and say it's because of doctor's orders."

Ramsey turned back, sneering. "You think you know me. You don't know anything about me."

Cheng paused. Could that be true? What were the odds he had calculated everything all wrong? Maybe, but if that were the case, Ramsey's psychology was truly unknowable. "On the contrary, Colin. I know you better than anyone else does. You are my life's work. I've watched every second of every interview you ever gave. I've listened to every recorded word you've ever said. I'm confident that I'm the only technician you would even allow to engage you in this conversation. I know you. I know how you think."

"You really don-"

"You think you're a god."

A stunned silence.

"You said it yourself. You said my life is yours and everything I do counts as your accomplishment. Who else can say that about their people? Only a god."

"I do not think I'm a god," said Ramsey.

Cheng started inching toward Ramsey. "No. You don't believe in gods. You think you are like a god. The closest thing to a god in the universe. A close facsimile."

Ramsey backed away a little.

"But here's the problem," said Cheng. "You started to believe your own propaganda. You started to worship yourself a little. You stopped believing you could fail." He was crazy to be saying this, but he couldn't stop it now. "But you can fail. And if you fail, the consequences will look very much like the failure of a god. Its people, your people, will be lost forever to the merciless flow of time. Humanity will die anonymously."

Ramsey's eyes were hard, but he kept inching away from Cheng.

"There is only one thing you can do now. Get help. We, the technicians, understand the necessity of you waking up every year. We get it. We won't betray you, even on doctor's orders."

"I don't believe you."

Cheng registered with some satisfaction the implicit admittance of Ramsey's concern over technician loyalty, and plowed ahead. "My life's work has been to demonstrate my trustworthiness and loyalty to you."

"No, your life's work has been to pretend — to study

and learn about me like a voyeur doing a perverted science experiment. You aren't interested in me, Cheng. You are interested in the role I perform, and frankly, you're not nearly intelligent enough to understand it. How could I possibly trust you?"

"Because I'm the one who has been protecting you from outside forces that wish to force their will on you!" Cheng regretted it immediately. Ramsey's eyes narrowed, and he halted his subconscious backward drift. Cheng's forward momentum ground to a halt.

"So you waited until now to tell me that there are conspiracies against me, and you dare to call yourself a loyal friend?"

Cheng raised his hands in front of him in an attempt to deescalate Ramsey's new aggression. "Everyone just wants to survive, Colin. We want you to survive, we want us to survive. I told them that it wasn't what you wanted. I told them we should let you make the decision on your own. I did not anticipate it being this difficult to persuade you."

"You should have told me, Cheng. Give me names."

Cheng considered his options. "Why? What are you going to do?"

"Put them back in cryo and deal with them when we get to Ithaca. The names?"

"You can't do that!"

"I can do whatever I want, this is my ship. The names."

"Listen to yourself! This is not your ship. This is humanity's ship, and humanity's last hope. If you can't see that, then you truly are lost, and we are all going to die."

"Everything is under control. Just give me the names."

Cheng realized how close Ramsey had come to him now. The great man stood before him, now nearly thirty years his junior, with madness in his eyes.

Behold, the savior of the human race.

"No, sir. I won't tell you. I have no wish to be your enemy. Everything I have ever done has been an attempt to serve you. Forty-five years here, and six years before that back on Earth. After all this time trying to give you what you want, I see now that the only way left to serve you is to resist you."

Ramsey's eyes narrowed. "You do not want to be my enemy."

"I know. If that is how you must think of me, so be it. I have sought only your benefit my whole life, and I can hold my head up with integrity. But now, as I draw near the end, I see that what you really needed, all along, was someone to tell you 'No.' So I'm telling you now. No. I will not put your paranoid desires before the real needs of every other human on this ship."

Ramsey grabbed him by the shirt and pushed him against the wall. Cheng allowed it to happen, but they both seemed to realize how weak Ramsey's body was. After a tense moment, the hand on Cheng's collar released. With one last poisonous glare, Ramsey stalked away.

Cheng stood there for a long time.

He wondered if he had just torn down the lifetime of progress he had made with Ramsey. Then again, he reflected bitterly, he hadn't gotten anywhere, so it was no great loss.

He turned back to the serene face of his beloved. "What has my life been for, my darling wife? I have accomplished so little, and it has been such a long, long road."

If she had moved at all during his waking years, it hadn't been much. Those same loose strands of hair still hung over the side of her face. That Mona Lisa smile was still etched on her lips.

But there seemed now to be a different brightness to her. She felt closer, somehow, even as time pulled him further from her, like he could reach out and touch her. For a moment, he thought he could. His right hand drifted delicately to the glass, anticipating the warmth and softness of her cheek, and instead meeting the cold metal of her sarcophagus.

En Route to Ithaca - Year 383 of 504

CHENG AHN INITIATED THE CRYO-EXTRACTION SEQUENCE. A digital countdown began on the display screen. It had been a year since his falling out with Ramsey. The remainder of the previous Ramsey week had been full of cold shoulders and hot tempers.

The usually silent hall of the crew cryo chambers hissed with the introduction of Somnithaw into the long-static environment in Ramsey's chamber.

In the intervening year, Cheng had thought a lot about how to proceed. His previous plans had revolved around dealing with a frightened person. Instead, what he really had was a delusional and frightened person. And entrenched delusion at that. It seemed the only possible solution was to demonstrate the truth of his loyalty and the need for medical attention in a way that revealed its objective reality. There were no words in human persuasion that Ramsey would hear, not now. The human mind, and Ramsey's in particular, cares too much for self-preservation to let biases about existential threats to be reconsidered.

Cheng ran through his mental checklist for Ramsey's waking. The mat, the bucket, the gloves, the sponge, the cot. Check, check, check, check, and check.

The countdown indicated another two minutes. Ramsey himself showed no sign yet of stirring.

While waiting for the Somnithaw to have its full effect, he paced down the corridor to his right, stopping to observe the old faces of his previous coworkers, frozen and motionless, ghostly portraits of nearly forgotten men. The flickering purple light illuminating the curved ceiling amplified the impression. Cheng considered each of them — Santos, Maurice, Manny, and the old man Cheng had replaced. Dean, he remembered after a long moment.

He retraced his steps back to his own empty chamber.

Three years left. Three years until he could wake the next technician, Moussa Adekugbe. He had learned the name long ago, longing for the day that the mantle of the fate of humanity could be passed from his shoulders to those of the young Ivorian. Three years until the end of his long labor, then training Moussa, then sleep, then Ithaca, then Lin.

The old man felt almost boyish again, grinning at the thought of her. He pushed down the unbidden anxiety that followed soon after.

With a gentle pop, the vent on Ramsey's cryo chamber opened. The neutralized gasses began to escape from the chamber in little puffs before vanishing into the air return above. Cheng shuffled back to the terminal. He watched the contorted face inside grimace and flinch. The indicator light illuminated, and Cheng entered the command to open the chamber.

Nothing happened.

He entered it again. Still nothing.

Ramsey palmed the glass in front of him. Cheng looked up to see the man trying to push the door open. Ramsey was in his hell now, and Cheng couldn't touch him.

Cheng watched the display screen as he followed the command tree progression for a third time. Then he saw it: the last tree was corrupt. He glanced up to look through the cyro chamber glass, now partially coated with that thick yellow-brown of Ramsey's stomach acid and bile. Behind it, Ramsey's eyes had closed again. Fainted.

Cheng's pulse pounded. He placed his palm on the screen. "Administrative Access."

"Access Granted," replied the cool, feminine voice of the AI.

As he scanned the code for a way to circumvent the command trees to initiate the opening sequence, the screen glitched, and the terminal went black. The cryo chamber resealed its vents with an emphatic click. Cheng looked up. Ramsey remained unconscious. But even so, with the vents to the chamber closed, he'd use up the oxygen and asphyxiate. Quickly.

Cheng threw himself to his knees to access the underside of the ancient terminal. His arthritic joints protested. He ignored them. He touched his earpiece to speak to the other technicians. "Emergency in crew cryo. I need help. Power failure in Ramsey's chamber. Run."

He'd removed the back panel while he spoke. Examining the wires, nothing stood out as the source of the problem. His practiced fingers examined each connection on the panel. He detached the control board. Nothing seemed broken, overloaded, or singed.

Frantic footfalls in the adjacent hallway materialized into Randy, his Junior Technician. "What can I do?" Randy asked, his voice shaking.

"First, stay calm. We need clear minds to solve problems."

Randy nodded and took a deep breath.

"Second, tell me what's wrong with this control board."

Randy hustled over. He sized up the complex piece of technology in an instant. "Everything looks ok here. What actually happened?"

Cheng summarized.

Randy ran around the control panel and peeled up the black meta-material coating on the floor. A drill was suddenly in his hand, and a moment later the floor access was open. "Yeah, just like I thought. This connection between the control board and the unit is fried."

"Fried? How?"

Randy shrugged. "Probably just overuse. There are extra precautions in Ramsey's unit because of the extreme number of times it needs to be used, but I think it just burned out."

"How do we fix it?"

Randy flashed a nervous smile. "Err, we don't. It's unfixable. This unit will never work right again, and that terminal will need some major repairs."

Just then, a desperate banging began. Ramsey was awake again. Through the viewport, his eyes looked animalistic, his cries for help dampened by the metal tomb around him.

No. Not a tomb.

This wasn't over yet.

Cheng racked his brain, "There must be some kind of emergency override."

Randy furrowed his brow and nodded. "I have an idea, but we need to restore power first. Let me take a look."

Randy returned to the terminal. Cheng removed himself to accommodate his younger, more nimble colleague. Randy's hands vanished into the mess of wires in the back panel.

"Let me know when power comes back to the screen," said Randy.

The old man labored to his feet.

Ramsey's second round of vomit brought a reprieve from the frantic pounding, but replaced it with a sickening, if distant, retching. Cheng looked through the transparent port where Ramsey's beleaguered eyes were still wild with fear. He tried to signal what was happening to Ramsey, but the pounding continued.

Cheng watched the screen for several long seconds. The pounding on the chamber slowed. He glanced up from the terminal.

Ramsey stared back, his cold rationality subduing the terror in his hindbrain. "You did this." His voice was muffled, and much quieter than when he had been screaming, but the movement of the lips and the accusation in the eyes left little room for interpretation.

Cheng stepped to the center of the viewport and looked up into Ramsey's eyes. He shook his head. "No. Never. We are trying to help you."

Ramsey lifted his hands up in front of his face in a silent mockery of applause. "Well done, Cheng. You've killed us all. Me, you, your wife, everyone. I hope it was worth it."

"You are not going to die, and neither are we." But he saw Ramsey's eyelids begin to droop as the oxygen in the tiny chamber quickly depleted.

Another round of vomiting. Cheng returned his focus to the control panel.

Just then Fabian rounded the corner to the cryo room, panting for breath. "I got here as fast as I could."

"Wake Dr. Miller," Cheng directed him.

Fabian rushed to find her chamber and begin the process.

Two tense minutes ticked by. Ramsey was fading fast. Asahi arrived, but could provide no further assistance. Cheng sent him to prepare the medical room for Dr. Miller.

The screen burst back to life. "Power!" said Cheng.

"Good." Randy stood and began entering commands on the screen before Cheng had even finished moving out of his way. "I'm setting up a feedback loop in the power supply to supercharge the circuit. There should be a subroutine in place to prevent catastrophic overload. If we can trip it, it should complete the extraction process automatically. And if not..." He trailed off as though he had just considered the possibility of failure.

Cheng offered his grim reassurances: "If we do nothing, he will die anyway."

Randy gulped and nodded, then returned to his work. After just a few more seconds, he said, "There. Feedback loop established."

"How long will the overload take?," Cheng asked.

"I'm not sure, to be honest."

"Guess."

"Uhh, two minutes? Three maybe," Randy guessed.

A dull thud sounded from the cryo chamber as Ramsey gave in to the lack of oxygen and collapsed.

"I do not think he has that long," Cheng observed.

Randy's eyes widened. "I don't know what else to do."

Ramsey was dying now. Each moment grew closer to when that brilliant and tortured mind would cease to think, cease to be — at least on this plane of existence, where it was needed. Three minutes was far too long. Two minutes was far too long. Cheng spun, searching his mind for inspiration even as he searched the room.

His eyes fell on an old crowbar that had been left by the exit door during maintenance two weeks earlier.

A grim determination seized Cheng as his body marched toward the crowbar.

He turned back towards the failing cryo pod, crowbar in hand, desperately searching for some other option even as he realized there wasn't one.

"Get back," Cheng commanded.

"What're you doing?!" Randy backed away.

"What I can."

Fabian said something, but Cheng's ears had started to ring as he charged for the console. Randy's eyes went wide in the realization of what was about to happen, and he scampered for cover.

"I'm sorry, my love," Cheng said aloud, imagining Lin's face even as he raised the crowbar above his head.

"Wait! No!" screamed Fabian.

Cheng plunged the crowbar into the console. Sparks flew. Pain erupted in every paralyzed inch of his body. A pungent, acrid odor enveloped him.

Then, nothing.

18

ORPHANS

14 APRIL 2214 CE - 2 MONTHS BEFORE DEPARTURE

Cheng Ahn had never been to space before. Troy Orbital was a marvel unlike anything he had ever seen. Located at the Earth-Moon Lagrangian Point L1, a gravitationally neutral region between the Earth and the Moon, *Troy* had once been a hub of international business, and home to nearly four thousand people, with Ramsey Technology Enterprises at the center of it. Over the last decade, it had transitioned to become the staging ground for CIV. Its other uses had been discontinued for security reasons and the population reduced to a few hundred.

The quiet halls, uphill in both directions due to the wheel-like design of the station, unnerved Cheng. Footsteps echoed, voices carried, and a dull, ubiquitous hum suggested a life support system in disrepair. Out of professional curiosity, he speculated about which of the three possible components was likely at fault for a sound like that.

The beginning of training later that day brought respite from the eerie emptiness.

———

CHENG SAT NEAR THE FRONT OF A SMALL AUDITORIUM filled with about forty other men, nearly all of whom seemed to be in their twenties. Dr. Ramsey entered to whispers of admiration from the technicians and he began with neither introduction nor ceremony.

"You are here," Ramsey said, "not because you are the best in the world at the work set before you, but because you possess a rare combination of mental stability, technical skill, and excellent predisposition towards natural health and long life. It falls largely on your shoulders to keep my ship operating over the next five hundred years. So, if you want our species to continue, I suggest you take notes."

English wasn't Cheng's native language, but he was pretty sure he had just been insulted.

"Nice opening, eh?" the man in the next seat whispered.

Cheng smiled politely.

It didn't get much better from there. Ramsey reminded them of their commitments, the importance of their role (although he never quite used the word "important"), and of the basic responsibilities they would each have during the four phases of their fifty years of service.

Ramsey continued to speak for a long time, and then dismissed himself for the day quite suddenly. One of the instructors stepped in and suggested a short break.

As many of the technicians began to filter out of the room, the man in the next seat extended his hand to Cheng. "I'm Dean, from the RamTech Winnipeg branch."

"Cheng Ahn, Beijing." He shook Dean's hand.

"Beijing? Haven't made it to your part of the world, hate to say. And, uh, I guess I never will now, eh? The wife always wanted to take me, seein' as how she went once when she was a kid." He shook his head. "Never made it, I guess."

Cheng had practiced speaking English with Lin for months, ever since he first applied. His fluency had improved dramatically. He focused. "She will see Ithaca. China is beautiful, but not as interesting as another planet, I am sure."

Dean's shoulders slumped. "Yeah, well... Haven't seen her since I got the letter. She didn't want me to choose between her and our daughter, Kelly, so she ran off. Police couldn't spare the personnel to try finding her. So, Kelly it is. That's life, though, eh?"

"I am sorry. I do not mean to open your wound."

"No harm done that weren't done already. You got any kids, Cheng?"

He shook his head.

"Count yourself lucky. I bet half these guys had to make the same choice as me. Wouldn't wish it on anyone." Dean's expression grew heavy. "Ah, damn." He sniffled. "Sorry. I just need a minute." He excused himself and joined the line exiting the auditorium.

———

20 May 2214 CE - 2 Weeks Before Departure

THE EXPLOSION OF A MOLOTOV COCKTAIL ON THE OUTSIDE of the thick, cold armor of the military transport started Dr. Damian Cartwright's pulse pounding in his ears. Through a small, narrow window near the top of the cramped passenger compartment in the rear of the vehicle, he caught glimpses of the tops of buildings zipping across the dreary backdrop of a cold spring's morning just north of London.

Damian wrung his hands. "Are we nearly to the launch site?" he asked the soldier who sat opposite him.

"Nearly."

Gunfire erupted outside. Damian ducked his head and whimpered.

"Nothing can hurt you in here," the soldier reassured him. Damian caught the note of impatience in his voice.

Damian righted himself in his chair, tried to sit still, and ended up fidgeting with the buttons on his overcoat as the roaring crowds and muffled announcements over megaphones serenaded him. "You know, I applied to go to Ithaca on a whim. My therapist said it would be good for me to have an adventure. I teach history at Cambridge; never expected to be chosen to become part of it."

The soldier grunted.

"I'm not much for travel, you see. I've a delicate constitution. And a touch of claustrophobia from an unfortunate childhood incident. Must have been thirty years ago now, but some things stay with you, you know?"

Outside the transport, gunfire rang out again. The

multitude who would remain and die with the Earth roared in protest.

Damian shivered.

More gunfire. More screaming. The voice on the megaphone grew louder and more persistent, but the words were still indecipherable.

"It's not my fault these people weren't chosen for Ithaca," he continued. "And there's no guarantee we'll even make it. We may get stranded in the middle of nowhere three hundred years into it. Or the whole ship could blow up. They probably wouldn't prefer that, would they? Or, worst of all, what if we get to the planet and discover all the analysis was wrong and the rock isn't even habitable, or is filled with massive predators, or–"

"Enough, Dr. Cartwright!" the soldier yelled, "I don't care one bit, not one bloody bit, what happens to you. The Earth is dying, you prig! Do you not understand that? All those people outside applied for a spot on CIV, same as you. Any one of them would gladly take your place. You've got a chance to live. That's one thing the rest of us don't have. So shut your bloody mouth or get out of the vehicle and make room for someone else."

"Sorry," said Damian, after several seconds.

They rode the rest of the way in silence, surrounded by periodic shouting, explosions, and gunfire on the other side of the armor.

———

"WHAT'S THIS?" DEMANDED THE SECURITY OFFICER, HIS finger pointed at Damian's breast pocket.

Damian's transport had arrived at the launch site. Chosen people from much of Northern Europe, as well as some who had been transported from other parts of the world, were gathering at the launch site just north of Bedford. All around, security officers were investigating the personal effects of the chosen before they could board the shuttle to CIV.

Damian pulled his tweed jacket tight over his chest. "A family heirloom. A very expensive antique pocket watch I inherited from my great-grandfather. Surely you won't be taking that away from me, too? You've already thrown out half of my rare book collection, and I won't stand for any more."

The officer stared at Damian, wide-eyed. "Half? Have you got more hiding somewhere?" When Damian didn't respond, he addressed his colleague with a sigh, "Gerry, make sure we got all the books out of this bloke's bags." He turned back to Damian, "Look, mate. All of these books have digital copies stored in the ship's database. You can print new copies later if it means that much."

Damian sputtered. "Some of those are three-hundred-year-old first editions! They can't just be replaced. I'm the expedition's historian, for Christ's sake! Don't you know that?" The two officers exchanged a bemused look between them. "Dr. Damian Cartwright? Professor of History at Cambridge University?" They shook their heads. Damian sighed in frustration "Well, whether you've heard of me or not, I was promised that I could bring some of my collection with me."

"Sir," the first officer said, his tone very cross, "I don't have any special exemptions regarding you. What I do have is two hundred people trying to get on this shuttle to Troy. Each of you has a ten-kilo weight limit for personal items, beyond the clothes you're wearing." He checked the number still displayed on the scale and his eyebrows shot up. "And you brought ninety-five kilos. Mate, almost everything will have to stay behind, and there's no two ways about it. If you really want to bring a few books instead of extra clothing, be my guest. That pocket watch needs to be put on the scale, too, though."

Damian sighed. "It's just not right," he muttered as he removed the pocket watch and handed it over.

———

THE TRANSPORT DOCKED AT TROY ORBITAL STATION. Stains marred Damian's tweed jacket where weightless particles had escaped his sick bag during the flight. The return to simulated gravity through the spin lock had been just as uncomfortable. He retched again as he exited into simulated gravity, at least managing to catch it all this time as it, reliably, fell down.

As he stood back up, his weakened knees buckled. A young Asian woman rushed to his side and knelt next to him.

"Are you alright?" she asked in clear, but accented, English.

"I–I'm not entirely sure," he confessed, "All these changes in gravity, and the G-forces of the launch, I'm not sure I'm quite well."

She offered him some bottled water, which he sipped gratefully.

"Can you stand up yet?" she asked.

"Yes, I think I can do," he said. "The nausea is passing."

She helped him up and offered her hand, "I am Cheng Lin, or Lin Cheng, as you say in the West."

"Damian Cartwright," he shook her hand, "or, I suppose, Cartwright Damian, if you prefer."

She laughed. "That will not be necessary."

He smiled for the first time all day. He looked off to the side, embarrassed and not sure what to say next. Sterile white and silver hallways extended uphill in both directions and his vertigo returned. The smile vanished from his face as he remembered the ordeal ahead of him.

"What did you leave behind?" she asked.

"I'm sorry?"

"You look as though you carry a great burden," she said, "And we have all left much behind to be here. Do you want to talk about what you left?"

"It's just that... I'm not at all certain I want to do this. What if something goes wrong with the ship and we all die? What if we get there and find out Ithaca is just a rock? What if it's all for nothing?"

"It is not for nothing. My husband is one of the technicians who will work on the ship. We were not among the chosen, like you. But he has chosen to trade fifty years of his life to bring us all safe to Ithaca. Even if you are right and we do not survive, his willingness to sacrifice is still honorable."

"So, you're not afraid?" Damian stretched his aching legs.

A sad smile. "When we arrive, I will be the same and

my husband will be an old man. It is hard to imagine. I am afraid, yes. But..." She hesitated and put her hand on her abdomen, tapping it absentmindedly as she collected her thoughts.

His sister had done something similar before his nephew's birth. "My God. I don't mean to pry, but are you pregnant?"

A series of expressions came over her face before she finally looked away shyly and made a small nod.

"Traveling in your condition... How can this journey possibly be safe for you?"

"The doctors said we will be perfectly safe." She shrugged. "Fear, worry. These things will not change truth. If we stay on Earth, my baby will die. Now, either my baby will be healthy, or he will not. But he has a chance. It is always better to hope than to fear."

"Well, what about your husband? What does he think of this?"

"He... he does not know. He left two months ago for training, before I found out. I have not told him."

The shuttle pilot exited the spin lock then, and ushered Damian and Lin on their way.

After checking their assignments as they walked, they discovered that their cryo chambers were close to each other. Together they passed through the disorienting hallways of Troy Orbital, following signs until they found the proper umbilical connection and crossed over onto CIV.

Recessed LEDs made the white, arched canopy dance with alternating greens, blues, and purples. The bullet-shaped corridors, twice as tall as they were wide, gave the impression of catacombs, and the black latticed floor seemed to be made of a durable, rubbery meta-material. The sterile air noticeably lacked a smell.

"Lin!" a voice called out.

Lin turned and, with a grin, ran into the outstretched arms of an onrushing man. Her husband, Damian assumed.

He lifted her up, spun her around and placed her back on the ground, delight in both of their eyes. He traced the line of her jaw with his thumb, then placed a loose strand of hair behind her ear.

They spoke in Mandarin, and Damian understood none of it. The man kissed her deeply for a long time before someone called him back to his prelaunch duties. He said a few more words to her, kissed her fingertips. They held hands until the last possible moment as he departed looking like the happiest man Damian had ever seen.

Damian realized he'd been staring. When Lin turned around, he feigned distraction as a very belated courtesy.

They took several steps in silence. "Did you tell him?" asked Damian.

She shook her head. "How could I? I must not add to his sorrow."

"He didn't look sad to me."

"My husband can always find joy, even in sorrow, but I know him, and the sorrow is still there. I, too, will choose joy, even in my sorrow."

A crew member appeared from around a corner and ushered them forward. He issued them ID cards from a console on a nearby wall and, with little regard for gentleness or warning, injected each of their necks with a vital signs monitor. The injection stung, and then throbbed.

Damian rubbed his neck as the crew member led them down to the lowest, innermost level of the ring where the cryo chambers were. Each cryo chamber, little more than a vertical coffin with a small window, contained an eerie, frozen face. The death mask faces did little to lessen his impression of coffins lining the walls. Damian's pulse echoed in his ears at the thought of the enclosed space. He took a deep breath, like he had practiced.

The crew member directed them into their respective chambers, right across from each other. The door closed, leaving Damian isolated in a silent, claustrophobic tube. Through the glass, he watched Cheng Lin. She smiled at him. The corner of his lip went up, as if it wanted to smile, which made him aware of his furrowed brow, sore from the many trials of the day. He blinked to reset his face, then smiled at the intriguing woman. Her eyes had already closed.

A soothing voice came through speakers behind his head, "Please try to relax. The more relaxed you are now, the better you will feel when you awaken. The cryo-sleep induction process will begin in twenty seconds. Please remember to keep your eyes closed..."

Damian shut his eyes hard and tried to calm himself. His mind drifted to Cheng Lin. How could she be so calm? Her husband was going to be as good as dead the next time she saw him.

And suddenly, the fear resurfaced. If something went wrong, these could be his last thoughts. He tried to think of something good and noble, something fitting of last thoughts, but his brain would only repeat a chorus of "oh God, oh God, oh God."

But, Lin was calm. He cheated his eyes open as the countdown ticked to fifteen. Lin's face was peaceful, her hair falling slightly over one side of her face in a portrait of acceptance.

She was right about one thing, Damian realized, shutting his eye again. Somehow being here on the ship, in the cryo pod, had made it real to him. The Earth was dying. Had he said goodbye to everyone?

Had he said goodbye to anyone?

Too late he realized the gift he had been given. Not too late for him, but too late for all those he would leave behind. Better to be an orphan of planet Earth, adrift in space but with hope for the future, than to fall in anonymity in the death throes of a failing world. Not that he could have done anything to save those left behind from their plight, but perhaps, as the official historian, he might have better recorded their stories before they became a mere memory of the Ithacans-to-be. He would have to do better once he got there. The stories of so many were soon to be erased, but he swore he would record as many as possible from the first generation of Ithacans. He could do that much.

All those things he had spent so much time and effort pursuing in his fledgling academic career — chasing book deals, being interviewed, growing in prestige, all of it — were soon to fade, along with all the people he had tirelessly tried to impress. He took another deep breath and...

He slept for five hundred years.

————

1 June 2214 - 8 Days Before Departure

Six weeks into training, Cheng was feeling confident in his abilities. Most of the actual training would come during his waking tenure on CIV, but everyone had now been trained together in the basics. They'd also been extensively tested to confirm their suitability for the role — the last checks among dozens that had been done beforehand. Digitized copies of their genomes had been uploaded to the MedAI to ensure any injuries or conditions were treated with genetically customized solutions.

With just over a week until launch, the technicians were getting close to being put into cryo. Ten technicians had been selected to assist with launch duties — the four technicians that would work the first twelve-year shift plus six other subject matter experts. Most of the technicians, like Cheng, had connections to RamTech that predated their selection for their current role, and the six additional experts awake for launch had all helped in the construction of CIV or the Ramsey-Alcubierre Drive that would propel them through the galaxy.

But today was a big day. Today was the day they would receive their order of duty. There were forty-three slots, the first three had been pre-selected by Ramsey.

Everyone had worked out the math. They all knew that technicians forty-one, forty-two, and forty-three would arrive at Ithaca without having to complete the full fifty years. They knew their odds were long, but everyone hoped, including Cheng.

They gathered in the small auditorium they had often used for large group lectures during training. One of their instructors explained the process to them, and then called each row, one at a time, to come forward.

To remove any sense of bias, the selection process would be as basic and un-hackable as possible: forty-three numbered strips of paper had been poured into a bucket, and the technicians drew their numbers one by one. Your fate was in your own hands.

Cheng's row was second-to-last. He grabbed at random, without deliberation, his heart pounding. He unfolded it, read it, read it again. Relief washed over him. He showed it to the technician next to him.

"You lucky son of a bitch," he whispered. "Forty-two? You just got yourself out of twenty-one years of work, my friend."

Cheng smiled. "My wife will be delighted."

"Wife, huh? Well, better you than me, I guess. I'm not sure my brother cares much if I'm young or old when we get there."

Cheng nodded, suddenly feeling awkward about his good fortune. "What number did you get?"

"Nothing special. Thirty-four. Would have rather been in the first half, I think. But what can you do, right? I'm Randy, by the way."

"Cheng Ahn." They exchanged a warm handshake.

"You keep that close to you, Cheng. Some of these guys might jump you for it." Randy patted Cheng on the shoulder and headed toward the registrar.

Cheng took another delighted look at his slip of paper and was about to follow Randy when he quite accidentally noticed the last technician grab the last slip of paper. However, instead of following the flow of his colleagues, he circled back to a chair and collapsed, head in his hands.

Cheng considered ignoring him and continuing on his way. He even took a hesitant step in that direction before deciding he would want someone to check on him if they found him in the same situation.

He excused himself as he cut across two other technicians to get out of the registrar's line.

As he approached, he heard the man taking calming breaths, muttering to himself in a tongue unknown to Cheng. Cheng sat down two seats away, and the chair creaked.

The other technician looked up and hastily dried his tears away. "I am fine, do not worry about me," he said, waving Cheng away. His Middle-Eastern accent matched the gentle brown of his skin.

"It seemed like you needed to talk to someone," Cheng offered.

The man eyed Cheng through the gaps in his fingers. "We have psychologists for that. Leave me be."

"I may not be a psychologist, but I know what a broken heart looks like. What number did you get?"

The man did not respond, but tossed the piece of paper he had set on the chair beside him toward Cheng. It wasn't heavy enough to cover the distance and fluttered to the floor.

Cheng retrieved it from under the chair and unfolded

it tenderly. The man shifted his weight off of his knees and leaned back in the chair, arms folded across his chest, face turned away from Cheng. "Thirty-one," Cheng read aloud.

"Yes, I know what it says."

"Who is it?"

He made eye contact with Cheng for the first time. "Who is who?"

"Who did you bring with you, who sleeps in the cryo chamber?"

He averted his eyes again, but not so angrily as before. He hesitated, then said, "My daughter, Adilah."

"I see. How old?"

"Three years. Her birthday was just before she went into cryo."

"Very young. The youngest I have heard of. She must be very brave."

"She is a small child," he snapped. "She is terrified."

Cheng bowed his head. "Of course, I apologize."

He sighed, "No, no. It's ok. You mean well."

Cheng offered his hand. "Cheng Ahn."

The man took it slowly. His grip was strong. "Mohammed Samaras."

They sat in silence for a moment. In the far corner of the room, the young doctor with the brown hair still had a long queue of technicians to register and tag with their bio-tracker for the cryo chamber that matched the number they had drawn.

"Why has God done this to us?" Mohammed said.

People had been asking why God had allowed this to happen to the Earth a lot over the last several years.

Cheng's opinion was that humanity had done this to itself. But that didn't seem to be Mohammed's question. "Done what?"

Mohammed seemed to catch the ambiguity of his question. "Us, the technicians, I meant. It would almost be easier to start over on Ithaca with nothing than to face that child again after fifty years, knowing that my strength is all but gone and my heart is all but empty. It is a cruel fate, to survive the coming disaster on Earth, only to arrive in a new paradise too old and used up to enjoy it with our loved one."

Cheng considered this for almost a full minute. The line trickled down to its last few technicians. "It might be easier to arrive without attachment, but harder to leave, I think. And harder to live with yourself in the meantime. It might be easier, but it would not be better."

Mohammed looked at Cheng for several seconds before turning back toward the front of the auditorium. "You are right, of course. Thank you, my friend."

"Gentlemen?" the doctor called out. The line was gone. They were alone.

Cheng held the scrap of paper up to Mohammed. "Make Adilah proud, Mohammed."

He nodded solemnly as he took the paper. "Thank you, my friend."

They proceeded to the doctor's station by the room's exit. Cheng hurried to take the spot in front of Mohammed.

"I'm Dr. Miller," the doctor said. "I'm probably the only ship's doctor you haven't met yet. I'll be there to assist with any medical needs that the MedAI can't handle during your journey."

They greeted her politely. Cheng handed her his slip. She read it, crossed his name and the number off the list, grabbed the unsettlingly large subcutaneous transponders, loaded them into the gun and unloaded them professionally into Cheng's neck and right forearm. It took only seconds, but the pain, Dr. Miller warned, would last for an hour or so. They would be in cryo long before that.

As Mohammed braced himself, Dr. Miller said, "Ah, so you're one of the lucky ones then."

Two subtle hammer blows, Mohammed winced, but bit his lip. Then he said, "Lucky ones?"

"Yeah, number forty-two. You've only got twenty-nine years instead of the full fifty. You'll be bringing us into Ithaca."

Mohammed smiled, "I am sorry, but you are mistaken. I am number thirty-one."

Her eyebrows narrowed as she cocked her head. "No, he's thirty-one." She pointed at Cheng, who smiled sheepishly.

Mohammed looked at Cheng inquisitively. He thanked Dr. Miller and followed Cheng out of the room. "What have you done?" he asked in the corridor.

"I drew number forty-two, Mohammed."

"But, why did she think I was number forty-two."

"Because you were. You are."

He blinked. "I... I don't understand."

"I switched my drawing with yours when you weren't looking."

Realization dawned on his face. "You... But... Why?"

"I did nothing to earn that number. It came to me through luck. I was free to do with it whatever I wished."

"So you gave it to me?" His lip quivered. "You gave up twenty-one years of your life for a stranger without a second thought? Just like that?"

"You are not a stranger, Mohammed. We do not have those anymore. No, you are my brother."

"Brother," he repeated quietly, nodding. "No. This... this is too much to accept."

"It is already done. You must accept it."

A solemn nod. "I will never forget what you have done for me. For my family. I make this vow today: your family is my family, forever."

Cheng clapped him on the shoulder with filial affection.

As they continued on their way, Cheng said, "Do you believe that everything happens for a reason?"

"Difficult to say. Things happen. We can find a reason in them later, but you can never know what would have happened under different circumstances. In science, yes, but not in life. So, is the reason determined ahead of time, or do we make the reason for ourselves after we see the outcome? It is impossible to say."

Cheng considered this. "I do not know why I saw you take your seat in that chair, Mohammed. I do not know exactly what drew me to your side. I do not know why I felt that I must switch my paper with yours. But I did." He paused. "Whether we find the deeper meanings of events or we create their meanings as we go, most decisions in life, I have found, end up with some meaning attached to them. I do not know what meaning this has beyond the years you have won back to spend with your daughter... But I can't help but imagine that there is some higher reason for all this."

"If that is true, why did we need to swap? Would it not have been more straightforward to have us each draw the opposite number?"

"Perhaps the significance is in our meeting, or in the act of the giving and the receiving." He pondered this himself. "We will find out," Cheng smiled, "in time."

Mohammed nodded, but was quiet.

They proceeded to the umbilical connection between Troy Orbital and CIV. Though Cheng had made the journey many times over the past weeks, there was a certain finality to it this time. The next fifty years of his life would be on CIV. That was real now. For a short time, before he had traded his spot, the sentence had been partially commuted, and that made the weight of the full thing somehow harder to bear. The other technicians were still being sorted into their respective tubes when Cheng and Mohammed arrived. They shook hands, hugged, and stood in front of their respective units while the launch crew readied the pods.

Just a few spots down the line from Cheng, Randy waved to him. "Hey, Cheng, I thought you were number forty-two?"

"Oh," Cheng said. "It did not work out. That is ok. I am happy to be where I am."

Randy shrugged. "If you say so. Well, it looks like you'll be my Senior Technician when I wake up now."

Cheng smiled. "Looks like it."

He greeted the men on either side of him — Santos Pantagiatis to his right and, to his left, the exceptionally-named Fabian Luis Da Silva Caceda. He tried to wrap his mind around the idea of each of these immediately adjacent men being his coworkers for thirty-seven of his fifty years, but could not.

Soon, the chambers opened, and Cheng stepped into his. From across the room, Mohammed watched him, and when he caught his eye, the Middle-Eastern man smiled a genuine, but sad smile and nodded his respect. Cheng inclined his head in mutuality.

Then the pods closed. It was real now.

He thought of Lin, of course. Her eyes, her hair, her smile, the warmth of her touch. He thought of Mohammed and the young daughter who would no longer be as-good-as orphaned when she arrived on Ithaca. He thought of the other sons and daughters who were not as lucky as Adilah Samaras and wished the pain did not have to be so.

He knew Lin would understand. She believed in building the same sort of world that he did. She would stand beside him, bent and grey as he would be, with pride.

Twenty-one years he had given away. Twenty-one years of a life with Lin. Perhaps they would still be able to have a child. Perhaps he would even be fortunate enough to get to know that child some before his age overtook him and he went the way of all things.

Or perhaps he was just a fool.

A tear rolled down his cheek. He wiped it away hastily.

The countdown started, as he had known it would. He concentrated on his breathing.

"I'm so sorry, My Love. I'm so sorry. Please forgive me."

In the last seconds before the sequence completed, Cheng experienced a sudden calm. Somehow, he now knew, he was exactly where he was supposed to be.

19

ACCOMPLISHED

S erena had started having dreams while being awoken from cryo. Fantastic visions of sweeping landscapes and rushing waters flitted through her subconscious.

And she was flying, always flying.

In waking life, she of course realized that these were drug-induced interpretations of her own neurological activity as it revived from the slumber of cryo, but the colors! The views! The smells! They were unlike anything she had known on Earth.

And even though she knew it was impossible, part of her wondered, and half-hoped, that somehow, some way, these were dreams of Ithaca. It was a good hope to hold on to, even for those fleeting moments before they faded into the insipid reality of life on CIV.

As the latest visions of deep blues and greens faded, Fabian's face appeared. He was worried about something. No, just older. Yes, older, but also worried. Or distracted, perhaps? He kept looking over his shoulder toward the entrance to the room.

Her thoughts began to coagulate. Cheng's plan. Her role in it. Had he succeeded? Was Ramsey ready to be examined? Her head was foggier than usual.

Fabian shouted, "Wait! No!" and then there was flash. A flash like lightning. The lights in the room dimmed, then returned to full brightness.

Fabian had vanished. Where had he gone?

Five, ten, fifteen seconds. A whooshing noise as the chamber vented. Fabian was back. He looked in through the window, terror etched on his face, just long enough to see that she was awake. He disappeared for a moment. The cryo pod hissed open.

Serena raised her hand against the brightness. "What's-"

"It's Cheng! And Ramsey! We need your help!"

Adrenaline sucked the cobwebs from the corners of her mind. Her pulse quickened, echoing in her ears. "Show me."

Fabian backed away, offering a hand to help her out of the tube. It shook as she took it.

Her eyes immediately found the scene. A technician, she didn't know his name, was performing CPR on a still figure, another lay face-down beside them. The new technician turned to her, eyes pleading. She stumble-ran to the bodies.

Not the bodies. The people.

Ramsey lay face down, motionless. Cheng was receiving the CPR. The smell of singed flesh hung in the air. Serena knew it too well.

"What happened?" She asked, rolling Ramsey onto his back. His nose was bleeding. It looked broken.

"Ramsey's cryo chamber," said the technician. "It sealed shut during extraction, and he passed out."

Serena checked Ramsey's pulse. Erratic, but there. And he was breathing, now.

Fabian took over the CPR from his colleague, whispering as he worked, "Come on, Cheng. Not today. Not today, my friend."

"You," she motioned to the new technician. "Get the defibrillator from my office."

He nodded, and took off running, touching his earpiece as he left.

Fabian said, "Cheng put his crowbar through the console to engage the failsafe and... well, look at him."

Ramsey let out a groan. He would survive. Serena rolled him onto his side and switched her attention to Cheng.

His hands were charred and mangled. Her stomach turned and she fought to compose herself. Flashbacks of Brazil played across her mind's eye. She checked Cheng's pulse as Fabian pumped his heart.

There was nothing. There was a chance that there was still electrical activity in his heart, and that's what she was banking on. But the situation seemed grim.

"Come on, Cheng. Come on, buddy," Fabian breathed between compressions.

"Keep going," she encouraged him. The initial rush of adrenaline was wearing off, and she felt how dense and foggy her mind and body still were. Better to let Fabian continue.

Serena looked up at the destroyed console. Cheng lay fifteen or twenty feet from it. A large metal crowbar protruded from the scorched terminal, half of the head buried in the circuitry. Black lines, preserved in a pattern like flame, surrounded the base of the unit. The pod itself looked dead; all of the usual ambient lights indicating system status were dark. A viscous yellow-brown liquid dripped from the inside of the open pod doors.

Ramsey heaved and vomited, barely coming out of his stupor. Serena returned to his side to help him. "Is this his typical Somnithaw reaction?"

Fabian nodded as he kept compressing.

"Poor devil." She rubbed his back for several long seconds and felt his muscles relax.

Ramsey mumbled something.

"Say it again?" she prompted, leaning closer.

"Thank you, Cheng." He collapsed back into unconsciousness.

She wasn't sure if Ramsey was confused and thought Cheng was rubbing his back or if he was having a surprising moment of lucidity and recognizing what Cheng had done, his sacrifice.

No, not sacrifice. He wasn't dead yet. Maybe.

Right on cue, Asahi and the new technician arrived with the defibrillator. "We got it," one of them said. She didn't notice who; it was time for action.

"Fabian, remove his shirt," she said, checking the charge on the unit, "cut it down the middle."

Fabian stopped his compressions and his mumbled prayers, pulled his knife from his utility belt, and had Cheng's chest exposed in seconds.

"Asahi, make sure Ramsey doesn't choke if he vomits again," Serena commanded as she turned toward Cheng's still form. The small Japanese man rushed to Ramsey's side.

She peeled the applicators from their pouch and stuck them to their respective locations on Cheng's torso.

Someone sniffled, suppressing tears.

The machine calibrated itself to read where his heartbeat should be, guessed his weight and dimensions, and indicated itself ready with a green light. Serena flipped the safety.

"Clear!"

She pressed the button.

Cheng's body jumped.

The machine prepped itself again. It had not detected a pulse.

Another jolt.

"Come on, Cheng."

Again.

"You can do this."

Again.

As it charged again, Serena looked up to face the technicians. Fabian paced back and forth across a twenty-foot stretch of the chamber, fingers interlocked behind his head. Asahi sat crouched beside Ramsey, one hand on his slumbering shoulder, the other covering his own mouth. The new technician sat with his back up against the wall, red eyes peeking over the top of his arms as they hugged his knees to his chest.

A final jolt.

Fabian's pacing stopped. He looked at Serena expectantly.

She shook her head.

"No, keep trying," he said. "Keep going."

"Fabian..."

"He would never give up on any of us."

"Fabian, I'm sorry."

He fell to his knees. "No, you have to keep trying."

She shook her head again. "I'm sorry. He's gone."

EN ROUTE TO ITHACA - YEAR 383 OF 504

RAMSEY AWOKE TO TOO-BRIGHT LIGHTS. HE SQUEEZED HIS eyelids closed to shut it out.

"Shh," soothed a man's voice. "Don't try to move."

Ramsey's throat was dry. "Water."

Almost immediately a straw was at his lips. He took a few sips, but it felt like all he could manage. He tried to open an eye, but it was still too bright. "Where am I?"

"Ah..." the voice trailed off.

"Who is that?"

"It's Fabian, First Technician. And you are in the medical observation room."

Ramsey's eyes flew open and he immediately found that he was strapped to his bed, tipped up to about a thirty degree angle. The room was white, clean, and brighter than most of the rooms on the ship. An IV and various sensors ran from his body to a medical station at his bedside. His eyes found Fabian and his fury burned.

"What have you done? Where is Cheng? Let me out of here!"

"I'm sorry sir, but I need you to calm down."

"Let me go and I'll show you how calm I am."

"Soon. I promise you, soon. But you need to cooperate first."

Ramsey jeered at him. "You're making demands? You? On my ship? I don't think so. Let me go before I-" he stopped himself. He really had no way to discipline the technicians. That had been perhaps his worst oversight. "Before you do something you'll really regret." He injected his tone with as much menace as he could.

"Ok, I didn't want to have to do this..." He touched his ear, talking to someone else. "Orange button, right?"

A moment later, Ramsey felt a chilling sensation run through his arm and spread through his body. Against his will, his body began to relax. "What did you do to me?"

"Just something to take the edge off," said Fabian.

"You're not a doctor," said Ramsey.

"No, I'm not."

"Then how..." Ramsey couldn't remember what his question was supposed to be.

"Uh, we might have gone a little too heavy with it," said Fabian, again touching his earpiece.

But then the world faded into...

RAMSEY AWOKE AGAIN.

He flexed his arms, and they pulled at the restraints that still bound him.

"He's coming back," said Fabian's voice.

Ramsey opened his eyes, trying to find the energy to be furious, and failing. "Let me go," he said, with much less authority than he had intended.

"Soon. I promise."

Ramsey closed his eyes and turned away.

"I'm on your side, Dr. Ramsey."

"Then why am I tied down?"

"We need to monitor you for at least 24 hours. I know you don't want that, but you did almost just asphyxiate. Speaking of, how are you feeling."

"You're not a doctor."

"No. We know how you feel about doctors and wanted to respect your wishes."

Ramsey scoffed. "You would have no idea how to set all this up. Where is she?"

"Where is who?"

"That woman doctor."

Fabian hesitated. It was all Ramsey needed to know he was right.

The door hissed open in confirmation of his suspicion. "I'm here."

Ramsey lifted his head.

"I don't know if you remember me. I'm Dr. Serena Miller."

Ramsey laughed bitterly. "Oh, I remember you, Dr. Miller. Congratulations! You and your coconspirators have won. I am at your mercy at last."

She frowned. "What do you think this is about, Dr. Ramsey?"

"Control. The technicians don't want me to be in charge, and neither do you." He said more than he meant to. He reminded himself that he was under the influence of an unknown substance and that his words should be more measured. They had won this pivotal battle, but the war was still there for the winning. He wasn't defeated. Not yet. No, not yet.

"So Cheng was right." Dr. Miller sighed. "Dr. Ramsey, no one wants to keep you from your work. My job is to keep you healthy so you can *complete* your work."

"What was Cheng right about? And where is he? Isn't he your ringleader? Isn't he the one who contrived this whole situation?" It was the only logical conclusion. He was an insightful one, that Cheng. Sticking his nose where it didn't belong. Guessing at things unknowable.

Fabian and Dr. Miller glanced at each other, trying to coordinate their lie.

Dr. Miller was the one who spoke. Fabian bit his lip and turned away. "I regret to inform you that Cheng Ahn passed away from the injuries he sustained in saving you."

Ramsey chuckled. "Bullshit." Dr. Miller held his gaze. He chuckled again, more nervously. "It's been almost four hundred years and no one has died yet. We have too many precautions. That's impossible."

"Well, it happened," said Fabian. "I *saw* it happen. We have *surveillance* of it happening." His voice took on a threatening edge as he turned back toward Ramsey, "Would that make it less funny to you, if you got to watch it?"

"Your lies do not interest me."

"Lies?"

"Fabian," cautioned Dr. Miller.

"No. Forget it. I'm done. I don't care what we talked about." He raised a finger at Ramsey. "I don't care who you think you are. I don't care about any of that. My best friend sacrificed himself to save you. The best man I ever knew is dead, and the worst one I ever knew," he motioned derisively, "is left here instead. I tried, *Colin*. I fucking tried. All Cheng ever talked about was how important you were. That we had to overlook your cruelty. That we had to forgive your anger. He said you would come around eventually. Well, you know what? He was wrong, and, in the end, he died for nothing. You're a cruel, petty, selfish tyrant, and that's all you'll ever be."

The room echoed for a moment. No one had ever spoken to Ramsey that way before. Ever.

"Fabian," whispered Dr. Miller.

"I don't care," he said to her. Then, turning back to Ramsey, "You want to be the way you are, Ramsey? Fine. But if I ever hear you spit on the memory of my best friend like that again, I swear to God, I'll kill you myself." He held his position, then turned and stalked out the door.

The silence hung in the air again.

Ramsey found himself less sure than he had been mere moments ago. He turned to Dr. Miller. "Is Cheng really dead?"

She nodded somberly. "Electrocuted."

He let his breath out slowly. He had never considered that he might lose a technician. "I... I'm sorry to hear that."

"Yeah," was all Dr. Miller would commit to.

Cheng's death presented a dilemma, an unforeseen

contingency. Fortunately, he had been close to the end of his term as Senior Technician. Perhaps the team would just have to carry on with three members for a few years until they could get back on schedule.

The other option would be to awaken a new technician now and shift all the subsequent ones a few years earlier. That would extend the four-year period at the end of the journey with only three crew members by a few years.

No, probably better to allow the technicians to be understaffed temporarily on two occasions than to overburden the technicians at the very end of the journey.

The question remained of what to do with Cheng's body. CIV was not equipped for the disposal of human remains. The only thing resembling an airlock was in the colonization module on the other side of the ring. That was probably the most viable option, but it would be a major distraction, especially for a now-understaffed technician crew.

"This is a major inconvenience," he said aloud.

"Excuse me?" said Serena. "I'm sorry, what's inconvenient?"

"Cheng. It will take quite a bit of logistical work to accommodate his loss."

"Dr. Ramsey," said Serena.

He looked up. Her eyes had narrowed, her lips drawn into a narrow line.

"A man has just died," Dr. Miller said. "A good man. A great man, even. I don't think it's appropriate to be complaining about the logistical problems right now."

"You see, this is why I can't trust anyone else." He

stared Dr. Miller down. "This mission is bigger than Cheng, Dr. Miller. It's bigger than everyone. Do you not understand the scope and significance of what we are accomplishing day by day, century by century? Do you not understand that the lives of any of you are meaningless in the scope of the grander plan? This is about the life or death of the human race. We don't have the time or the bandwidth to pause and mourn the loss of any individual, good man or not."

Dr. Miller lacked the self-control to conceal the look of disgust on her face. He'd seen it before. "You and I have very different ideas about what it means to save the human race," she said.

"Oh, spare me your moralizing. I've heard it all before, and from wiser minds than yours. I have one mission. *We* have one mission, and that is to get this ship to Ithaca with our cargo intact. Cheng's death is a hindrance to that target, and therefore a nuisance to be overcome."

"How can you say that?" The finely controlled persona the doctor had put on had all but vanished under Ramsey's probing. Her fists shook at her side. "After all that Cheng has done for you, sacrificing his life, his time, his future. This is how you show your gratitude?"

Ramsey scoffed. "You don't really want to talk to me about sacrifice, but since you brought it up, I'll indulge you:

"I was the richest man in the world. I had everything I ever wanted. What did I do? I liquidated it to save five thousand people.

"I could have spent the prime years of my life building a legacy on Earth and living in the lap of luxury. What did I do? I worked endless shifts at all hours of the day to ensure that the one project that really mattered was completed in time.

"I could have broken my own rules and saved my best friend and his family. What did I do? I stayed true to the rules and principles that have guided this mission from the beginning.

"I invented a dozen technologies that made this ship possible a century ahead of its time. And what happened to me? One of them turned against me and has put me through hell for almost four hundred years.

"I saved these forty-three technicians and a loved one for each of them, sacrificing room for far more qualified passengers. And what became of that decision? Four centuries of enmity, conspiracy, and strife.

"I have sacrificed and suffered more than you can possibly understand, and I believe my accomplishments have earned me the right to conduct myself and this expedition however I damn well see fit."

Dr. Miller's face had softened some at this. Compassionate people were always easy to persuade. However, when she spoke, there was still an unexpected resoluteness to her voice. "Everyone on this ship has suffered, Dr. Ramsey. Maybe not in the same ways you have. But all five thousand of us have suffered something. Every last one."

"And what about you, Dr. Miller? What have you suffered? I place you at thirty-one, thirty-two. You're a young and largely inexperienced doctor who was probably fresh out of medical school when you joined RamTech, no doubt with the objective of securing passage to Ithaca. You're white, American, and based on the way you speak I'm guessing West Coast, upper-middle class family. Statistically speaking, you're probably an only child, which combined with the rest of it means you probably had most of your accomplishments handed to you, including your education. By the time I was your age, I was already building CIV. I've spent the last seventeen years of my life dedicated to this vision." He put all of his derision into his final accusation. "You're barely more than a passenger."

Dr. Miller's arms had crossed; her moistened eyes glistened in the still-too-bright lights. Her words had the same venom his had had. "You know nothing about me. Yes, some of what you guessed was true, but most of it couldn't be more wrong.

"My parents were basically destitute after my dad lost his job to a RamTech acquisition. I graduated high school at fifteen. College at eighteen. Full ride academic scholarship to UCLA. I finished my residency at twenty-four and joined the Global Health Project. I did a two-year stint in Mozambique before being recruited for a new project in Brazil. That was where I met the love of my life." Her eyes met Ramsey's. "He was brutally murdered by terrorists. He lied to me and sent me away to protect me. He saved my life, but that wasn't what I wanted. I wanted to be with him, come what may. I never really got a chance to say goodbye, and I haven't really forgiven him yet.

"After that, I used my connection with Dr. Daniels to join RamTech. My father nearly disowned me, but I couldn't stand to be on Earth anymore; a world that would destroy my Philippe was not a world worth living in. My mother died about six months before we left. Cancer. I wasn't allowed to go to the funeral and my Dad stopped talking to me after that. I've lost and sacrificed everything to get here, just the same as you have, Dr. Ramsey. And I'm not the only one.

"Have you ever really talked to any of your technicians? Any of them? Even Cheng? Every one of those men feels deep anguish about the years they've lost on this ship. Their whole lives, sacrificed and used up in the blink of an eye, just to do their small part to keep the ship moving and operating, hoping against hope that their loved ones will still recognize them when they get to Ithaca, praying that their sacrifices and their suffering was worthwhile. Everything Cheng ever did was for his wife, Lin. And now she will be a widow on Ithaca. Not to mention the technicians who have children sleeping in cryo. Some of them are not even five years old, and now they've lost their mothers back on Earth and their fathers will be replaced by old men who haven't seen them for half a century!

"But maybe they're still the lucky ones. Every single person in cryo left everyone and everything behind on Earth. Every person they ever knew is gone, dead, and likely dust by now. All of their friends, spouses, children. You are literally going to have a planet full of people who know what it means to sacrifice and suffer. It's built into the very DNA of this mission, but I'm starting to wonder if you ever even considered that."

He hadn't. That was the honest answer. His pulse pounded as he considered what he had just admitted.

She was...

She was right.

But there was another suffering. One that only Cheng had ever glimpsed, and that one eclipsed all the others. He hardened his heart. "You have no idea what I've endured."

"I can't know your suffering, just as you can't know mine. We're all just drifting through life, hurting, hoping we can find someone whose wounds will help us understand our own. And then, if we're lucky, we both can heal."

Ramsey sighed heavily. She did not understand what he knew to be incomprehensible.

"I know what you've endured, Dr. Ramsey."

"No, you don't, Dr. Miller."

"Please call me Serena."

"Fine."

"I do know, Dr. Ramsey. On top of your weekly battle with Somnithaw, you have suffered the agony and isolation of immortality."

"If that's supposed to impress me, you've failed. I already know that you and Cheng have been long-term coconspirators."

"I know something Cheng could never know, and that's what it actually feels like."

He raised a skeptical eyebrow.

"I'm another immortal, like you."

He looked her up and down. "You're not like me."

"I'm not the same as you, no. But I am like you."

He looked away.

"I know that you're lonely, Dr. Ramsey. I'm lonely, too. What I've had to go through, watching these men grow old, it's been harrowing. Sometimes I wake up and they've aged thirty years. Young men's lives are all used up while I sleep."

He hadn't considered that from her perspective before. "But you have the luxury of being able to pretend they are different people. You don't see snapshots of every year. You don't watch the life and youthful vigor evaporate out of them like a grape in the sun."

"And you don't see the ship deteriorate before your eyes. Your contact with it is too frequent. Every time I wake up, the doors make different sounds, the walls are a different shade of faded, the air is that much more stale. There are entirely different trees in the primary life support."

He stared at her.

"You see, Dr. Ramsey. I'm more immortal than you are. Compared to me, you've aged a lot. I see the pull of time dragging even on you."

Could it be?

She held his gaze as his eyes bored into her, seeking a shred of deception or duplicity.

He found none.

The way she spoke about it rang true to life. And there was something in her eyes, a certain tiredness that he felt, too. And a longing.

"Like me," he whispered.

She nodded. "Just like you. Or, at least, enough like you that, maybe, my wounds can help you understand yourself better, and vice versa." A sad smile flickered across her face.

And then she began to unbind him.

In seconds, his hands and feet were free.

Ramsey sat the rest of the way up. "I... I don't understand," he said.

"It was never my intention to force you to submit to an exam. But I did need you to listen. And you did. Thank you. If you want to walk out now, that's fine; I won't stop you. You've recovered enough that I feel comfortable pulling out your IV... But I hope that you will stay and let me examine you."

He glanced at the door of the room, then back to Serena, who looked at him hopefully, compassionately.

"Promise me you won't lock me back in cryo. Truly, the ship needs me."

"My goal is to find a solution to enable you to complete your work. I promise."

He stared at her for a long time.

Then he nodded.

As Serena began her scan, Ramsey's attention was drawn elsewhere, despite the stakes. Like a curtain being opened to let in the brightness of day, the realization dawned.

"You said that Cheng saved me back in cryo. How, exactly?"

"He drove a crowbar through the control panel of your cryo unit after you passed out. It activated the failsafe and the doors opened."

Ramsey nodded, then he laid his head back and thought for a long time. Finally, "Why?"

"Why, what?"

"Why would he save me?"

"He's Cheng. That's just how he is."

"I wouldn't for him."

"He's not like you."

"No. Obviously not."

Serena smiled. "He loved you."

"Did he, though? Most of the time it seemed like he wanted to *use* me. He wanted to *manipulate* me. And here I am, talking to you. So I guess it worked."

"He was a flawed and broken person, just like everyone else. He made himself a student of you. That was his life's work. He may not have been the right person, or used the right methods to win you over, but I know that everything he did, he did with pure intentions."

"I suppose."

Serena returned to her work. She attached a biometric scanner like a weighted sweatband around Ramsey's head.

"Do you know that you thanked Cheng, after... after what happened in there?" she said.

Ramsey shook his head, his thoughts far away.

"You were a little delirious, but you said, plain and simple, 'Thank you, Cheng.' I was rubbing your back at the time, and I wasn't sure if you thought I was Cheng or if you realized what he had done."

Ramsey didn't recall.

"Well, I know what it's like to be a survivor. After everything that happened with Philippe, my fiancé, even in my anger, I've always felt this thread of gratitude. It's bittersweet. I'm not done being angry, or lonely. But I recognize that every decision I make now bears more weight. My Philippe made the ultimate investment in me. And that's what it is, ultimately, to lay down your life for someone, right? You're telling them that you're betting your entire life, all that you are, all that you could ever have been, on them accomplishing something amazing, or at least showing them their value to you. Philippe cashed his chips in on me, and Cheng cashed his in on you."

Ramsey nodded. His brain felt foggy. The Somnithaw must have been still wreaking havoc, or possibly he was feeling some effect of the scanner on his head.

Serena continued, "The rest of your life, you're living for two. Whether you want it to or not, your life now bears the burden of Cheng's love. His interests are now yours, his goals. They're a part of you now."

"I... I can't."

"It's not a question of will, Dr. Ramsey. It's a fact about you now. Cheng lives on through you. You have to make him proud, honor him."

"But, my responsibilities. They're so much bigger than that."

"That may be. But the fact remains. Your life is Cheng's now. I know that's not easy for you to accept. So maybe, try to believe him about all that stuff he talked about: that he loved you as a brother, that he wants to save his wife, that he wants to see everyone, including you, make it to Ithaca and thrive there. Think about things he told you. Remember his values, and try to live them out."

Ramsey nodded his understanding and sat up on the side of his bed. "What should I do? What did you do first?"

She flashed a sad smile. "You get up tomorrow and you keep going, somehow. We get to Ithaca and find a way to make life work."

"It's what this guy, Philippe, would have wanted?"

"I don't know. But it's the best I can do. He told me to live my life. To try to love again. I'm not ready for that yet, but I've been trying to live as best as I can. As best as we would have."

"And, uh, what about Cheng?"

"What do you mean?"

"I'm just realizing that, for all the time I spent with him over the last year, I don't really know him that well. What am I supposed to do?"

Serena removed the scanner while she considered the question with a far-off look. "You could see to it personally that his wife is cared for on Ithaca. Make sure she has everything she needs."

Ramsey nodded noncommittally. "I'm not accustomed to being in someone's debt."

"I know." Serena smiled. "It'll take time."

They sat in silence.

"Come on," Serena said. "Just a few more test to go."

FAREWELL

6 JUNE 2214 CE - 5 HOURS BEFORE DEPARTURE

The day of days had arrived.

A decade of destruction and rebirth, negotiations and proclamations, but mostly of industry and innovation had led to this moment.

CIV spun freely now, released at last from the umbilicals that tethered it to Troy Orbital, and, symbolically, to Earth. Ramsey Technology Enterprises had been reduced to nothing. The last Earth-side assets had been sold, along with all the other colonies that orbited that dead world. Only these two rings, Troy and CIV, remained of the empire of the late Dr. Ramsey the Elder.

His son, the victorious conqueror at the end of history, watched the soon-to-be-forgotten world rotate below him. Strands of lights like golden spider webs illuminated parts of Europe as Earth spun that continent through the night, oblivious to the sufferings of those living on her surface. The night looked so dark. The lights were so few now compared to what they had once been. The world's infrastructure was collapsing everywhere, and the hub of Western civilization was no exception.

CIV's clock said it was late, but Ramsey wasn't tired. He couldn't remember the sensation of a time governed by the flow of day and night. There was only ever the right now, and what could be accomplished in it.

But this right-now was particularly significant. The RAD had just been activated, and would spend the next few hours creating and preserving the remaining exotic matter it needed to generate the energy-density field that would propel it across the stars.

There was no turning back now.

There was also nothing to do now. That was a novel sensation.

Ramsey sat in the command center, a grandiose name for a room barely twenty feet in each dimension, filled with sensors, view screens, and monitors. It would seldom be used during the next five centuries, but would be at the center of the action during departure and arrival.

The technicians were there, too. Old John, Miroslav, Kemal and that punk, Zeke. They were busy with their own responsibilities, but everything had been checked and triple-checked meticulously.

They were ready.

Ramsey excused himself from the command center, deciding to get an hour of rest before the next status update from the RAD. It was a familiar process, and his mind was calm.

It was a short walk to his quarters on CIV, where he

would stay during his working week each year. They were efficient, sparse accommodations, smaller than the technicians' more permanent lodgings. He lay down on the bed, and his mind drifted from the previous ten years to the next ten. He had felt more optimistic about his waking weeks when he was only supposed to be awake for five years. But Ty's resignation had left no other option but for Ramsey to take sole responsibility for the maintenance of the RAD and other complex systems.

Ramsey would handle it, though. Like he always handled everything.

He lay in bed, sleep retreating from his attempts to seize it. The thought of Ty had unsettled him.

Five Minutes.

Ten minutes.

Twenty.

When it became clear that sleep would not obey, Ramsey let out a heavy sigh. "Damn it, Ty."

He removed his covers.

Activated the light.

Took a deep breath.

———

6 June 2214 CE

THE LATE AFTERNOON SUN POURED INTO TY'S OFFICE IN Cambridge, Massachusetts. It was just past four on a Thursday afternoon, and his research assistants had already left for the day.

The return to academia had been a liberating one.

After leaving RamTech, he had immediately been offered positions at most of the world's top surviving universities, and when Harvard came to call, he couldn't turn it down. The university was on summer break now, which meant the real work of research could get done.

In New England, where the effects of the environmental and socioeconomic catastrophes were substantially less severe than in most other parts of the country and world, it was easy to forget that this was a doomed world. Or, it would have been easier, if he hadn't been continuing to refine his Earth Systems models with the latest data, each day further confirming the hypothesis.

But today, they were alive. Today, they were ok. Now was not the time for thinking about everything that would happen soon. Instead, he was taking a long weekend in New Hampshire with Clara and Izzy. The air quality was still good there, and they were going camping. As soon as the model that hovered above his workstation updated with the week's latest data, he was going home.

A notification appeared in the bottom corner of his display, indicating a call. He was expecting a call from Clara soon, so he answered it absent-mindedly.

A pale, tired face with curly hair in dirty blond greeted him instead. The man looked as surprised as Ty felt.

"I, uh. I didn't think you would answer," said Ramsey.

"I… I wasn't expecting to hear from you," Ty replied.

A silence stretched.

"We're getting ready to go," said Ramsey. "Just a few more hours."

"I know. We're heading to New Hampshire to do some camping and get a good view of your departure. It'll be the perfect time of night for it."

"There won't be much to see. We'll just, sort of, disappear."

"I know. But we had to mark today somehow."

The projection of Ramsey took a deep breath. "It's not too late, you know. We could delay the launch a few days, get you on a shuttle."

Ty hesitated. Everything in him said to go. The planetary model projection hovered behind Ramsey's face like a portent of ill fate. It was easy to forget here – where life was still happening more or less as usual - what the data meant for the future. Nothing good could come of staying on Earth. And here, at the end of any hope of human civilization surviving to the end of the century, came a lifeline from the black. "You know I want to, Colin."

"Then come!"

"Clara and Izzy?"

Ramsey's shoulders slumped. Frustration and disappointment oozed out of the way he licked the corner of his lip, then set his jaw. "You know where I stand."

It wasn't worth the breath to defend Izzy; Ramsey would never understand. "Look, Col. We have a life here. I know better than anyone, better even than you, how bad things are going to get down here. Maybe I'm making a mistake in staying, but, please try to sympathize, I would never be able to live with myself if I abandon her."

"You know I don't understand."

Ty nodded. "Yeah. I know. You never did."

"It's just not right, Ty. For you to die meaninglessly down there."

"Well, maybe that's the biggest difference between us."

"What is?"

"To you, meaning is determined by results, by outcomes, by recognition and accomplishment."

"What else could it mean? Nothing is meaningful if it's forgotten."

"But it is, Col. Don't you see? Maybe no one will remember my name in the far-flung history of the human race. Maybe my accomplishments will all come to nothing. But all that makes me is human. Most of us are forgotten, eventually. Even you might be, someday. At the very least, the universe will fizzle out in a few trillion years, and there will be no one left to remember anything at all. And yet, we still went to the trouble of building CIV. You're going to go through the trouble of setting up the first human colony world, even though humanity will eventually be extinct, one way or another. And yet we did it anyway. What actually makes something meaningful has to be decided by each person. Maybe for you, it is exactly what it seems it is. For me, my reason has always been to do right by the ones I love. I'm here with Izzy and Clara because traveling to Ithaca is meaningless to me in itself, as amazing as it would be."

"Well then, what is your higher calling, if not the salvation of humanity?"

"To keep humanity worth saving."

Ramsey blinked, processing. "Shouldn't we just save them first?"

"No."

"What do you mean, 'No'?"

"I mean it matters what we do, Colin. If I leave my daughter to die for my own selfish gain, I bring a worse humanity to Ithaca than the one being left behind. If I stay, I demonstrate that we are a species that cares for the other, even to the point of laying down our own lives."

Ramsey just shook his head.

Ty's heart pounded. He had thought a lot about this over the last nine months. In this conversation, though, his calculated rationale had to stand up against the unexpected hope that, just maybe, he could be saved after all. His heart was persuaded, but his mind railed against the rejection of this one last spark of possibility as it begged and pleaded to live.

"You never do cease to surprise me, Ty."

"Thank you."

"Listen, there's almost nothing left of the company, but after selling everything off except for what we needed, we're actually in the black financially, and we've still got Troy Orbital. I was going to surprise you, but I guess I may as well tell you now. All remaining RamTech assets will become your personal property at midnight tonight, your time. You can do whatever you want with them, if they're even worth anything. I know it's going to get rough there, and I certainly don't need them anymore. I hope you can do something great."

Ty's heart continued to pound, but with a very different reason. "Oh my God. Are you... Are you sure?"

"Definitely."

"I... I don't know what to say. Troy Orbital alone is

worth billions. You've just made me one of the richest people in the world." Not that it would matter soon.

"Well, don't let it go to your head. There's no one else I would want to leave it to."

Ty suspected that Ramsey had no one else he even could leave it to.

"I have a lawyer who will be in touch with you tomorrow."

"Thank you, Colin. Truly, thank you."

"I'd rather have you here with me. But, you and your damn principles. This is the best I can do." Ramsey hesitated, like he wasn't sure if he wanted to say what he was about to say. He looked away from the screen. "You're my best friend, Ty. My only friend, really. And, I don't know, I guess I'm realizing that I'm not going to see you again after this. And I want you to be ok."

Ty didn't know what to say either. "Thank you."

"Yeah. Well, listen. I probably need to go."

"No, of course. I have to get going, too. No problem."

"You take care of yourself, Ty. I know Clara probably hates me, but say hi from me, if you can."

"I will." Ty smiled, and found that it came more naturally than he thought it would. "Godspeed, Dr. Ramsey. Bring those people home."

Ramsey's lips flicked up in a brief half-smile. "Good luck, Dr. Daniels. I wish you well."

The screen flashed three times and evaporated, exposing the data and the charts Ty had been working on.

RamTech was his. It was probably not as generous of a gift as it had seemed. Almost nothing was left, and the billions of dollars that Troy Orbital was worth mattered little without infrastructure to travel to it or a buyer to take it off Ty's hands. But he already had a few ideas for how to use it for advanced Earth systems modeling. It sounded like a lot of work, but maybe he could do something interesting with it before it was all moot anyway.

Even in the foreknowledge of the looming end of the world, there was still that piece of him that refused to lay down, refused to acknowledge the fact. And that part of him would fight with every available mental, physical or financial resource until his last neuron fired.

But for now, there was time. A little bit of it at least. Time he had bought so he could share it with his loved ones.

The data set could wait until he got back on Monday, or Carl, his research assistant, could take a look at it. He added Carl's username to the report distribution list and gathered his jacket and personal items.

Ty pushed his chair in, but before he could turn to leave, his script alerted him that the latest batch of data had been processed. Unable to stop himself, he pulled his chair back out and returned to his seat.

The model swam before him in threatening reds and oranges and yellows, each strand represented a different story, a different course of events, all leading to the end of human civilization. He motioned for the visualization to include the latest dataset.

A single strand of pale green cut through the middle of the projection field, almost invisible among the adjacent yellows. He motioned a command, and the model zoomed in on this thread of faint, distant possibility. He stared at the data for a long time.

"Interesting," he said, at last.

----

6 June 2214 CE - 3 Minutes Before Departure

GREEN.

Every light on the board is green.

It's time to go.

Farewell, Earth.

Farewell, Ty.

Farewell, birthplace of the human race.

Farewell, only one I ever loved. If only I could have told you. Perhaps my parting gift will show you, a little.

I go now on a journey that none have walked before. I prepare to take on a legacy no less than the fate of sentience in our galaxy.

My ten years will be their five hundred. Like a god shall I outlast them.

And you, Ty. Even you.

Be well, best of mortal men. Ithaca will be worse off for your absence.

And so will I.

A voice interrupts. "It's time, sir."

Green.

Every light on the board is green.

I nod. "Here we go."

The technicians type and press and pull.

My display changes.

I take a deep breath.

Ten years of work, all I've done, all I've sacrificed, everything has led to this moment.

I authorize.

The RAD activates, and Earth disappears into a blackness that even light cannot pierce.

Within moments, we are traveling faster than light.

And yet, we feel no new forces on the ship as space expands and contracts around us.

We are away.

And if we are ever to return, it will be a long, long time. Beyond even the end of my days.

No, this is the final chapter of the world that birthed us.

Now we go home.

Ithaca, immortality, come to me.

21

SAFE

EN ROUTE TO ITHACA - YEAR 383 OF 504

"According to my report, you've lost twenty-five pounds, your blood work is way out of whack, your immune system is compromised, your sleep patterns are erratic, and, if I may say so, you look like hell."

Ramsey blinked. "I see."

It had been two days since the incident in cryo, and nearly twenty-four hours since Ramsey had agreed to testing. He had spent most of that time sleeping. Whatever Serena had given him, it was good stuff. He didn't feel good, per se. He couldn't go that far. But he felt less horrible than he had in quite some time.

"I know you want to put me back in cryo," he said, probing. A thread of well-trained anxiety tickled his mind.

"Of course I do," she said, placing her tablet down on the counter of the medical room and settling into the chair by Ramsey's bedside. "That's what's best for you.

But I also understand why it's not a choice. Something has to change, though."

"Like what?"

"You won't like it."

"I already hate everything about this. Just spit it out."

"Okay. I recommend a strictly controlled nutritional supplement, anti-inflammatory and immune-boosting injections, and to increase your recovery time each year from one waking week to two."

He laughed incredulously. "No. That will add more than two years to my work. I can't do that."

"The technicians work for fifty years. We've got a hundred and twenty years to go, so that would add about an extra two or three years for you. And even with those extras, you'll have put in, what, eleven or twelve years total? So why can't you do it?"

She had a point. He hated when people had a point. Unsure what to say, he resorted to folding his arms and scowling while avoiding eye contact.

"It's harder than you pretend it is, being the only god in a world of mortals." Her voice was soft, but intelligent. "You're barely hanging on, aren't you? Cheng said you liked it at first, but now you've become the loneliest person in the universe."

Ramsey averted his eyes.

"I believe him, you know. I can't imagine what you're going through. But I can imagine how impossible it must sound for me to ask you to add two more years of suffering. If you want to talk about it, I'll listen."

He let his eyes drift back in her direction, but never met her gaze. He'd come this far, already, he realized. It was too late to say anything but the truth. "I've spent the last four hundred years entering the mortal world fleetingly. I never touch the surface of life long enough to connect with it, like a well skipped stone across calm water. All my life I've longed for immortality. But every time I return to this decaying place, it's different than the one I left. I see entropy increase with every beat of my heart. I feel ancient. Beyond the scale of human reckoning." He met her eyes then. "I am the only god in a world of men. Alone in all the universe." He buried his face in his hands.

A reassuring hand rubbed his back. Like Cheng used to.

"And now you've lost your only friend." She sighed. "I'm so sorry, Dr. Ramsey."

"Colin. Please."

He could almost sense a smile in her brief hesitation. "Colin. Of course."

Serena hesitated before speaking again, gathering her thoughts. "Last time I saw Cheng, he had an idea. It took me a long time to think about, but I've made my decision now. I know that we've just met each other in any sort of helpful way, but I think I already know you better than anyone else on this ship does. So, if it suits you, I could keep you company whenever you're awake. We'll tell the technicians you need to be monitored, which is partially true. I'll take care of my patient, while he takes care of everyone else. Seems like a worthy use of my time."

It was a good idea, but he resisted it. "Thanks, but the ship isn't designed to handle more than five waking crew members for very long. We don't have the resources."

"Already thought of that. I had Fabian run the numbers. It'd be a little draining, but doable for two weeks at a time."

"I'm sure that prospect thrilled him."

"Not so much. But we'll leave your H.R. problem for another day." She smiled.

"Well... but... where would you sleep?"

"I was in Brazil, remember? I can rough it here in the medical facility. Look, Colin, do you want my help or not?"

He considered for a moment, then nodded.

"Good." She patted him on the shoulder. "Let's start with some breakfast."

———

THE OPTIONS FOR DISPOSING OF A BODY WERE PRETTY limited in space. Most of the ideas for how to handle Cheng's remains were too gruesome to consider. Eventually, everyone agreed to preserve his body in cryo for a proper burial on Ithaca.

Fabian's pod was cannibalized to restore Ramsey's, and, to compensate, each technician for the remainder of the expedition would have to inherit the cryo pod of the technician who came after him. It was as elegant of a solution as they could have hoped for, given the circumstances.

They put Cheng's body into cryo without much ceremony. It seemed wrong to everyone to say goodbye now. They would save their words, save the ceremony for Ithaca.

Fabian overwrote the biometric sensors that insisted there was no one in the chamber, and one by one everyone returned to their work.

————

En Route to Ithaca - Year 400 of 504

FABIAN LUIS DA SILVA CACEDA CLOSED HIS EYES AND leaned into the headrest of the cryo chamber. Asahi, three minutes away from becoming Senior Technician, showed the new guy, Javier, how the cryo chamber worked.

Fabian had already said goodbye to Randy and Mousa, who had urgent work to complete elsewhere on the aging ship.

The chamber doors closed. This pod had originally been Asahi's, but each technician would need to shift down one spot to accommodate the pod they had cannibalized to upgrade and repair Ramsey's.

Fabian did not let go of grudges easily. Less and less as he had aged. He still hadn't forgiven Ramsey for surviving at the expense of Cheng. He knew it had been Cheng's choice. He knew how essential Ramsey was. He saw that Ramsey was doing better now, both physically and relationally. He didn't begrudge him that. But he still couldn't accept the way things had happened.

Ramsey had tried to make it up to him. He'd been kinder, but not kind. Gentler, but not gentle. He wasn't so dismissive, but he still didn't listen. Serena was probably helping, but she had looked tired the last time Fabian saw her.

But none of this was his problem anymore. He peeked at the digital timer inside the pod. Thirty more seconds until he slept, and then it would be Ithaca at last.

He'd given so much, for so long. He'd taken over as Senior Technician in the absence of Cheng and led a shorthanded team until Mousa awoke to replace the long-departed Cheng. Even that had been almost thirteen years ago.

The fifty years had inched by, and yet, where had they gone? It seemed impossible that so much time, so much life, had passed by so quickly.

Ramsey's Ithaca awaited. Where Fabian would spend the rest of his days in the peace and beauty of a new world.

And, who knows? Maybe Ramsey would do an alright job leading things there after all.

————

En Route to Ithaca - Year 464 of 504

Serena waited outside the door for Ramsey. He had made a habit of visiting the tube where Cheng's body rested every few weeks. She liked to give him his privacy. When he exited crew cryo he looked shaken.

"You didn't need to wait for me," said Ramsey, turning away and down the corridor.

"You were in there a long time. I didn't know if you wanted to talk."

"Not really."

They walked back toward the medical room through the gray, nondescript corridors in silence. Despite his previous insistence to the contrary, Ramsey made little noncommittal noises, like he wanted to say something.

"What's on your mind, Colin?"

"It's nothing."

She didn't believe him. "We've been friends for three years now and I know you pretty well. You can tell me."

"I know I can, I just... I'm still not good at this yet."

"You're getting better, though. Cheng would be proud."

"I wasn't thinking about Cheng, actually. I was... thinking about my Dad. And when he died."

"Flashbacks?" She stopped in the corridor and turned to face him.

"Not exactly." Ramsey matched Serena's body language. "He was a brilliant man, my Dad. Kind, too, but hard at the same time. We were on good terms, but even as a kid I felt like an employee. I got my drive from him."

"I think you got a lot more than that from him."

"I'm not so sure they were all good things, though. I was sad when he died, of course. But, more than that, I saw it as my big chance. I fought for the company, made it my own, and not five years later Ty came to me with the information that led us to where we are today. I was so distracted with the opportunity his death represented that I'm not sure I ever really understood he was gone."

Serena nodded, encouraging him to continue.

"And now, this thing with Cheng. It's been three years for us, but I don't know. It's all becoming real in a way it wasn't before. There's a sanitization of aging that happens here, because the technicians aren't supposed to die. They go back to sleep before that happens. And then I think about Earth and all the people we left behind. Like Ty. Like Clara and Izzy. My mother. And every time I see a technician grow old, it's like losing Ty all over again. Even if he was lucky enough to grow old while the world fell apart around him, my best friend has been dead for centuries..." The last word took the air out of Ramsey's lungs. "Centuries," he repeated, battling for composure.

Serena said nothing.

"I killed them," said Ramsey, his mind and his eyes suddenly afire with the tragedy. "I may as well have murdered them myself."

The corridor was quiet for several seconds.

Serena spoke first. "I don't know many details of what happened between you, beyond the speculation in the media when Ty left his post. I haven't asked you before, and I won't ask you to tell me now. But I know enough that I won't absolve you of your responsibility."

"I'm not asking for absolution." He started walking again, leaving her no choice but to follow.

"I know." She jogged a few paces to catch up. "You're allowing yourself to be seen, like Cheng tried to teach you."

Ramsey shrugged. "I suppose so."

"I've thought about it, too, you know," said Serena. "My parents. My friends. My would-have-been in-laws. Everyone is gone now."

"But you aren't responsible for what happened to them. I am."

"What do you mean?"

Ramsey sighed heavily. "I'm the one who told Ty he couldn't bring his daughter, and so he stayed behind, too. I may as well have shot him. It's my fault he's dead. I killed him."

"Colin-"

"And," he half-suppressed a bitter laugh, "That's not to mention the billions of people who applied for CIV and were turned away. A lot of them would have done fine. Maybe one in ten. But I'm the one who decided on five thousand. I could have done more. I could have made the engineering work. I could have saved more people. But I didn't. I picked a few and threw the rest away. When I started building CIV, it was because I wanted history to remember me." His voice cracked subtly, "But not as a monster."

"You're not a monster."

"You're the one who showed me that I had to live my life for two because of Cheng. That I have to learn to carry him with me in everything. Well, what about Ty? What about Clara and Izzy? What about the billion names I never learned who reached out to me for help and I turned them away? I can't carry a billion people with me, Serena, I just can't."

"No one's asking you to. And none of that makes you a monster. Just the opposite. It's only the people who actually try to save lives who feel guilty about the ones they couldn't save. The effect is well-documented at least as far back as the middle of the twentieth century, during the Second Great War."

"Maybe. But the question remains. How do I carry on for a billion lives?"

Serena stopped walking again. Ramsey took another few steps before stopping and turning back towards her, avoiding her eyes like a schoolboy about to be reprimanded. "You keep forgetting," she said, "You're not alone. I'm here. The technicians are here. And soon there will be five thousand of us to carry them with us into the future on Ithaca."

Behind his cheek his tongue rolled indecisively. "Is that really enough?"

"It has to be. This is where we are now. This is the story of the human race."

"I know you're right. It just seems... insufficient."

"Maybe it is."

His eyebrows shot up. "Helpful. Thanks." His arms folded across his chest.

"Well, what are you going to do about it, then?" She kept her voice carefully level. "Are you going to keep complaining about how insufficient it is? Are you going to spend the rest of your days wishing there was something you could do when you know there's nothing?"

"No, of course not."

"Then what? How are you going to make it up to them?"

"I'm going to make Ithaca the best damn place it can be, so their sacrifice isn't in vain." His own words seemed to surprise him.

Serena took a tentative step towards him, placed her hand on top of his shoulder. His sickly body swayed under her touch. "Make Ithaca the place Ty and his family, Cheng, and all the ten billion people who stayed behind would have wanted Earth to be. That's how you do it."

He sighed. And embedded in that sigh was a depth of tiredness that only an immortal could know. "First we have to get there. Then the real work can begin."

————

En Route to Ithaca - Year 476 of 504

"MY BROTHER. MY FRIEND. TRULY THERE IS NO MAN LEFT alive who is like you. I see in the scars you bear on your body, both of age and of hardship, that you lived your life well. That you fought for the good. As it is written, 'Whoever saves one life, it is as if he had saved the lives of everyone in the world.' With you, perhaps it is even true.

"I know not what to say to you, to express my gratitude for your sacrifice. I am in your debt in a way that cannot ever be repaid. Even less so now that Allah has brought you into his rest. May your path bring you peace.

"Salaam, my friend," said Mohammed Samaras. The new Junior Technician placed his hand over his heart and bowed respectfully before the cryo chamber where Cheng Ahn rested.

There were twenty-eight years left until Ithaca.

22

HOME

DAY 1, MONTH 1, ITHACAN YEAR 1

A hologram planet of lush greens, sandy browns, patches of white, and vast expanses of deep, rich blue loomed in the center of the command room of CIV.

Ithaca.

She was too beautiful to be real.

Ramsey sat at the central console, drinking in the alien coastlines, the patterns and motions of the clouds. And the color. Oh, the color was unlike anything he ever remembered seeing, hues so rich and deep that he lacked the vocabulary to describe them.

His technicians faced him, each busying himself at a smaller console in a semi-circle around him. A series of beeps from his screen signaled the conclusion of the planetary analysis from the probes they had dropped to the surface a few hours earlier. The technicians exchanged nervous glances as Ramsey accessed the report.

He looked at each of the men through the projection of the planet. A smile crept onto his lips. "Ninety-Eight percent of Earth gravity, twenty-five hour and thirty-eight minute days, proteins and carbohydrates close enough to work with... Analysis confirmed. She's habitable!"

The technicians erupted in celebration, embracing each other. His senior technician — his final senior technician — approached to shake his hand. "You did it, sir."

Ramsey's hand trembled as he grasped Kaiden's hand. "We did it together. Thank you."

The old man smiled and turned back to his colleagues. A gentle touch found Ramsey's upper back. He looked over his shoulder and found Serena beaming at him through tired eyes. He returned the smile.

Ramsey quieted his technicians. "I'm running the program to identify our optimal landing site. The result should come back within an hour or two. I need you to do a final inspection on our shuttles and start waking the first wave of sleepers. Shuttle crew, engineers, xenobiologists, you know the list. Let's get on it."

Ramsey continued his work as the technicians finished their tasks and filed out of the room.

Serena approached the projection, admiring it as she took a deep breath. She turned and flashed a grin at Ramsey. "You're home."

Day 24, Month 1, Ithacan Year 1

CHENG LIN SHIVERED AS SHE BLINKED THE SLEEP AWAY.

Through the small pane of glass, a pretty, brown-haired woman in a lab coat, a doctor, observed her. She turned away, saying something to someone Lin couldn't see. The curved doors of the cryo chamber parted, rotating into place behind her. She squinted one eye against the brightness.

The hallway was gloomier than before her slumber. It was jarring to awaken and have the world suddenly look different around you. Motes of dust drifted in the stale air and the white plastic ceiling had yellowed. The once-bright green and blue hues of light that alternated across the ceiling were dimmer now, shades of white rather than actual colors. Something rattled intermittently nearby. The ship seemed to groan with the weight of its years.

The woman in the white coat extended her hand, her striking brown eyes warm and sad. "Mrs. Cheng?"

A man who looked to be in his fifties stood close by. His dark hair was flecked with grey, and he wore a well-groomed beard. He smiled at her with the same sadness that the doctor carried in her eyes.

The corridor was quiet. Across from her, that peculiar English historian rested, still asleep in his pod. In fact, none of the other pods' occupants were awake.

A quietness beyond a lack of sound left the ancient hallway strangely empty.

Lin stepped out of the vertical tube, grasped the doctor's hand and bowed. "You may call me Lin."

She smiled, "I'm Serena."

"What has happened? Have we arrived at Ithaca?"

"We have. We arrived a few weeks ago and the first colonists are already on the surface. Your section is scheduled to wake up later today. However, we wanted to wake you up early because..." she glanced at the bearded man, and Lin's heart began to sink.

"What has happened?" she repeated, one hand rising to her mouth, the other resting on her abdomen.

"Mrs. Cheng," Serena began. She sighed, then began again. "Lin. Toward the end of your husband's service, there was an accident while he was extracting Colin — that is, Dr. Ramsey — from cryo. He saved Colin's life, but received a massive electrical shock in the process. I, um... I regret to inform you that he died of his injuries almost immediately."

Fire erupted in her chest even as her knees collapsed and strong hands caught her.

Gone. Her Ahn-Ahn was gone.

Removed from her not only by the unequal passage of time, but also from one life to the next.

Gone. He couldn't be gone.

But he was.

Hot tears streamed down her face as she attempted to gain control of herself.

Serena and the man helped lower her to her knees. She pulled the doctor close, not knowing why, but needing something, anything to anchor her to reality.

Serena embraced her respectfully.

Through the nauseating waves of unspeakable sorrow, Lin's reason began to return. It was not many minutes until she disengaged from the hug with a feeble, "I am sorry."

Serena rubbed Lin's shoulder, tears in her own eyes. "Please, don't be. He was a great man, so full of love and kindness. And he loved you deeply, right until the end. That much was always clear."

"That is... kind of you." Lin sniffled. She was not ready to hear her Ahn spoken of in the past tense. Not yet. She had been prepared to see him old. She had been prepared to lose him before too many years passed. But she had never envisioned a version of Ithaca entirely bereft of him. "May I see him?" she asked.

Serena looked to the man, who nodded, then back to Lin. "Sure."

———

THE BEARDED MAN, A TECHNICIAN NAMED MOHAMMED, LED them up into the main crew habitat. Once again the faded colors and worn walls and floors surprised Lin. She hadn't seen this part of the ship before, but it was in a similar style to the interior of Troy Orbital, but so run down. It seemed like the ship had barely held together.

"Crew cryo is just ahead," said Mohamed, gesturing towards the door ahead of them.

"Thank you," said Lin, her voice barely more than a whisper.

The doors retracted, revealing a large room with an open space at the front with one cryo chamber facing the door, and behind that, lined with two corridors of cryo chambers.

"This way," said Mohammed, gesturing to the right.

Just beyond the central chamber, a handsome old man rested in a pod.

She recognized her Ahn immediately. His hair was

silver, his face wrinkled, his skin tough and pale. But her eyes removed half a century of use from his haggard frame. The man she had kissed goodbye yesterday stood there before her. Eternally youthful. Wise and distinguished beyond his years. She'd recognize him if he were a thousand years old.

She observed him for a long while, a smile flickering across her lips. She placed a gentle kiss on the glass in front of his forehead. "I'm here, my Ahn-Ahn," she said in Mandarin.

And though he did not move, and the doors did not open, he came to her. Her eyes never left that silent, sleeping face, but nevertheless, he was there in a way that she knew was only in her mind, yet was much more than mere imagination.

That vision of Ahn stared into her face for several silent seconds, his rich brown eyes dancing with life and love, searching her, seeing her, knowing her. A smile like the rising of the sun materialized across his wrinkled features. "My darling," he said. He burst out in a laugh, his eyes never leaving her. "You are as beautiful as ever, my sweet Lin."

The sound of his voice removed the weight of the years they had been apart. In that mystical not-place where she now saw him, she had lived through those years, too. She was ancient, his peer again. "And I love you more than ever, my beloved husband."

He made a small nod. His eyes brimmed with tears. "I'm glad you are here, my darling."

She smiled, her own tears threatening, then spilling over. "I miss you."

"Me, too."

"There is something I must tell you, my husband. And I am ashamed, now, that I did not tell you before."

"I know, my darling."

She paused, wiping her eyes. "You do?"

"I've met him... in my dreams of Ithaca. You must name him *Weilai*."

"'The future'?"

"The firstborn of Ithaca. The future of us all."

She smiled. "It suits him."

A long quiet followed. They gazed into each other's eyes.

"Be at peace, my husband."

He reached out toward her face. "I love you."

She reached up to press his hand to her cheek, though she knew it wasn't really there. "Always, my Ahn-Ahn."

And he was gone.

She let her hand fall back to her side.

She gazed into the kind and dignified face of the real Ahn, who rested before her.

Then she kissed the glass over his forehead again. "Goodnight, my husband." She took a step away from the chamber. "Dream beautiful dreams of Weilai and of Ithaca. I will see you when you wake up."

———

Day 25, Month 1, Ithacan Year 1

DR. DAMIAN CARTWRIGHT, FORMER PROFESSOR OF

History at Cambridge University, awoke. His shoulders were stiff, like he had fallen asleep at his desk and slept there for far too long. The cryo chamber's seal broke. The doors retreated into the sides of the unit and bright light flooded in. He blinked as his eyes adjusted.

Someone made an announcement about not trying to move too quickly, but Damian found himself searching for the intriguing woman he had been speaking with just before the chamber closed. The pods around him were also open, their inhabitants stretching. Across the corridor, Cheng Lin stood outside of her open chamber, her eyes closed. Her lips moved subtly, like one of his students rehearsing facts and dates before an exam.

He smiled, opened his mouth to ask what she was doing, but noticed a tear on her cheek. Peculiar. She fiddled with the simple silver band on her left hand.

He'd forgotten about her husband while he slept. His uncomfortable night hadn't felt like one year, never mind five hundred. Cheng Lin's husband would be old by now. He found it hard to imagine.

Looking up, she spotted him. Her lips and eyes curled into a small, sad smile.

Damian waved as nonchalantly as he could. "Hi."

"How are you, Dr. Cartwright?"

Taking stock of himself, he said, "I'm all right, I suppose. How are you?" His insides cringed. He shouldn't have asked.

"My baby and I have made it to Ithaca. We are safe. My husband's work was not in vain." Her proud voice failed to compensate for the joy that had vanished from her eyes since he last saw her the day before.

A long silence stretched between them. Someone in a uniform came over to check his pupils and manual dexterity, part of the waking process.

Noticing that the uniformed crew member did not check on Lin, he asked, "Have you been awake long?"

"Just a few hours."

He was going to ask why she had been awoken early, but they were directed to begin filing through the corridors before he had the chance. The other passengers exchanged nervous conversation punctuated with bits of laughter and excitement.

"That passed so quickly."

"Are we really at another world?"

"Are you feeling ok?"

"I'm hungry."

"Five hundred years in the future!"

"I can't wait to see it."

"Can you believe this is really happening?"

"So, everyone on Earth is long gone by now, huh?"

But Lin remained silent.

Against his better judgment, Damian asked, "When will you see your husband again?"

She held her head up, that same pride radiating from her. "I will see him daily in the face of my son. He will visit me every night to comfort my dreams. And one day I will find him again in the life yet to come."

Damian wasn't entirely sure what she meant. He began three different questions, stopping each one after a few words.

Lin put him out of his misery. "He did not survive," she said, "but I was able to say goodbye, in a sense, and that will have to last me many long years without him, as he endured many long years without me."

He had more questions, but swallowed them. He settled on saying, "I'm sorry," and he was.

"I am not sorry," Lin replied. "I am sorrowful, but not sorry. He was an honorable man. A good man." She looked Damian in the eye. "It is up to all of us to make his sacrifice worthwhile every day."

Damian's line stopped abruptly, and Lin was swept away from him.

Alone at the edge of the universe, Damian's heart flooded with gratitude.

————

Day 4, Month 3, Ithacan Year 1

COLIN RAMSEY MADE A POINT OF BEING THE LAST COLONIST to set foot on Ithaca, about three months after the first colonists awoke. The site the computer had selected was a warm, grassy plain close to a freshwater river and a hearty forest. Hundreds of shelters had been constructed and the initial infrastructure for their small community had been completed.

As he waited to disembark the last shuttle to Ithaca, he looked through the window at all the colors of the outside world. The natural sunlight and flowing grass looked alien to him after twenty-some years of metal walls and LEDs. Memories of Earth rushed through his mind, like remembering a beautiful dream from a childhood he thought he had forgotten. Ithaca was nearly indistinguishable from the home they had left behind. Even most of the alien plants and animals bore resemblance to those of Earth — new, but not entirely strange.

Ty had done very, very well.

"Ready?" asked Serena from the seat next to him.

He nodded, but didn't take his eyes off the window until the hiss of the shuttle door on the opposite side of the cabin told him it was time to disembark.

New, unidentifiable smells, indescribably rich and wonderful, poured into the cabin. He pushed himself to his feet with his cane and headed for the door. It seemed centuries since he had smelled the outdoors.

As he exited the craft, a roar of applause greeted him. Colonists gathered around the shuttle in the thousands. They began to cheer his name. "Ramsey! Ramsey!" Hundreds more ran to join the worshipful masses as Ramsey the Colonizer set foot on Ithaca for the first time.

An empty pit formed in his stomach.

Serena put her hand on his upper back to urge him forward.

"I was such a fool to desire immortality," he said, taking a hesitant step, "I spent twenty-two years working for this, and now I don't want it."

"History will always remember your name. There's no way around that now."

"If history must remember names and deeds, it should remember Ty, who found this world. It should remember Cheng, who saved me, and saved us all. It should remember you, Serena."

She spoke gently. "That's not how history works."

He nodded. "I know."

To his right stood a group of old men. His technicians, save for one. Many of them refrained from clapping, but some of the more recent ones chanted his name along with the masses. The way Ramsey had skipped through the years as they plodded through them made him feel paradoxically much older and much younger than them.

He gazed out at the masses again. Their slumber insulated them from any sense of the time that had passed, what had been done, what had been sacrificed. Only he understood. Only he was alone.

Ramsey glanced at Serena. Her eyes met his reassuringly, like she had been reading his thoughts. "Time moves the same for all of us now," she said. "You aren't alone anymore."

He considered her words for a long time, scanning the crowd and waving as they walked. "I suppose that makes me human again."

She took his hand in hers. "It certainly makes you mortal."

A smile materialized on his face. He gripped her hand tighter. "That's enough for me."

The End

RAMSEY'S ODYSSEY IS OVER...
BUT THE STORY IS JUST BEGINNING
Exclusive offer:
Join the mailing list, get *One Small Step* for FREE!

davebrunetti.com/freebook

A new world. A new home. A new struggle for the future of the human race.

For Commander Aziza Tantawi and her crew of forty, the mission is simple: Establish a base of operations on Ithaca and ensure the planet is safe for the rest of the colonists.

But when now-ancient equipment on CIV and on the planet malfunction, Aziza and her crew find themselves in mortal danger. It will take everything Aziza's got to see her mission through to completion, and live to tell the tale.

We've come so far. Will we fall at the final hurdle?

Find out what happens in this thrilling short story continuation of *Dreams of Ithaca*, available exclusively to mailing list subscribers! Join at the URL below and get *One Small Step* sent to the device of your choice!

davebrunetti.com/freebook

Thank you!

Did you enjoy this book? Just a moment of your time can make a HUGE difference!

Dear friend,

I loved sharing *Dreams of Ithaca* with you! If you made it this far, you probably enjoyed it, too!

If you have a moment, a review on Amazon would mean the absolute world to me and my ability to help new readers like you discover my stories.

Unfortunately, I'm not at the point just yet where my name is included among those famous authors who need no introduction, so reviews like yours are absolutely ESSENTIAL for readers to take a chance on me: the new guy they may never have heard of before.

Reviews may be as short as you like, and it only takes a moment. Share the love! If you enjoyed *Dreams of Ithaca*, head on over to the Amazon page, and help other readers discover it, too.

Thank you,

Dave

ACKNOWLEDGMENTS

This story was five years in the making. Born in a humble coffee shop in Billings, Montana thanks to the ever-brilliant insights of my ever-brilliant wife, Amanda, this story emerged as little more than a ten page treatment exploring the idea of time passing differently for different people on a colony ship.

Amanda, without you this idea would never have been born. The importance of your encouragement and insight over the last five years as I began my author career cannot be overstated. You have been a constant companion, a trustworthy sounding board, and a kind shoulder when I needed one. But for you, I would still be wondering if I had it in me to write a novel, let alone launch this career. You are the light in my world.

Before that came my parents. Dad, you spent countless hours reading to me at my childhood bedside, fanning the sparks of my fledgling imagination into flame. I would not love stories if it weren't for you. Mom, you spent countless hours listening to me prattle on about whatever new story caught my fancy. Without your patience, I may never have become a story teller.

This book would not be possible without the dozens of people who have influenced it in some way. Thank you, Mark Dawson, who made me believe that this was a worthwhile pursuit, and that it might even be a career. Thank you Beta Readers Nan and Travis Pond, Danielle and Ryan Kellison, and Elliott Warden. You told me what I needed to hear to make this book the best I could make it and the final product is far better for your help. Travis, thank you again for your help designing CIV and for your photography skills. You're a brilliant man to whom I am deeply indebted. Elliott, you have been my biggest cheerleader. I think I'll keep you around.

Thank you Jeannie for your insightful and illuminating editing. I learned so much from you.

Thank you also to Stuart Bache for your cover design and your great patience.

To my friends at SCFW, thank you for the laughs and for the community. You helped me believe in the stories I wanted to tell.

To all the many, many people who expressed interest in my stories and encouraged me, and especially to the dozen or so of you who asked to buy the first copy: You are far too kind. Thank you for everything.

To anyone whose contributions I have neglected on these pages, I truly and deeply apologize. Thank you.

And finally, dear reader: thank YOU for reading. All these others made it possible, but ultimately I did it for you.

19971726R00187

Made in the USA
Middletown, DE
08 December 2018